BLOOD MATTER

M. V. Ghiorghi

DIVERTIR
PUBLISHING
Salem, NH

BLOOD MATTER

M. V. Ghiorghi

Cover design by M. V. Ghiorghi

Published by Divertir Publishing LLC
PO Box 232
North Salem, NH 03073
http://www.divertirpublishing.com/

ISBN-13: 978-1-938888-13-7
ISBN-10: 1-938888-13-8

Library of Congress Control Number: 2015955202

Printed in the United States of America

Contents

"Love us when we are dirty. Any fool can love us when we are clean."
Nikolai Gogol, *Dead Souls*

Prologue

Execution

It was the eve of his death, but the fiery hatred streaming through his veins filled him with savage life.

Outwardly, he was calm and cool. He chatted with the three guards docked on the bench across from his cell, telling stories suited to the occasion—like the one about Billy, his minor-offender, hapless acquaintance from the county jail where he had waited for his trial. And not just telling it, but role-playing it, different voices and all, with Billy as a high-strung, depressed country bumpkin.

"…So he climbs on the upper cot and tells me, 'I'll see you in haven!' An' I tell him, 'I don't know 'bout that, Billy,' sad kinda-like. An' he says, 'Don't despair, Sammy, God will forgive us.' And I just wait and watch 'cause the rope is way too long. Sure enough, the moron jumps and screams his head off, 'cause he broke both his legs. Spent all his time before the trial in the jail's infirmary, cursing his luck."

The easily impressible Jimmy, who had always been kind to Sam, laughed.

Dan, the worthless turn-key cockroach, snickered. "Yeah, but who is lucky now, huh, Sam? The moron or the smart ass?"

The laughter died. The oldest of the three, a Russian guard named Michael, stared in front of himself, uncomfortable. Jimmy glared at Dan.

Sam leaned his back against the wall, eyes half-closed to dim the murderous fire in them, smiling a bit for the guards' benefit as if he was not perturbed. Thus, resting, he went over every detail of his plan.

"It's time, Samuel," said a strained old voice.

Sam Horowitz, or 'Sam the Slasher' as he was known for most of his adult life, opened his eyes to see, on the other side of the bars, the somber lined face of Father John. Dan sprang up, weasel-like, to unlock the door.

Sam arched his back, yawned, and rubbed his knees. As he rose, they cracked loudly. "How ya feeling, Pop?" he asked the chaplain. "Nervous?"

Jimmy shook his head with a smile. The uncooked, sphinx-like face of Michael remained impassive. He never went further than what his job required. Him and Jimmy, they were okay.

"I'm fine." Father John stepped inside. He waited as the eager beaver Dan snapped handcuffs tightly on Sam's wrists. "Did you think about our talk?"

"I tell ya what," Sam said. "I've one wish left. If there's a God, he'll know what that is. And if he grants it, you can call me a Believer and save my soul, if you still care to."

Father John looked at him, puzzled, but Sam's intense, mocking stare discouraged further inquiry.

The guards ushered the condemned man into the corridor. The chaplain led the group, with Michael on Sam's right and Jimmy on the left, a step ahead due to the narrowness of the passage. Danny-boy followed with a spring in his step and, Sam imagined, a smirk on his face.

Earlier, Sam had asked Michael and Jimmy—beseeched them, as if the two were his last friends on Earth—to walk his final passage with him. "No offense, Daniel," Sam had said. "We weren't on good terms, so you be so kind as to walk behind."

The Russian and Jimmy, as Sam long observed, didn't care much for their partner and told Dan to honor Sam's last request.

Once they started walking, Sam waited a bit then casually moved his cuffed hands to the belt of his gray trousers. He pretended to scratch himself as he reached for a shank beneath. He had made it from a stolen fork, wrapping it in a ribbon torn from his sheet. He carefully shaped it over the course of three months preceding his execution, hiding it in his anus whenever his cell was searched.

Turning the corner…slowing down…

Sam spun around—and Dan walked straight onto the shank.

They fell together as Sam stabbed, twisting the blade again and again. In the brief stunned silence of the other three, Dan shrieked. His blood sprayed the walls, the floor, and Sam's clothes, turning the dull prison grays a vivid red and coloring the meager shreds of time that Sam had left in abandonment and truth.

Michael and Jimmy screamed and fell on him. They kicked him and slammed his head against the linoleum covered concrete, pulling him away from his enemy who was writhing his last. They pinned Sam down, their sweat dripping on his face, their knees crushing his chest. His ear pressed to the floor felt the pounding vibration even before the sound of the footfalls of more guards racing along the hallway reached him and his captors.

Sam twisted his head, and his eyes found Father John standing frozen as Lot's wife, the old terrified face salt-white above the white collar. "I believe!" Sam hissed, grimacing at the chaplain, "I believe!"

§ § §

They bundled him up and carried him like a rag doll to the death chamber, their hearts beating so wildly he could hear them. In the gray, cinder-block room where the witnesses and the execution team waited, they stood him up on his bound feet.

The executioner's assistant, a young guy with a shrewd face, attended the big oak and leather contraption, while the blank-faced executioner by the controls tried to appear as inconspicuous as part of the device. Two somber newspaper reporters, dressed in dark suits wrinkled from traveling in overnight cases, watched from the corner partitioned by a wooden barrier: the Witness Box.

Hiding behind them was a scarecrow of a man, the custodian of the orphanage where Sam grew up and the one witness he had requested. The old alcoholic was the single person from Sam's childhood that Sam remembered with some goodwill for sharing an occasional bottle of shine with a loner kid. The pasty-faced warden, the clean-shaven doctor, Father John and the guards made up the rest of the public.

"Howdy!" Sam said to all with a broad smile. "Sorry, can't wave." He looked at the custodian. "How are ya my good man? Glad to see ya. Hope ya have fun."

Sam's old acquaintance shrank even more, mum as a mouse. The puny guy had aged badly. Not that Sam cared. The old fart had one use, to watch and remember Sam's last show and blabber about it afterward to all those Sam hated. And Sam hated plenty. All those miserable foes of his inglorious bed-wetting childhood, his humiliating past. They would all know. All except for the orphanage director, his wife, and his two whiny little girls—Sam's first four victims.

Sam's feet and hands were untied and they propped him into the chair, where he sat like a king on a throne. Jimmy and Michael placed leather straps around his legs, arms and chest. The executioner's assistant shaved a patch on Sam's head, cut Sam's pants up to his left knee, and shaved his calf.

Throughout the process, Sam's hungry, feverish gaze wandered. He savored every breath of the stale antiseptic air, every crack on the walls. He took in the grainy finish and noted the rough imprint right above the entrance, probably left by one of the builders—a palm in the cement, offering the doomed a high-five.

The doctor handed over sponges soaked in brine, which were placed on the shaven spots of Sam's body. Father John stood in the corner, eyes averted, lips moving in prayer.

"Samuel Horowitz," the warden said. "Do you have any last words?"

"Nah. Let's do it."

Michael stared hard at Sam, urging him to look at him, and Sam did. The Russian nodded slightly and, unnoticeable to the rest, gave the dead man a thumbs up—the one and only signal of approval Sam had received in his entire life. *Sailing off well, kiddo!*

Sam grinned at Michael as the black hood fell over his face. He felt the surprising weight of the helmet on his head and its straps being adjusted under his chin. At that moment, a bright thought struck him. If there is a sequel after death, he would come back as a glorious avenger, a hero at last! He would make a great spectacle of his time on the Earth and scratch the coarse hide of history so deep the scar would take centuries to heal—

The executioner threw the switch.

§ § §

That same night, an angry rain descended on a bleak town sprawled in the low hills a hundred miles west of the prison. At the town's train depot, the rain's dull melody mixed with agonizing moans coming from a desolate old boxcar rusting on the back tracks.

Another bout of moans came and went. Then, a howl ended humanity's oldest song. But inside the boxcar there was a continuation, a newborn's mewling as it mourned its entrance into the world. The tiny baby squirmed between the legs of a young woman sprawled in the depth of the car, away from the twisted patterns of yellow, sickly light cast on the dirty floor by a security lantern outside.

Exhausted, the woman rose on her elbow to glare over her hiked-up hospital gown. Her offspring, covered with birthing muck, its genitals hidden by the bloody placenta, looked deformed and ugly. With an effort, the new mother hauled herself onto her knees. Without showing any curiosity about the child's gender or making any attempt to clean it, she scooped it into a filthy rug. Moments later, hair plastered with the rain, losing her soggy slippers every few steps, she waddled along the tracks. Without thinking, she cradled the child in her arms just like any mother would. The baby, secure in the closeness and the feverish heat of her body, cooed.

"Shut up!" she said. "Don't you act cute on me, you devil's blood! You joinin' your damn father soon enough."

Approaching the depot, an incoming locomotive slowed in preparation to enter the depot's gates.

The woman hurried toward the rising sound.

Chugging through the depot's front gate, the locomotive released a mighty shriek in a burst of steam into the wet air.

The wail of a police siren answered it, as the black and white screeched to a stop on the other side of a row of resting boxcars. The woman gawked in the direction of the car and then peered eagerly into the red eye of the Cyclops coming her way.

A man's voice rang out. "Mary? Are you here?"

A great beam of light washed off the features of the woman's face. She dropped her bundle onto the vibrating tracks and fled over them and into the darkness away from the rising drone of the locomotive and the cop's voice.

§ § §

The sheriff, a grizzly man of fifty, climbed over the slick connecting platforms and jumped down. The engine was approaching, still going at a good speed, and in its glare he saw a figure sprinting away behind the curtain of the rain. He noticed a bundle on the tracks between him and the woman. At first, it looked like some rag she dropped. But then it wriggled.

The heavy man rushed, grabbed the bundle, fell, and rolled off. He huddled still on the wet gravel, his heart thumping, hot dangerous air rushing above dragged by the steel Goliath surging past with an earsplitting screech.

Chapter 1

Standoff

Los Angeles, end of September, 35 years later

Gun fire from the front was answered by two shots from the house. A short barrage followed, covering the sound of breaking glass as Joe smashed through the window. Steve and O'Neal's team were hard at work distracting Gonzales.

He reached for the latch and nearly lost his footing on the retractable ladder. His headache, the result of another ill-slept night, was back, and his Kevlar vest and helmet seemed hotter and heavier than usual. More blasts rang out while he pushed the frame open and climbed inside. The ratty, marital bedroom was in disarray, the mattress missing on the bed, a pile of beddings on the floor, a dresser overturned...

Joe drew his TRP and exited into the small landing. A quiet 'neh-neh' froze him in his tracks. *Alberto,* he thought, and his heart lurched with anxious, crazy hope before he remembered.

He listened. An outgoing gunshot from downstairs—and another lonely, kitten-like, muted 'neh-neh' from behind the closed door across the landing. Only this time, Joe's aware, ever-recalling ear discerned that the cry wasn't Alberto's. A similar baby sound, but not the same. Still, his perception longed to be tricked.

His legs carried him to the second door, and his hand turned the knob. He stepped into a child's bedroom, clean and unadorned except for a white ceramic cross entwined with pink roses above the empty crib. The queen mattress, dragged here from the parents' bedroom, leaned against the wall. He kneeled and peaked into the space formed behind it. The round eyes of a two or three month old baby stared back from the car seat packed with pillows, semi-safe from a stray shot. A pink knitted blanket...Joe thought about the agents with their rifles behind fruit trees and the sniper on the neighbor's roof.

"Hey," he whispered. She 'neh-nehed' at him, urgent. He found a milk bottle stuck in the seat's corner, gave it to her, and she started sucking on it right away. At the back of his mind, the clock ticked off its hurried seconds, but he watched her for a little while. At last, he got to his feet.

He thought about the unfair fate that would give such a beautiful child to such worthless parents. A shame came on the heels of this jealous bitterness. What did he know about them—and who was he to judge? *He's a good father,* Gonzales' teenage wife had said—the one sniveling at the back of the patrol car parked outside—and Joe thought her dim-witted at the time. She also said, when Joe had asked her what weapons her husband owned, *I never saw a gun in the house.*

Another shot came from downstairs where the said husband, twenty-five year old Manuel Gonzales, was holed up with his hostage, the SWAT Second Element's brand new leader, Marcus O'Neal. So, Joe reasoned, when O'Neal went in to try and talk Gonzales into giving up the child, Gonzales didn't have a gun…*They'll kill him. The stupid son of a bitch will run out of ammo, and they'll go in and shoot him.*

Joe Vasquez, or 'Hound' as they nicknamed him at the department, closed the door of the bedroom and started, on cat-paws, down the rickety stairwell.

§ § §

It occurred to him, right before he came into the open, that a bullet into his head would end it all—and it would be okay. If those Catholic tales he was fed from childhood contained some truth, he might even see Alberto again.

"Don't shoot," he called in Spanish raising his hands, the TRP in his right in plain sight. The son-of-a-bitch did shoot at him, shrieking, losing his footing, and sliding on his ass, forcing Joe to lurch under the insufficient cover of the stairwell. Another bullet hit the wall above Joe's head. "I'm not going to shoot back! Don't shoot!" Joe hollered.

There was a pause.

Joe came out, hands raised. The young, wild-faced Mexican man cowering by the front window stared at him from behind O'Neal's Sig quivering in his skinny hand. Out of the corner of his eye, Joe detected O'Neal's form underneath the small kitchen counter.

Joe said, in Spanish, "Don't destroy your life because of this asshole. I know he drove you to it." Then, in English, "Put the gun down! It'll be alright, I promise! I'll vouch for you! You're off your meds, Manuel. You're not all here!"

Their eyes probed each other—Gonzales' scared, Joe's insistent.

"The meds made me dead inside," Gonzales said, his face mournful, the Sig in his limp shaking hand pointing at Joe's midsection.

"They'll put you on the right meds. You' won't be locked up for long. You'll see your daughter."

"She'll see me in heaven," Gonzales quipped and brought the pistol to his temple.

Shit! An icy hand gripped within Joe's ribcage. The gun clicked, once, twice—empty. Gonzales threw it on the floor and closed his eyes. Poor bastard just wanted it to be over.

O'Neal's scream lashed at them. "Shoot! Waste the wetback!"

Joe gritted his teeth. "You'll be alright," he said to Gonzales, picking up the Sig. "This is not the end of the world."

He went to O'Neal, took out his clip knife and cut the duct tape binding O'Neal's hands, knees and feet. He wasn't gentle. O'Neal rose, red-faced and cursing, and grabbed his gun from Joe. As Joe glanced around at the surprisingly orderly house, he heard O'Neal load a new magazine.

"If you care about procedure so much, Vasquez, I'll waste this fuck."

Joe turned and promptly stuck his Springfield in O'Neal's ear. O'Neal, pointing his Sig at Gonzales, froze.

"Stand down," Joe said.

The snake who had breathed down Joe's neck ever since coming fresh from Quantico to the L.A. office a year ago and had already curried favors from the Criminal Division's Senior Acting Commander, Don Cowell, obeyed. Joe lowered his gun as well. He could imagine the lashing he would get if he committed any of the many screw-ups that O'Neal had sailed through. Their old SAC must have felt nostalgic, seeing himself in the young, ladder-climbing asshole.

The designated golden boy sneered, "I almost forgot. You're the 'offenders defender,' aren't you, Vasquez? Especially of your own breed. Just like your daddy."

A blast of rage hit Joe, and before he knew it his Springfield was aimed at O'Neal's face, which started to melt and quiver. Then Joe dropped his arm and discharged the gun into the floor at the yelping O'Neal's feet. When he finished, his voice came out calm enough. "I serve the law. What do you serve, O'Neal? The Klu Klux Klan?"

"You fucking psycho!"

"What did you tell him? How'd you insult him?" Joe did his best to get his internal shaking under control.

"You think you're so high and mighty! Everybody in the department, all but your dumbass sidekick, hates you. Cowell can't stand you," O'Neal spat.

Now that O'Neal had lost it and turned to school-girl taunts, Joe regained his grip. Funny how it worked. "How did this milk sucker get your gun? Enlighten me."

"He snuck up on me! Stuck his rifle into my back!"

"What rifle?" Joe glanced at Gonzales in disbelief.

O'Neal waved curtly at the corner. Joe went there. A toy pellet gun lay on the floor. "You've got some cojones, boy," he said to Gonzales.

O'Neal stared at Joe with hatred. "He assaulted me!"

"Shit your pants, Marcus?"

Gonzales laughed like a hyena.

§ § §

A squad car bearing Gonzales' baby daughter and her mother pulled away, en route to the grandparents' home. The cops packed Gonzales into another sedan, heading for the county jail.

Joe took off his helmet and slumped against the apple tree. Now that the pressure to keep things together released, he felt weak, his insides trembling like guitar strings. It was getting bad, he thought. He needed to get more sleep. He could make an appointment, ask for pills…Nah, he decided. They'd want to send him to a shrink, force him into evaluations and counseling, and might deem him unfit for duty. All while his work was the only thing keeping him on an even kilter. He'd have to do with something over the counter, like Benadryl.

Joe took a few deep breaths. The breeze dried his sweaty hair, and the mild October sun caressed his face. The gnarled limbs of the tree opened welcoming, and the tangy stench of rotting apples that spotted Gonzales' front yard crisped the air. It wasn't bad to be alive. Then Joe remembered the two who would never again enjoy the sun or smell the apples, and an immense, habitual guilt descended on him, shattering his one moment of contentment.

Steve Mallow walked over, a giant of a man, Joe's partner and second in command of his SWAT element. He put his broad arm across Joe's shoulder and gave him a brief squeeze. Others nodded or shook his hand as they made their way to the van. Joe, not wanting to drive with the rest of the team, waited for the cop who promised him a ride.

Steve leaned on the same tree. Joe was grateful that Steve could come along when they called him in to clean up O'Neal's mess. The men, both about to turn forty, looked strikingly different. A tall, broad-shouldered white guy and a medium-height, wiry Latino. The square-jawed Steve clung to his wheat-blond buzz cut, while Joe's neglected visits to the barber let his wavy, streaked with premature grays black mane reach halfway to his shoulders.

"How are you holdin' up?" Steve asked when no one was around. Joe realized that the question didn't refer to the shootout.

"I'm alive."

Steve studied him. Whatever he saw apparently satisfied him, because he nodded. Joe sensed that Steve was gathering up for something. He waited, and Steve said, in a discomforted voice, "Cristie's making fish tacos tonight. Asked me to invite you."

"Is her friend coming too? I'm not up for extra company." By extra company he meant a pretty blond accountant Steve's wife had slipped into their tight little circle at Mallows' two weeks prior.

"Hey, I'm sorry. That girl, Sandi, asked for your number. I told her you are not…in the right place right now. Did she call you?"

"Yeah," Joe said. The girl called a couple times, playing the buddy card, trying to get him out of his shell with small, bubbly, annoying talk.

"She's a nice gal, smart, independent…" Steve said, clearly disgusted with himself.

"I'm sure she is."

"I'll tell Christie that you are busy." Steve sounded relieved, his marital obligation to support his wife's matchmaking effort fulfilled.

"Wanna grab a beer after work?"

"Sure."

They stood in a comfortable silence, their very vibes synchronized it seemed, the way it was always between them since the day they met years ago. Joe stared without seeing. The sunny yard and the smell of apples faded away. *Just like your daddy*, the bastard had said.

He expected that a couple people at the department would be privy to his family history, those who read the personnel files as a part of their job. And Steve, of course, who knew everything there was to know about Joe. Except that telling Steve a secret was the same as burying it. The fact that O'Neal knew about Joe's father was unsettling, but not that surprising. As Joe's mother always said, *What two people know, the pig knows too.*

One of the officers who handled Gonzales approached, motioning over his shoulder. "The shithead wants to talk to you."

Joe walked to the van as the driver lowered the back window. "I got something for you," Gonzales said in Spanish. He looked broken, though still wild-eyed. "Remember that black kid they found a few months ago?"

Joe did remember—the Blake Johnson case. A brutal killing handled by the East Side police with no progress so far.

"I delivered some rock back then to an apartment. This guy went to get his money, and I saw some kid with him on the couch—he looked like he was sleeping. A week or so later, I saw a kid that looked a lot like him on T.V., missing. In a few more weeks, they said somebody offed him bad."

Gonzales glanced toward the driver and lowered his voice to a whisper. "I remember the place, but I won't tell the cops or your mother fuckin' feds—only you."

Chapter 2

Pale Eyes

The murder of Blake Johnson didn't make many headlines or keep the public's attention for long. A 16-year old black student from the projects, he had disappeared a month before hikers discovered his head and leg in the forest near Wilmington in a shallow grave revealed by a strong rain. The following search recovered the remaining parts, some dragged away by animals, some buried.

Joe learned the facts of the case from the overworked detective, Ron Stout, who handled it. The autopsy report was unusual, and not because of the presence of cocaine in Blake's tissues; before being chopped with most likely a chain saw, the body was drained of blood. Also worth noting was Blake's canceled criminal record, an arrest for dealing drugs in his high school followed by a few weeks in a juvenile hall before the charges were dropped.

Testimonies of the boy's friends were of no help. No other witness came forward as Blake's mother couldn't offer a reward. As far as detective Stout was concerned, there was no hope to find the killer, and the case went stale.

Joe didn't anticipate any problems taking over if he gleaned any new leads with a search of the apartment where Gonzales claimed to have seen Blake last. And so, on the second afternoon since the stand-off, he and Steve paid the place a visit. They obtained a warrant but, out of caution, didn't contact the landlord.

The neighborhood was quiet and appeared unpopulated, most denizens being at work at this time of day mid-week. Cars in different stages of disrepair decorated the dry lawns of the seedy block. The apartment was in a one-level duplex, the entrance hidden from the street on the alley side of the building.

They donned disposable gloves and picked the easy lock, listening to freight cars passing by a quarter-mile away. Stepping inside the tiny living room, they closed the door and waited for the rumble to die off.

The furniture was sparse—a small table, a lawn chair, a crooked blind blocking the view from the window, a tattered couch, and an old refrigerator in the corner. The place looked rarely occupied. Joe was sure the tenant had another residence somewhere for his other, overt life. Nevertheless, it was prudent to stay on guard. Easy too—the walls were thin. If anyone approached from the outside, they'd hear. And as long as they didn't make much noise, they wouldn't scare the returning tenant off.

Steve disappeared into the apartment's only bedroom. Joe checked the refrigerator first—empty and, according to the smell, not turned on for some time. From under the table, he pulled out a plastic garbage bag, full and tied up—seemingly containing mostly paper waste.

He went to the bathroom, put on a disposable mask, and sprayed the place liberally with a solution of Luminol. Then he turned off the light, shut the door and waited. There was no luminescence on the walls, floor, or the bathtub, meaning no traces of blood or recent treatment with bleach.

He took the mask off and went to the bedroom. "The shithouse is clean," he said to Steve.

His friend crouched by the queen-size bed that had a dirty mattress and no sheet, pulling out empty beer cans and crusty pizza boxes from beneath the metal frame. He used his flashlight one more time and got up. "Something's there…"

They pulled the bed away from the wall. A yellow baseball hat wedged behind the mattress fell. Steve fished it out and passed it to Joe. "Wasn't the kid wearing something like this when he disappeared?"

Joe kneeled, examining the spots on the mattress. He sniffed a few places.

"You do look like a hound, you know."

"Old semen," Joe said. "Seeped through the sheet, which he discarded."

"Didn't the report mention cotton fibers on the body?"

They flipped the mattress, and a mid-size manila envelope lay on the slats. Joe picked it up. The envelope wasn't sealed. He shook it, and three photographs fell out.

He and Steve examined the glossy images. In the first photo, an old patrician-looking man stood on the steps of a stately building addressing a large rally of some sort. The second photo depicted a country road by a corn field, with a barn in the background and a wooden post in the foreground. In the third, a close-up likely taken with a telephoto lens, the same man listened to a dark-haired, pale, willowy woman. Joe studied her. She looked to be in her mid-thirties. Even in the picture, the intensity of her eyes was striking.

"A looker," Steve said.

"Arresting," Joe agreed.

"Arrested you," Steve chuckled. He turned to the bed. "Got the stickies?"

Joe pulled a pad of sticky notes along with a Ziploc baggie out of his old leather jacket's overburdened pocket; he always had a few of those baggies on him. Steve took them and went to work collecting the particulate.

Joe put the photos back into the envelope and walked out. He stopped in the living room and listened. The silence here was eerie. Not a sound came from the bedroom where Steve worked. A dismal pang of complete loneliness, in the drab apartment and in the world, struck Joe.

He shook the insidious sensation off, but the vague evil of the place persisted. He marched to the couch and removed the cushions to check the accumulated grit underneath, then went to the table, pulled the garbage bag from below, untied it, and dumped the contents on the table, some falling to the floor.

The first newspaper he lifted from the pile had a big square missing in the front page. A second had a hole also. Someone clipped the articles. The first rag, *The Daily Carrier*, hailed from Colorado; another, *The Standard Recorder*, from Arizona. Both were dated last year, a few months apart.

Joe sorted through the rest and found a piece of white, crumpled paper among the remaining whole newspapers pages. Joe flattened it. Letter-sized and printed on it in big bold script were the words, 'Back off or I'll lay you out.' It had all the appearance of a draft, a first take of a blackmail message he thought. He laid it aside and returned to the remainder of the pile.

Among the paper scraps and wrappers he fished out a photo. Someone attempted to rip it and half-succeeded. It must have been discarded because of the lousy resolution. At first, Joe couldn't quite make heads or tails of the elongated object, light in the dark background…And then it dawned on him and he drew his breath. He put the picture on top of the reviewed stack and became aware, without knowing how, of a hostile presence.

He stood still, facing the door, his 'Hound' senses sharpened. Outside, a twig snapped beneath weight…He pulled his Springfield from its strut holster. Sand grated underfoot…moving closer…Joe clenched his teeth and raised his gun. A key slid into the lock…

A floorboard squeaked behind. Joe turned and shook his head at Steve. His friend froze at the bedroom entrance. The key withdrew…

They stared at the door, the silence ringing in their ears. The realization dawned. Whoever tried to enter was stealing away. Joe tore for the door, threw it open, and jumped out into the narrow alley. Steve ran out after him. A tall wooden fence overgrown with elderberry blocked one of the alley's ends—two dented garbage containers in front, purple flowers stirring in the breeze. They ran to the other end, which opened into the street. Deserted as far as they could see in both directions, it was, on the right, just two houses short of the block's end.

"I'll check the garbage cans," Steve called and hurried back.

Joe sprinted toward the corner, reached it, and eyed the crossing street. It was open and straight to his left, and to his right crooked and treed. He started moving when a gunshot whipped him into a one-hundred and eighty degree turn. "Steve?!" he yelled.

No answer. The mute windows and deaf fences were silent. He ran back.

He burst into the alley and saw at once that one of the garbage cans was on its side, no longer concealing the gaping hole in the fence behind. He went for it and dived through. A gurgling sound came from a ditch between two rows of houses. A few feet ahead, Steve lay on his back, his quarry, whoever he was, nowhere in sight.

Joe kneeled by his friend's side but didn't dare lift him. Unable to think, he pressed his hand over Steve's neck below the chin where the bullet entered, as if he could arrest the spurting blood. It quickly soaked the front of his shirt. Steve's eyes bore into his. The big guy was trying to say something.

"Shhh…," Joe said. "Lay still. It's gonna be alright." Tears streamed down his cheeks.

In Steve's last willful effort, words came. "Pale eyes…like silver fish…" Then the face of Joe's friend slackened, his eyes staring past Joe and absorbing the blue of the sky.

Chapter 3

Dante Gayle

I mpressive," SAC Cowell said, leafing through Dante's transcripts. The head of the Criminal Division was the only eyesore in a model office sagging with catalog-perfect furniture; a fat bureaucrat with piggy eyes compensating for his unfortunate genetics with a forceful display of dominance and importance. "Your field counselor and class supervisor think highly of you. The key now is to pair you up with someone you can learn from. I suggest Marcus O'Neal."

"If you don't mind, sir, I would like to work with Agent Vasquez. I heard he just lost his partner," said the newly minted Fed standing in front of Cowell's desk. Young, black and super-sized, with the relaxed muscles of an intelligent face and heavy eyelids giving him a sleepy expression Cowell suspected to be misleading.

"Why Vasquez? I don't know what you were told, but I'll tell you, between us, he's a loner and inhospitable. With O'Neal you'll learn the ropes; he'll set you right. And he can certainly use someone like you. As your SAC, it's my duty to put you where your abilities are best utilized."

"If I can speak freely, sir?" Gayle's stare was respectful and his speech unhurried. "I heard Agent Vasquez has solved all the cases he's been given. They even call him 'Hound,' right? I gather he's not popular, but everybody agrees his work ethic is exceptional."

"Yeah, he spends a lot of extra hours on the job," Cowell said. "Although, to tell you the truth, none of his cases were much to speak of. The problem with him—he doesn't like anyone treading on his domain, which is not a good quality in an agent."

"They say he's an excellent SWAT leader, good at negotiations, and treats minorities with respect. Plus, he has 12-years of experience."

"So you like how he treats minorities?" Cowell's sarcastic stare measured Dante's hulk. "Have it your way, then. His partner's death is still under investigation. But if you want to take the dead guy's place, so be it. Maybe you'll be luckier."

§ § §

"The murder of a federal agent is not a local matter."

"I didn't say the case shouldn't belong to us. I'm saying *you* shouldn't handle it. You've been running amok," Cowell said. "Get some rest. You are overdue for a nice long vacation, Vasquez. When you're back, work on some routine stuff; nothing to overheat the old apparatus." Cowell tapped his forehead with his finger. "I'm sorry about Steve. But we don't need any more screw ups. The time of the lone cowboy is long over."

"There won't be any screw-ups," Joe said. "I give you my word." He stared darkly at his boss. "If you don't give me this case, I'll resign."

Cowell leaned back in his chair, appraising Joe. Joe didn't care what the SAC saw. He avoided mirrors lately. The haggard, aged man reflected in them was unfamiliar to him.

"Well…" Cowell gazed around in pretend thoughtfulness.

Joe tried to quiet his internal tremble.

"Have at it then," the magnanimous blowhard expounded. "I expect you to keep your promise. Also, we've got a new guy, a new grad, recently finished SWAT training too. He needs a mentor."

That was just great. Just what he needed—a babysitting gig. Joe nodded curtly and headed to the door.

The SAC spoke to his back, as if in afterthought. "By the way, Hound."

Joe turned, his hand on the knob.

"The A.D.C. considers the last operation successful and your conduct commendable. The correction's shrink says Gonzales had a paranoid episode. He wouldn't be much of a loss, but the press would have a field day if he was shot. We got a nifty article instead. Check the L.A. Times today."

§ § §

His work was his crutch and his salvation. His knack for it ensured his addiction from the time when, as a little kid, he would recover household items misplaced by his mother, or help their neighbor to retrace steps to find the twenty dollar bill the old guy dropped.

Since the day after Steve's death, Joe holed up in his tiny office. He slept in the recliner across from his desk piled with papers. There were also piles on the floor. The computer screen hurt Joe's tired eyes, so he read print-outs. The

18

papers multiplied and spread to his recliner, turning his office into a messy nest no one else could navigate.

Mallow was not just Joe's best friend, but also the only one who broke into the prideful, shabby castle of solitude Joe had lived in since childhood. They both hailed from fatherless families and met in the navy where they earned their college scholarships. They struggled through their studies together and together applied to the FBI. Unlike Joe, Steve had other friends, but Joe was by far his closest. From the get-go, they were tighter than most brothers.

By the second day after Steve's funeral, and the first day of the Blake Johnson case being officially assigned to him, Joe had learned a few things. The discarded Polaroid from the apartment on Garden Lane pictured a human thigh matching in proportions and general appearance the right thigh of Blake Johnson found near Wilmington. Of course, a smart-ass defense lawyer would say it could be a picture of any thigh, or something made to look like a thigh. The picture, as well as Blake's hat, could have been placed in the apartment by the real killer, a good lawyer would point out—perhaps Gonzales himself. It didn't matter that Gonzales had no faculties to pull off such a killing and a cover-up; he was still an imbalanced and violent offender. And the murder of Steve, the smart-ass lawyer would argue, was likely self-defense considering that, while in hot pursuit, Mallow likely had failed to demonstrate to the perp that he was a federal agent.

But for now, Joe didn't care what the lawyer could say. What mattered was Joe's belief that the Polaroid was a picture of Blake's thigh, that more pictures of murdered Blake made it into a blackmail package of some sort, accompanied by a warning along the lines of the crumpled note, *Back off or I'll lay you out*, and that the killer of Blake and Steve sent the package to one or both of the people in the photos found under the mattress. Joe searched for recent crimes involving dismemberment in the NIB Reporting System database. After he came up empty-handed, he called Ron Stout to see if the detective unearthed anything through other means.

Stout bristled at the implication of being expected to perform such a search. His resources were limited, he told Joe. At the moment, he was busy looking for a guy who raped a student at a local community college. Joe guessed Stout was demoted to handling rapes after failing a murder case and wasn't happy to talk to the Fed who took over the latter.

Too tired for diplomacy, Joe hung up on Stout. The student, a white middle class girl, apparently deserved more effort. Joe got a feeling that some of the interviews Stout had conducted would need to be redone.

The lack of valuable fingerprints presented another challenge. Joe went back to the apartment with a couple of forensic technicians the day before Steve's funeral. They combed through the place and picked up enough prints, too many and mostly of bad quality, to keep the lab busy for a while. The manila envelope was clean and so was the Polaroid, the newspapers, the other paper waste from the garbage bag, and the bag itself. The only prints were on the photos and belonged to a technician from a busy photo-processing place close to the duplex, which Joe located simply by using his GPS. The killer wasn't taking any chances. The absence of food, linens, or even scissors at the apartment confirmed that he occupied it on an as-needed basis.

The photo lab technician remembered that the photos of the woman and the grey-haired man, as well as of the barn, came from a larger collection, but he didn't remember what was on the rest of the pictures, nor who brought them in for development.

The 80-year old landlord of the duplex, Mr. Crabber, lived with his son's family and rarely visited his property. The rental agreement between him and his tenant was arranged by phone about a year ago. The renter, who called himself Will Brown, was punctual in his month-to-month cash payments. The social security number he provided to Mr. Crabber belonged to a retired geezer who had no idea his identity had been stolen. In his rat-nest of hoarded receipts, Mr. Crabber managed to find the phone number the tenant supplied. It dialed a phone booth at LAX.

The editors of the two newspapers found in the garbage bag emailed Joe the missing articles. Upon his follow-up requests, both local correctional facilities faxed to him the related case pages the articles mentioned. Joe lifted a mug shot of an ugly, burly man from his desk. James McKee, nicknamed "The Strangler," incarcerated in ADX right before his untimely demise last November. He picked up the next print, an image of McKee stretched dead on his cot in a puddle of blood. Next, a close-up of McKee's face, a good deal uglier than in life, with a noose cutting deep into his neck. The killer, who the article said was never seen by anyone, penetrated McKee's cell, strangled him, and evaporated into the night. The body was found during morning roll call.

Joe believed that McKee deserved the isolation and misery of the Florence Maximum Security prison. But there was a particular brutality about the payback inflicted on someone already living in a close approximation of hell on earth. One would think they'd have the best security in a Super Max.

Joe read on. The execution almost matched the Strangler's own method of killing. Almost. McKee didn't cut his victims, and the primary cause of his demise was hanging. But the coroner's report mentioned a few cuts on McKee's wrists, behind the knees and groin matching the pattern of the cuts found on Blake's body. The cuts were done while he was still alive, hence a good deal of blood on the mattress.

Joe laid the mug shot back on his desk and lifted another. The victim presented on it was the subject of the second missing newspaper article. Conrad Bacholski of Arizona was ash-haired with close-set eyes in a bony face. According to his case papers, Bacholski and an accomplice would invite seasonal workers over for a drink on pay-day, drug and bind them, then drown them in Bacholski's bathtub.

Joe picked up another photo. Conrad again, but this time face down in the prison's gutter. 'Bacholski drowned in the sewer during what appeared to be an escape attempt,' the article said. Describing Bacholski's injuries, the Arizona coroner reported some deep forearms gashes, their presence attributed to the escapee squeezing through the narrow rusted sewer grate. Joe found the stipulation lame. There was no mention of the grate's material analysis to confirm the examiner's theory. Joe studied the photo of the cuts in the coroner's report. He wasn't a forensic pathologist but, to him, while their jagged appearance could result from an accidental laceration, it could also be inflicted by a killer or killers pressed for time. The blood loss from those cuts wasn't significant enough to warrant a special mention in the report. Still, he or they went through the trouble of executing Bacholski by drowning instead of simply killing him in some other, more convenient way. Joe's gut insisted—since he, unlike the Arizona's investigators, also knew about McKee's execution as well as Blake's murder—that those weird cuts were purposeful and possibly a hurried attempt of bloodletting.

No other injuries were found on Bacholski's body, except for some minor bruising. The relative ease with which Bacholski drowned could be explained by traces of chloroform in his clothing, although the evidence of the chloroform presence was deemed inconclusive.

It seemed likely the original blackmail package contained the two clipped-out articles, along with some photographs developed at the lab near the apartment and the pictures of Blake's body. The nature and timing linked the two prison executions, as did the fact the blackmailer and presumed Blake's killer collected the newspaper articles describing them. But was there a link between the body cuts present in those executions and Blake's murder? Could all three crimes be committed by the same individual or individuals? Joe imagined that a psychopathic bastard nervy enough to shoot Steve, a highly trained agent and ex-Navy

Seal, and twisted enough to kill a teenage boy by draining his blood and butchering the body, was equal to the task of dispatching two incarcerated serial killers in a manner matching their own modus operandi while bleeding them a little first. For the perv, the bleeding could have a symbolic meaning of some sort. Or he simply enjoyed the procedure. So, for now, Joe decided to assume that the killer of Blake was also the killer of the inmates. Besides the bleeding, the incarceration appeared to be the other common feature of all three murders—after all, Blake did spend a brief time in juvie.

So, how did the man and the woman from the photos fit into all of this?

Joe emailed copies of the photos to D.C. a few days ago, to the attention of Mike Berryhill, Steve's first mentor and partner in Washington when Steve and Joe graduated from Quantico and worked for a while under different bosses. After they finished their stunt in D.C., they both returned to L.A. Berryhill moved on to bigger and better things, but he and Steve stayed in touch. Joe knew he could rely on Mike's help if he needed to fast-track things or avoid official channels to get information, especially if any such help contributed to finding Steve's killer.

Still, he didn't expect for Berryhill to come through so fast. Hearing the familiar whistling of the fax, he got up, expecting more of the Arizona or Colorado case papers. But when he picked up the sheet and saw his mistake, he understood why it took Mike only two days to fish this one out.

An enlarged print of an official White House I.D was airbrushed and taken some years ago, but he recognized the thick mane of silver hair and the patrician composure of the face right away; he saw too much of it lately while staring at the woman's face alongside it. The old guy from the photographs was Texas Independent Senator Damien Sheppard.

§ § §

Joe was clearing space in the middle of his desk to build a new pile designated for the important person of politics connected to his case when someone knocked on the door. "Come in," he called, in a voice devoid of any welcome.

The man who entered was young, large and black. "Dante Gayle," he said in a rich baritone, "reporting for duty."

Joe examined his new partner morosely. Gayle's heavy-lidded eyes gazed back at him from an unperturbed, smooth-as-an-egg face. As tall as Mallow, but where Mallow was muscled, broad-shouldered and brusque, Joe's new partner was meaty and loose with male-boobs and sloping shoulders. The kid looked about twenty-five. Must have gone straight to college and then moved directly to the FBI.

In spite of the lack of actual likeness, Gayle's face reminded Joe of Bob Marley. Joe had nothing against Bob Marley—he even had an old Marley CD shuffling somewhere in the obscure bowels of his car. He just didn't want Bob Marley for a partner. For that matter, he didn't want any partner. He missed and needed Steve—loyal, even-minded, sharp Steve. Since Steve was no more, Joe needed no one.

The big boy's curious eyes, followed by Joe's jealous ones, went to the piles on the floor. "I think I can be useful," he said.

Like a small pox blanket, Joe thought.

To discourage visitors, he had removed all but one office chair. Dante's eyes stopped on the recliner hosting a pile of papers. With more nimbleness than his body shape suggested, he moved to the only chair behind Joe's desk and pegged his behind into it. He looked around for some means to break the ice and found none. That didn't deter him.

"I hear you're from Guatemala," he said with a big smile. "I've gone there a couple of times with my cousins, backpacking and such. Great country." Dante's expression grew startled at the sight of Joe's changing for the worst.

Joe gritted his teeth. He never talked about his origins and never visited his fatherland where his parents' families still lived, not even when he had traveled in Latin America with his now estranged wife. But the damn kid didn't know his reasons, he reminded himself. Joe picked up the folder with the collection of the case paperwork from his desk, slapped the Damien Sheppard ID picture Berryhill faxed to him to the top, and dropped the whole thing in Dante's lap.

"Why don't you redirect your curiosity," he said. "Make your own copies of everything and try to make sense of it, free style. Don't come back until you get somewhere."

He sat on the edge of his desk and folded his arms, short of saying, *Chop-chop, big slug; hope not to see you for a while*. His tension lessened as his new partner eased out of his small domain. And so ended Joe's first meeting with Dante.

Chapter 4

A Night at Home

Joe stepped inside the room and quietly closed the door. He waited until he heard only his own breathing. His eyes acclimated and made out the outlines of the crib. For a few moments, he thought he could feel his boy's presence.

Then a beam of light from a passing car broke through the sheer curtains. In one devastating moment, it illuminated the smoothness of the baby blanket inside. A cold hand in Joe's chest woke up and squeezed. His son was gone for eight months, his tiny body rotted in the bleak dirt hole next to the four year old grave of Joe's mother. Alberto would have been walking by now, talking a little, calling his father something silly. Joe's imagination rehearsed these over and over, without mercy.

The room was a mausoleum to Joe's fatherhood. He wouldn't let Lana, Alberto's mother and Joe's soon-to-be ex-wife, touch anything here. The baby clothes still filled the drawers, the tricycle Alberto never grew up enough to ride still stood in the corner, and his baby toys still overflowed the big basket next to it. Soon after their son's funeral, Lana wanted to donate all his things to her church. Joe would not let her. The toys, the clothes, and the crib remained. Lana, on the other hand, had moved out, and the arrangement sat well with him.

It had been almost five months since she left. She said she couldn't stay in the house or with Joe the way he was now. They didn't talk. A few days before she left, she dragged Joe out on a date and suggested they should try to get pregnant again. He used to appreciate his wife's even-tempered, habitual sweetness. Now, he found it to have the unwholesome aftertaste of confectioners' sugar and saw it for what it was—the incapacity for real love, real grief. After moving out, she emailed him demanding that he go through grief counseling as a condition for her return. Joe didn't answer the email. Instead, he filed for divorce.

For eight months, he immersed himself in his cases, however mundane and unrewarding they typically were. That's all he had—his work and Steve, whom he saw mostly at work too. Steve got married over a year ago, was expecting, and tried to spend more time home with Christie. Now she decided to stay with her parents in Bloomington until the birth. Taking her to the airport was on Joe's to-do list tomorrow.

He left Alberto's room and walked down the semi-dark hallway. This was his first visit home since his recent near-relocation to his office at Wilshire. He needed a little more comfort, a real bed for a change, and a hot shower in the morning. Much footwork waited.

He bought the house, the first he and his mother ever owned, a year after he started working at the bureau. It was old, and he put some good work into it. The hallway's entire length was lined with shelves he'd built before Isabel got sick to store all the books they collected: the mysteries and detective stories he favored, and the novels his mother devoured by Márquez, Benedetti, Rulfo, Casares, and other South American classics, almost all of them in Spanish. He hadn't bought any new ones in a long time. And the last volume, which he never finished, gathered dust in the guest bathroom, his customary reading room.

He didn't go to the master bedroom; it no longer felt right or good to sleep there, in his old marital bed, under the puffy, overly-warm comforter. Instead, he headed to his study. Converted from his mother's bedroom and located at the end of the hall, it greeted him with the permanently-open futon, the sheets which needed changing, and many months' worth of clutter on Isabel's old writing desk. He opened the window wide and deeply inhaled fresh air, the rain droplets spraying his face. When his chest was soaked, he turned on the ceiling fan. As of late, it became hard for him to cool at night; his body seemed to require freezing to help him fall asleep.

A desire to smoke came from nowhere—strong; not just a passing wonder about the almost forgotten taste in his mouth, but a craving, no longer tinged with a memory of nausea the very first inhale would likely bring.

He smoked his last cigarette at thirteen—or, to stand corrected, his last pack and half. It was the day his mother caught him in the bushes behind their old apartment building lighting up, not knowing what he was doing yet but trying. His whole experience up to that point came down to about five smokes, and he had quite a bit remaining, the wage a chain-smoking ex-military neighbor dude paid him for mowing his yard. Smoking seemed fun. It might help him fit in more, give him something to do during the breaks in school, and make his loneliness less noticeable; plus, he started to like the taste.

He thought the cigarettes he earned would last him a while, but found he was wrong when his mother caught him red-bogeyed. She didn't get mad, although her coolness scared him so he did what she told him. *It's okay, son, suck it in. Go on, don't stop!* He finished the cigarette up in one uninterrupted gulp. *Take another one. Here, I'll light it for you.* He smoked the next, and the next, fast, her quiet voice urging him on, her dark eyes never leaving his. He went through all his stash in less than a quarter hour, until a violent cough seized him and he was choking on his vomit.

Afterward, he missed three days of school and was sick for almost a month. All throughout his twenties, the mere thought of a cigarette would unsettle his stomach. Someone might call his mother's behavior child abuse, but he knew better. She loved him hard enough to be willing to hurt him in the short run to inoculate him against the insidious poison.

The inoculation worked till recently, but the desire was coming back, whispering that his mother's concerns no longer mattered and a shortened existence would be a blessing. And tonight, with his empty life in his empty house, the real urge returned. He almost wished he grabbed a pack at the gas station on the way home.

No, he didn't. He needed a clear, clean mind now more than ever, not addled and altered by addiction. Plus, smoking may bring pleasure, and Joe didn't want any. He had guilt enough.

He undressed and slid under the thin blanket. After a while he pushed it aside, leaving only a sheet. One great thing about his office at work was the air conditioning. He never got around to installing a unit at home because it didn't seem to be needed before. The time lagged, and he tried to get along with it by breathing evenly. He tried to empty his mind, but the memories kept coming into the void.

His little boy, soon after he was born, the brows arched in permanent surprise over big curious eyes that, in just a month after his birth, became hazel—the cross between his father's brown and his mother's blue. And his ecstatic grin whenever Joe's face was close. The boy almost never cried, never complained, and slept through the night, the parents rarely hearing a peep from him until 5 or 6 in the morning. The most easy, sweet baby.

Then one day, Joe woke up on his own around 6:30 a.m., alarmed by the break in the routine. Alberto was 6-months old, and they had moved his crib into the nursery and installed a baby monitor…The doctor said it was sudden infant death syndrome, a term they offered when lacking an explanation.

Joe drifted in and out of unconsciousness. Then, closer to dawn, he slipped into the dreams—one familiar, and another new.

He came to the crib and looked down at Alberto. He touched him, and this time, his son woke up, stared at Joe with the wide green eyes, and smiled. Isabel put her hand on Joe's shoulder, watching him and her grandson with immeasurable love. That's when Joe remembered that she was dead and never knew Alberto. As soon as he reached to touch her, a lump caught in his throat and she disappeared. And when he turned back to the crib, so did Alberto.

Then Joe rode with Steve as they always did while partners, but neither of them was driving. A shadow, a menacing presence, sat at the wheel. But nothing mattered, even that Steve was dead, because Steve was still around as long as Joe didn't make a move and kept silent. But Joe's longing was too strong. And as soon as he turned to see Steve's face, his friend was gone.

§ § §

He woke up crying.

Outside, Arleta awakened with the tires' screech of cars emerging from driveways. It was six a.m. Joe lay for a while, then got up and shut the window. Unhinged, he needed anchoring, even if it brought more pain. He staggered to the closet and kneeled before an old, maple-veneer trunk stored against the wall. He removed the shoe boxes from the lid and opened it for the first time in years.

He pulled his mother's things out one by one. Out came her blouses and a few pairs of slacks. She wore these whenever they had guests. He remembered the evening about five years ago when he first brought willowy, conventionally pretty Lana to dinner. He hadn't thought of marrying her, but he needed someone by his side. Isabel was sick, barely venturing out, and, they both knew, dying. After the dinner, when Lana was gone, his mother looked at him with her sunken, all-seeing eyes and stated, "You don't love this girl."

"It's too early to say," he had protested.

"We have hot blood, José. You've dated her for three months. If you are not sure now, you'll never be. It's hard to live your whole life with someone you don't love. Marriage is not something you try. Not in our family. Once you are in, you are in."

Isabel understood Joe better than Steve, and apparently even better than Joe understood himself. Lana didn't understand him at all. He didn't mind it before. He might feel content enough in his marriage, overall, if he had his mother and Alberto. He could get by.

No, that wasn't it, he thought, because if Isabel was alive there would be no marriage. Not to Lana. Isabel's death pushed him into it. He needed someone. Lana moved in a month later. They got married and in two years Alberto was born.

As devout a Catholic as his mother was, Joe knew she would understand him breaking up with his wife; she loved him too much not to. *She DOES understand me*, he corrected himself. He wanted to believe that Isabel was still around, still near somehow. This faith turned his pain into an enduring but bearable longing.

He pressed her old dress to his face, inhaling the lingering smell of rose oil she used in place of perfume, and then put it on the floor with the rest of her clothes. He found her reading glasses, some of his school papers she had saved, a tattered notebook of recipes in her Spanish handwriting, and a robe he bought her for her birthday with his first paycheck when he was eighteen, bundled around something…

Joe unwrapped it and took out, one by one, a framed photo of his parent's wedding…a stack of letters held with a rubber band addressed in Spanish to his mother from his father and posted with Guatemalan stamps…his father's old family album…Joe paused, holding the last object—Rafa's flannel pajama shirt, complete with a bullet hole and rusty spots of long-dried blood.

Joe stared at his findings. While growing up, he believed that Isabel had gotten rid of these objects. Their absence had sealed the silent pact between them, never to mention the man that Joe had struggled his entire childhood not to miss. Yet here they were, keepsakes of the dead, preserved lovingly for Joe one day to chance upon.

Numbly, he started placing everything back into the trunk then stopped, holding the letters. They belonged to his mother. He knew he should destroy them…But he also knew he couldn't. It was his professional habit compelling him to examine them, he told himself. He decided to keep them in his office.

Chapter 5

Asia Johnson

J oe ate at his customary spot, a hole-in-the-wall Mexican restaurant serving an excellent, if greasy, breakfast. He then drove his well-used Subaru Outback to see Asia Johnson, the mother of Blake. To his surprise, he found out she moved to one of the transitional suburbs. Her new place, only half an hour drive from downtown L.A., must have been a vast improvement over her former residence at a housing project in one of the oldest districts in South Central.

He left her a message the day after Steve's death, but she hadn't returned his call. He called her again yesterday afternoon, and this time she answered and they set up the appointment. Detective Stout had already asked most of the questions Joe had for her. But sometimes, the passage of time brings into focus elements muddied by the first shock. At least, so Joe hoped.

His GPS led him to a bucolic area populated by modest but clean homes. Low and middle of the middle class, he guessed. Teachers, plumbers, nurses, and the like. Asia lived in a one-story duplex. A police car was parked in the next driveway; her neighbor, a cop, was home for lunch.

Joe knocked on the door and Asia opened it right away, as if she waited behind. She had closely-cropped, wiry hair and more loose skin than her fifty-six years warranted, like someone who used to be plump but shriveled all at once. She didn't say anything when he introduced himself, but led him in, nodded at a worn chair, and sat herself in another. Joe took a seat, and she stared at him with her tragic brown eyes, her face impassive.

"I'm sorry I have to bother you with this again, Mrs. Johnson."

"I've been in the hospital near a month. Came home to a message on my answering machine. Called you back, and a lady said she'd let you know."

That would be McCollum, Joe thought. She must have told Cowell, and Cowell had treated Asia's call as unimportant.

"So you were sick for a month?" he asked.

"Longer. That's just the stay at St. Vincent. My heart's no good."

"I'm sorry to hear that." Joe reflected on how lame and commonplace his words sounded. He could do nothing about it. He was ill equipped to offer anyone solace. He took out his list and went over the routine questions first, and her patient answers matched her previous ones.

At last, he got to the worst. He opened the case he brought with him and extracted a gallon Ziploc containing the yellow baseball cap found in the apartment on Garden Lane. "Do you recognize this?"

Asia took the baggie. Her lips moved without uttering a sound while her hands rubbed the plastic, as if trying to feel the hat within. She nodded without giving it back to Joe. "Kids got no business dying before their mothers," she said. "When a mother dies before her child, she half-dies. But when a child goes before…both go."

Joe thought about the time she spent waiting for the cops to do something. She probably believed this FBI agent was no different, but still tried to guilt him into some kind of action. "You have another son, Adam," he said, and immediately felt stupid.

"He's my whole life. He's in Canada now."

"Canada?" Joe gaped at her. From what he knew, Adam Johnson, aged fifteen, went to the same school as his brother.

"In a boarding school," Asia clarified. "It's safer. I miss him badly. But I'll be moving there soon myself. He went a couple months ago. The pastor from our church flew with him. I was too sick to go. It's better this way. Before, I lived in fear every day that the man who killed my oldest will take this one, too. Every morning Adam stepped out that door, my heart was racing."

"How did you…Has your church helped you?" Joe asked.

"They did some legwork, but it was Gabrielle who started it all. She helped us a good deal."

"Who is Gabrielle?"

"Oh, a bit of a story there." Asia's face lit up a little. "Goes back to my Blake being taken to juvie. She was a shrink who talked to him, proved he was innocent. The lady is a certified angel. We didn't even know about the scholarship. All Adam's expenses are paid."

"He must be a good student," Joe remarked, flabbergasted.

"He is. Almost as good as his brother."

Another surprise. Blake Johnson a good student?

"She contacted me when…when they found Blake," Asia said. "We kept in touch after. I told her how I pray Adam would grow up and leave the projects. School there was bad, and I've got no money to help him. That good soul figured it all out. She found me this place, got some assistance. I'd never afford it on my disability. Doctors put a pacemaker in me, so I can't work. It's my own fault. Shouldn't drive myself crazy, thinking how Blake was before he died… Gabrielle told me about the boarding school too. Then the pastor helped us fill out all the applications. Adam will have a good schooling, go on to college."

Joe thought the story a small miracle, a reminder that there were some good, caring people in the world. Learning, in the midst of this depressing visit, that Blake's brother may have had a sunnier future warmed him up a bit. Still, his instinct cocked its ear and his Hound brain probed for a possible underlining to this development, even some connection to the crime. He'd need to look into this, he thought.

But his likely misguided misgivings aside, it was great to see a little light in Asia's worn face. He thought of his own mother. During his childhood, they lived in slums too. When he turned fourteen, on the brink of a boy's most troublesome years, she pulled all the stops, filled out piles of applications, found a second job as a night attendant in a hotel owned by a Guatemalan couple, and moved them into a tiny apartment in the suburbs—and him into a much better school. But his mother was healthier and stronger than Asia then, shrewder too, and she didn't go through the hardest heartbreak of all, losing her child.

"Let's hope, Adam will stay off drugs," Joe said.

"He does!" Asia said. "And Blake never touched the stuff, no matter what the cops say."

It was natural for a mother to be in denial. The tissues of Blake's battered body confirmed the cops' version of his character. Still…Joe thought of his own mother who not only adored him, but also knew him best.

His doubting expression agitated Asia. "I'm telling you, Blake was a good boy! You go talk to Dennis Bosko, his counselor at school! He'll tell you."

"Were any other adults in close contact with him?" Joe knew that Blake's father had been dead for several years.

"His uncle Darrel. He lives in Alaska, but they talked on the phone. His chemistry teacher, Mr. Potter, used to give Blake extra assignments. Blake got A's and B's all through that class. And of course, the counselor in the juvenile center, Don Selvage. He liked Blake. And most important, Gabrielle. She helped clear my boy; she saw right through him."

"Tell me more about her," Joe asked.

"She came from New York to do a demonstration for the other counselors. She questioned Blake some special way—to prove he wasn't involved in anything. And they reviewed his file and let him go. What's her last name? Something foreign sounding…Oh, Lord, my memory isn't so good. I call her Gabrielle. We don't misses or ma'am each other. Wait, I'll find it for you." Asia got up, still talking as she went to the bedroom. "She mostly calls me. It's hard to reach her sometimes."

Joe heard a drawer being pulled out and the rustle of papers.

Asia returned with a card. "Here." She read, "Dr. Gabrielle Lubovich."

Joe took out his notebook and wrote down the name, the phone and email, and the address, a PO Box in New Jersey. He also wrote, *ask juvie counselor about Blake's interview*. "You said you're planning to move to Canada?"

"In a couple months when I'm stronger. A place near Vancouver. Their child protective service needs help with the disabled children. I'll take care of some tiny ones. I can do it. I love lil' ones. They'll give me a room, and I'll be close to Adam."

A few more questions and Joe was done. He looked at the Ziploc on her lap, but instead of releasing it, she asked, "Where'd you get my boy's cap?"

"We found where the killer kept your son," and he told her about the visit to the apartment. When he got to Steve's death and needed to stop, she took his hand into both of hers, her eyes peering with compassion. His tears fell, giving in to the comradeship of grief. She just sat with him, quiet. Then, she gave him the Ziploc and walked him to the door.

"I'll find your son's killer," he promised.

"I know," she said. "You aren't like the rest."

He left with a wrench in his heart, much as he imagined her pacemaker might feel. *When a mother dies before her child, she half-dies*, Asia Johnson had said. *You get him*, Isabel Vasquez said in Joe's head as he got into his car. *Do it for me, and Alberto, and Steve.*

The day loomed crisp. Even meeting Christie, later in the afternoon, and the anticipation of their sad reminiscences on the way to LAX didn't weigh on him as before. He had his task and the right not to drown in wretchedness. He would tell Steve's widow she had a right to life, too, and a duty to her soon-to-be-born kid.

Chapter 6

Dandelion

Dallas—middle of October

With the piercing ring of the bell, the school day was over. If only he could sneak off without running into Coghill and his pimpled henchman, Middleton.

Brandon Mole grabbed his battered backpack and bolted out of the classroom while his teacher still dictated the homework in a monotone voice raised to overcome the end-of-class clamor. Brandon, aka 'Dandelion,' was a narrow teen of less than average height and athletic ability. His nickname was given to him by Coghill & Company, in spite of his obvious surname, because of the stiff yellow curls adorning his freckled face.

He emerged, one of the first out of C-wing, reached the corner of the building and peeked out. "Fuck," he whispered disheartened. Coghill and Middleton were hanging in the parking lot, a no-man's land that lay between the school and the bus stop. Were these two ever in class?

It would be a long way but a much better chance to be missed by the overgrown retards with itchy knuckles if he turned back and circled behind the school's portables. Dandelion stepped off the sidewalk to avoid the opposite current of the emerging teenage crowd and trudged warily to the end of the wing. When he reached it, there were no more people around, the din receding behind.

"Brandon? Hey! Brandon!"

He didn't know at first where the call came from. Then, he saw the police car parked on the street behind the row of trees. The car's nose pointed in the same direction Dandelion headed. The cop must have waited for him to come out and then followed. That was considerate of him. If he intercepted Dandelion in the parking lot, in everybody's view, it would have been a disaster. Not that Dandelion's denial saved him from harassment. But if Coghill and his stupid jocks knew for sure it was Mole who ratted out their cozy group to the principal, who in turn went to the cops, after they vandalized the library depository two weeks ago, they would fucking kill him. Dandelion trudged toward the idling police car. Its driver remained inside, in the shadows. He motioned the boy to the back seat.

Dandelion sighed and got in. "You should arrest the fuckers already," he said at the barred partition and the back of the cop's head. "Coghill has made my life hell. How long does it take to investigate something like this? Can't you guys figure out fingerprints and all that crap?"

"It's not that simple," the cop said without turning.

"The vice-principal promised that I wouldn't need to talk to the police. I told him everything. What else do you want from me?"

"Buckle up and keep your head down if you don't want anyone to see you," the cop said.

Dandelion did as he was told. The car took off and veered onto the road. The doors locked automatically with a click. There weren't any door handles in the back. *Treating me like a fucking criminal,* Dandelion thought.

The car turned onto another deserted street. The boy met his driver's eyes in the rear view mirror. They were unusually light, the color of burnished steel. Brandon looked back. His school disappeared swiftly in the back window. Suddenly he missed it all—the school, the crowd, the bus which would take him home, and even the bullies in the parking lot. And as if knowing that he had seen them all for the last time, grave misery touched his heart.

Chapter 7

Gonzales' Mission

Los Angeles

Not bald, not wrinkled, not fat, not thin. All around medium. Nothing prominent except for the eye color. That's why your guy can't recall much. Especially after so much time has passed," Bon Lee said.

The young Korean, a talented sketch artist borrowed from the LAPD, and Joe were looking at the color pencil portrait Lee and Gonzales worked on for over an hour. The man Gonzales claimed he sold crack to at the apartment on Garden Lane, seemed to be a mousy creature, unremarkable except for his narrow, light eyes. *Like silverfish…*

Joe sat across from Lee and Gonzales in the county jail's visiting room, reserved for their art session.

"I am sorry," Gonzales said. "I wish I could help more."

"It's better than nothing," Joe said.

Gonzales gained some weight, was clean-shaven, wore a blue jumpsuit, and seemed to be in good spirits. The new drugs the doctors prescribed for him appeared to be working. His court day was approaching and Joe intended to testify on his behalf.

Lee gave the sketch to Joe, gathered his pencils and took off.

"I'm really sorry about your friend," Gonzales said to Joe in Spanish. "If I can do anything, just ask. I won't snitch on one of my own, but anything else I'm your man."

Joe took a measure of the young man, thinking. The inmates' interrogation transcripts from the Colorado and Arizona prisons made him think of a code of silence surrounding McKee and Bacholski's deaths.

"How is your mood?" he asked in English. "Stable?"

"I can think straight," Gonzales assured him. "I stick to my meds. They're not downers like the crap I took before."

"Maybe you *can* do something," Joe said, "but think it over carefully." And he explained the gist of it.

"I'll do it!" Gonzales said after he understood what Joe needed from him.

"Remember, it's one of the worst prisons in the country, the Super Max. You'll need to mix with other inmates. I'll do my best to ensure someone watches your back, but at times you'll be on your own. You should think about it more."

"I've decided! It's good!" Gonzales' black eyes were bright.

"Okay," Joe said. "I'll set the wheels in motion. The sooner you become my ears, the better. And after a month or so I'll pull you out, even if you don't hear anything."

A few days later, Manuel Gonzales' trial was postponed. He was given a new, temporary identity of GD Martinez, a convicted cop killer, transferred to the USP in Tucson, and placed in the same wing where Conrad Bacholski was housed before his fatal escape attempt.

§ § §

Joe sifted through information on Sheppard he collected from the Vault, NARA's electronic reading room, and good old Google. A well-to-do Texas family, oily background, Yale education. A widower. One son deceased. The man didn't lead a happy life, in spite of his advantages and achievements.

Joe read on. He found it interesting that Sheppard, even though he ended up a politician, didn't seem to plan it this way. His degree was in psychiatry, and his area of interest forensic psychology.

Joe marked a number of Sheppard's articles, to order and take a look at later. He noted that, for the last twenty-odd years, the Senator hadn't published anything of significance. His name appeared for a while among the co-authors of the articles written by, most likely, his graduate students, and then even that stopped. Joe compared the dates. The last time Sheppard wrote anything scientific was two years before he first ran for the Senate. Which, of course, made sense. But Joe had a feeling he overlooked something.

He took a couple of pills to halt his budding headache and returned to browsing Sheppard's official website. He made another note to himself, *Obtain list of Sheppard's staff.* He came across a few pictures. There were women posing with the Senator in some of them, but not the one from the photographs he and Steve found.

As he worked, Joe's thoughts would occasionally turn to the Good Samaritan who helped Asia Johnson. He looked forward to talking to Dr. Lubovich about Blake. She could have some insights whether the boy had some secret life.

Someone knocked on his door.

"Go ahead," Joe called, and in came the young Dante Gayle, of big hulk and male-boobs, wearing a look of triumph and trying to cover it with a phony expression of humility. Joe occupied the only chair, so Dante remained standing.

"Let's hear it," Joe folded his arms.

Joe's new partner checked his notes. "First, Senator Sheppard. A Ph.D. in forensic psychiatry. Some interesting work on genetic links in psychopathic personality disorders. Was married for ten years to his college sweetheart. Lost his wife to cancer, never remarried. Had one son named Robert, or Bobby. Pretty much ditched science after his son's death. Some years later, entered politics…" Dante paused.

Joe was nodding, rocking his chair a bit to the rhythm.

Dante's face fell a little. "I wish you wouldn't send me chasing after things you already know yourself," he said.

"It's good practice for you," Joe said.

Dante continued in a voice that had lost enthusiasm. "His son was about the same age as Blake Johnson when he died. You probably already know how."

Joe stopped rocking.

"He was kidnapped in broad daylight, in Dallas. His chopped up body was discovered about a month later. They didn't have good forensics then, but they believed his blood was drained as the cause of death." Dante paused.

"Go on," Joe said quietly.

Dante perkiness returned. "I checked on women associated with Sheppard. I started with the most obvious ones, according to their age, Sheppard's students. Just a few of them fit, so it wasn't a big deal. I found this graduation picture on the Internet. It was taken about ten years ago." Dante placed a print in front of Joe.

The girl in the photo didn't look as sophisticated as in the photos from the suspect's apartment, and her face was younger and fuller. Joe wanted to applaud Dante.

"Gabrielle Lubovich," his new partner said. "Doctor Lubovich, after Sheppard was done with her. Has a long resume, writes articles on forensic psychiatry, speaks a few languages…I still need to find her present whereabouts."

"That's okay," Joe said automatically, his eyes on the picture. "I've got it."

"Damn!" Dante exhaled with exasperation. "I thought I got ahead of you at last!"

Joe shook his head and smiled. A sight Dante apparently didn't expect because he looked taken aback. "There's a storage closet at the end of the corridor," Joe said. "Mind bringing a second chair?"

§ § §

"Blake's killer could be the killer of Sheppard's son. Or it could be a copy-cat murder," Dante mused.

Joe, pacing to and fro in the tight space, shook his head. "The question is, *why* he sent the photos," he said. "That is, if he *did* send them."

"I'd say that hypothesis is pretty solid."

"It's still a hypothesis, Gayle." Joe paused, thinking. "I want you to make inquiries to all the major police departments about teenager killings similar to Blake's. If there's anything recent, you may find out quickly. If the same man killed Sheppard's son and Blake, he's been operating for years."

Dante made another note on his pad. "I'm trying to understand what motivates the killer," he said. "He drains a young doper of his blood; the motivation can be sexual. But he also executes two serial killers while they're incarcerated! What's his motivation there? Revenge? Or someone contracted him?"

"We don't know enough to come up with a motivation."

"Let's say he did kill Sheppard's son. The Senator gets something on him. Some implicating evidence. But the killer finds something about the Senator and sends him a warning. What could that be? An affair Sheppard is trying to keep secret with that woman?"

"Sheppard isn't married. And if the background records we pulled are recent, she isn't married, either. They wouldn't need to hide an affair." Joe stopped and gazed out of the narrow window. "You think they can be in a relationship? With that age difference?"

"He *is* a Senator. He used to be her advisor in grad school, and you know how it is with those charismatic professors and their adoring female students. The fact is they've obviously been close long after she got her Ph.D., which is unusual."

Joe was pacing again. "The interview she conducted with Blake..."

"Want me to look into that?"

"No," Joe said. "You've enough on your plate already." He met Dante's sly gaze. Joe appreciated the younger man's ability to connect dots, but not in this particular instance.

"Is that all?" Dante asked, innocently enough.

"Yes." Joe dropped into his seat. He caught himself folding his arms and his own defensive gesture annoyed him.

Dante, his good spirits departed once again, rose from the chair and grabbed it, about to take out.

For one weird, weak moment, Joe wanted to delay the rookie's departure. "Leave it," he said instead, "it's yours now."

Dante set the chair back and grinned. Discomforted, Joe waved him off.

§ § §

Joe's call was answered by Don Selvage himself.

"Yes, in part it was a demonstration for the L.A. Juvenile Justice counselors, but mostly we just wanted to help Blake," Selvage said. He sounded disheartened as if he was still affected by Blake's death. "That boy couldn't afford a lawyer. He should never have been detained in the first place. The evidence against him was all hearsay. You know how those young rascals are always trying to hang things on others and protect the real culprits. Blake was what you'd call a teacher's pet. Some of his more rowdy classmates resented that.

"In any case, I found out about this shrink, Dr. Lubovich, a rising star of some sort. She was coming to L.A. to demonstrate an alternative method of questioning to the forensic psychology graduate students. I contacted her myself.

"I offered Blake as her subject, told her about him. I even helped to organize the event. She was gracious, very sympathetic." His voice gained color at the memory. "Her demonstration floored us. And it sure cleared Blake. Too bad her method will never go mainstream. You can't train just anyone."

"Why is that?"

And Don Selvage explained it to him.

Chapter 8

The Polygraph and the Ice Cream Parlor

Dallas—end of October

Aslender young woman with dark, intense eyes walked down the second floor corridor of the Dallas FBI Headquarters. A gym hoodie and designer suit pants clung snug to her hard body. Her Italian shoes were sensible but elegant, and a roomy, sturdy, overpriced purse hung from her strong shoulder. While not much above average height, her confident posture made her appear taller. On a scale of horses, Gabrielle Lubovich was an Arabian.

She stopped in front of a door, listened for a few seconds to the nagging voice coming from inside, nudged, and the door opened a bit on its smooth, noiseless hinges. In the room, Professor James Weizlan, a withered man in his sixties, hovered over a barely out of his teens technician installing some new polygraph equipment.

Gabrielle stood in plain view but invisible, as if her vibes blended discretely with the background. After some tinkering under the discomforting gaze of the black spider eyes behind the Professor's gold-rimmed glasses, the young man clicked on start and several flat lines ran across a screen.

Gabrielle closed the door, went down the corridor, and into the women's restroom. When she emerged, her eyes were tearing, her face flushed, and her soft, stretchy jacket unzipped at the top revealing the upper thirds of her boobs, now hoisted to a maximum elevation. Her color turned to its normal pale hue before she made her way back. Reaching the door, she knocked and marched in.

The two men raised their heads and Weizlan's face hardened. "Miss Lubovich. To what do we owe the pleasure?" The icy glint in his eyes contradicted his dismissive tone.

"I would like you to reconsider signing my request to interview Baca," Gabrielle said, her English colored by a Slavic accent.

"I am not obligated to grant access to offenders kept in high-security facil-ities to independent researchers, even those with your connections. The last time I obliged, you got a confessed killer off death row." Weizlan tried to avoid looking at her jutted décolleté. "As you remember, it was my testimony that led to his conviction. Until you came waltzing in. Well, dear, no more. Find some other means to get your way. You have a talent for that, I'd say your biggest."

Gabrielle approached the table and inserted herself between the young and the old, making the former flush with her proximity. She gazed at the set up. "You should hire a fortune-teller instead, Professor," she said. "This thing can ruin a lot of innocent lives, as it almost ruined Brin James'."

"Only because he is guilty, Lubovich."

"*Doctor* Lubovich. You tend to forget my proper salutation, Doctor Weizlan."

Weizlan's face reddened. "A polygraph is an accepted method, *Miss* Lubovich. And ethical. Unlike the methods you employ."

"Yeah, I know, being ethical is so very important. I only wish it worked, too." She turned her friendly gaze at the technician, and he couldn't help smiling at her. "I tried polygraphs on my most interesting subjects, you know. Those bastards have no problems passing, as soon as they figure out how it works."

"That's not true," Weizlan said, looking less ambushed and more in the saddle. "Something I can demonstrate right now. Why don't we strap you in for a test drive? The equipment needs to be checked anyway."

Gabrielle arched an eyebrow. "I do have a weakness for virgins."

The technician swallowed.

"Let's bet," she said to Weizlan. "If you prove me wrong, you'll keep Baca out of my wanton clutches. If I prove you wrong, you'll sign my paper. Deal?"

Weizlan answered with a predatory smirk.

A few minutes later, Gabrielle sat across from the technician with the expendable bands around her thorax, electrodes attached to her palms, and a blood pressure cuff around her upper arm. He asked her all the usual control questions, periodically clearing his throat under her stare.

At one point, Weizlan's sharp eyes stopped at her feet. "Take off your shoes so we have no curling of the toes."

She nudged off her shoes.

"Do you own a dog?" the young man asked.

"Yes. A Doberman."

"Yes or no, please," Weizlan said.

"I feel like a criminal already," she complained to the technician.

"You have a very healthy pulse," he told her.

"Slow heartbeats are typical in people with under-developed conscience," Weizlan remarked.

"As well as in people who exercise a lot," Gabrielle explained to his sympathetic colleague.

"Concentrate on the test," Weizlan said.

"Are you married?" The technician asked another of the control questions from his list and colored.

"No." Gabrielle smiled. "Are you?"

He reddened more.

"Have you ever committed a crime?" The stern question came from Weizlan.

"No...Unless you count stealing a few coins from my mother's purse when I was little."

"I'm not married," the technician piped in.

"Have you ever assisted in a crime?" Weizlan asked, his eyes on the monitor.

"Not to my knowledge."

"Yes or no."

"No."

"Truth, so far," the technician commented.

Weizlan scowled. His coolness seemed to be dissipating. "Do you believe a punishment should match a crime?"

"Mmm...Elaborate, please, I don't understand the question."

"Should a murderer be executed with the same brutality he displayed toward his victim?"

Gabrielle stared at him, silent for a while. "I think it's a trick question, Professor Weizlan."

"Not at all. A rather simple one."

"A measure of brutality is subjective. One must take into consideration other factors, some mitigating, some aggravating. The answer can be given only on a case by case basis."

"You are being evasive, Miss Lubovich, but I've heard what I wanted to hear." Weizlan smiled.

"There was nothing to hear. I think you're trying to trap me, but I doubt you know what into yourself."

"Is your father deceased?"

"Yes." Gabrielle closed her eyes.

The technician nodded to himself at the steady lines running across the screen.

"Keep your eyes open. Was your father's death a direct consequence of his..." Weizlan made a show of searching for a word. "...behavior?"

Gabrielle's heart rate jumped. She opened her eyes. "What are you implying, Professor? That my parents deserved their fate?" Her words were deliberate.

"I only mentioned your father."

Gabrielle gazed at the wall. Her face was calm, but something savage lurked behind that calmness. "My father didn't bring his death on himself. Neither did my mother."

"So, no?"

"No!"

"This response can't be used," the technician said. "The subject's agitation is unrelated to the question itself."

Gabrielle smiled apologetically at him, turned her eyes back to the wall and took a few slow, deep breaths. Both the technician and Weizlan checked the screen. Gabrielle's heartbeat slowed down with promptness. The technician mouthed 'Wow!'

"Any more questions?" she asked. She seemed paler and drained.

"Do you believe that criminal tendencies are inherited?"

"Yes, to a degree. But you should stick to the actual test, James, instead of trying to rouse me. Give it a rest. It's been ten years."

Was the old lizard involved with her? Ten years ago he may still have been a man, the technician thought.

Gabrielle turned toward the open window and furrowed her brows. She rubbed briefly, absentmindedly, at her right upper arm. The technician recalled her doing this before. Must be a habitual gesture, he thought.

"Do you smell that?" she asked.

The men exchanged glances.

"It's pretty strong! Someone is smoking right outside!" Gabrielle gaped at them, as if not comprehending their dull senses. "Gosh, I can't stand it!"

"Don't you smoke?" Weizlan asked.

"Moi? No! Unless it's grass. And organic."

"Truth again," the technician said.

Weizlan peered at her with doubt, then at the lines.

"*That* was it?" Gabrielle asked. "Oh, well…you got me! I quit a good while ago. So the thing works, I guess."

"Still the truth," her young champion proclaimed.

Weizlan scowled at him. "Do you believe that Brin James is innocent?" he fired at Gabrielle.

"Shame on you, Professor. You know the answer." She sat upright and started pulling the electrodes off. The technician hurried to assist her.

She picked up her purse, walked to the window and got out a pack of cigarettes. She lit one and sucked in the smoke.

The two men watched her, engrossed. "Smoking is not allowed in the building," Weizlan muttered.

"What smoking?" She shrugged. "Don't you trust your lie detector?" She dropped the cigarette into the waste basket, pulled a paper out of her purse and handed it to him. "Pony up, Professor."

Without a word, grimacing, Weizlan scratched his signature underneath a few names already on the form.

"Thank you!" she said, and strode out of the room like a regal cat.

§ § §

Once outside, her proud posture crumbled and she fled to the restroom again. It was deserted when she ran in, ripped her jacket down her right shoulder and pulled an inch long pin out of the inside of her bicep. She dropped it into the wall receptacle, grabbed one of the sinks with both hands and gave it a furious tug. "You fucking shit, you bastard!" she hissed. Another jerk made a crunching sound, and the sink started to sag. Sobered up, she pushed against the sink, trying to force it back into place. She somewhat succeeded, but it careened.

She picked up her purse from the floor, stepped to the next sink, and got out her make-up bag. Out came a few wads of cotton and some Band-Aids, a bottle of hydrogen peroxide, and a smaller one with tea tree oil. She soaked a cotton ball in the tea tree oil, poured the peroxide over and pressed the cotton ball to the bleeding mark. She covered it all with a Band Aid. She straightened her top, pushed her hair away from her forehead, and, checking the mirror, dabbed off the beads of sweat with a paper towel.

A door swung open. By the time a woman in a business suite approached, Gabrielle dropped her supplies back into her bag and looked put-together. The woman stepped toward the lopsided sink and hesitated.

"I wouldn't risk it," Gabrielle said.

§ § §

It was the same October day and just as balmy in Deep Ellum, more than two decades earlier.

A shabby ice-cream parlor—'eclectic' they call them nowadays—was situated in a small Victorian building. The sunshine sparkled on the sky-blue ceramic floor of its petite, shaded patio. An elderly couple enjoyed strawberry Sundays at one of the tables. A young pair got up from another.

They were teens who knew the nooks and crannies of the Deep Ellum by heart, both dark-haired and dark-eyed, unrelated by blood but with a resemblance of siblings. At 18-years, the boy was almost fully-grown, tall and broad-shouldered. The lanky girl was yet to shed her 14-year old awkwardness, her scrawny frame and apprehensive bearing a far cry from the cool of her adulthood.

Hovering a head above her, the boy hopped down on the pavement and stopped her atop the patio's single step. She had a cone in her hand, plain vanilla. The light of first love, or first lust, if there is a difference, was in her eyes.

To the girl, Bobby, her soul brother, so diligent about taking care of her—first at his father's appointment, but soon of his own accord—was the best of humans; a boy of light and promise, and in addition, inconceivably, as full of faith in her as she was of distrust in herself.

"Nobody cares," she said, hungry for him to blow-away her doubts. "Your dad is only interested in me because I'm a freak."

He took her hand and she stared at him, wide-eyed. That was the moment; it was possible then. He could change everything because he was the only one who mattered.

"You are not a freak. You are fierce."

She shook her head and dropped her eyes, because that wasn't it.

"I understand you," he said. "I know you better than he does." He tried to catch her eyes again.

It still wasn't what she was after, but getting closer…

"I came up with something," he said. "It's too serious to discuss in a hurry. Let's talk tonight, when I come home, okay? I love my dad, but his whole approach… He's not the god he thinks he is."

She didn't know what he had in mind, but hope's wings fluttered in her narrow chest. She would guess it years later, and her futile longing grew stronger. He would know what to do, she thought. He was so smart.

Bobby likely saw the light in her face, because he cupped it in his big hands and kissed her—the only kiss they shared. The first and best she had, from the firmness of his lips and tongue, to the tremble of his fingers on her skin, to the desire spinning her head. She could never recapture that kiss, even as she blossomed into a sinuous, sophisticated shrew; not in all her years of screwing with a vengeance.

She was drunk with bliss when he got into his little VW bug. They waved to each other and he twisted his neck looking back at her, both his car windows rolled-down.

She still smiled stupidly as the VW rolled a few hundred yards and slowed down at the yield sign at the end of the block. A man lurking on the corner dashed to Bobby's car.

Wearing a jogging suit and a black ski mask, he held something in his hand—a gun, she later understood—which he stuck into the open passenger window. A second, and he got in and the little VW took off. No one else on the street, except for her, realized that the kidnapping happened.

She gaped for a few long moments that she later thought of as an inexcusable eternity, the unaware elderly couple chatting behind her. Then, the ball of ice cream plopped by her feet and she screamed.

When she saw Bobby months later, he wasn't whole. His severed head featured a hollow, decaying face, mummy-like because he was drained of blood before he died. The head didn't look like him at all.

Sometimes, she felt angry that Damien allowed her to see the body—but only sometimes. Often, she wondered if the delirium of their first kiss had dulled Bobby's usual quick-thinking, and if because of that, his death was her fault.

§ § §

As the new silver Corolla turned East along Commerce, the sun shone mellow in the gray-blue sky, and the city's air caressing Gabrielle's face through the open windows tasted of a burned Moroccan coffee, barbecued ribs, and occasional exhaust. She drove past graffiti murals, the old tea-room building, sign-posts plastered with advertisements of upcoming indie shows, and turned on a narrow side street.

Most of the shops here were shut down, with a few beaten cars parked along the curb at random. The ice-cream parlor was long gone, its patio stripped of the awning, the bright blue tile faded and chipped.

Gabrielle gazed at it from her slow-rolling car.

The patio's resident bum lifted his shaggy head but, by the time he raised his cardboard solicitation, the car had already passed. It slowed down at a yield sign near the intersection, while two other cars approached cross-wise.

A gruff male voice yelled into the right side of Gabrielle's face, "Open the door!"

She turned and stared at a silencer dressing the long muzzle of a Smith and Wesson 500, the 'Bone Collector,' pointed at her through the passenger window. A leather-clad hand held the gun, the face behind hidden by a black ski mask with light, dead fish eyes peering through the slits.

Fast as a snakebite, she seized the man's wrist, pulled his hand from her face, and floored the gas. There was a dry 'pop,' and a bullet hole marked the front glass, spreading shard petals.

§ § §

The bum, shook-up by the mad squeal of tires and honks, struggled to his feet. Shielding his eyes from the sun, he watched a white Sedan roll across the intersection and almost crashed into the Corolla's rear as it ran through, dragging along a man in a jogging suit. The Sedan screeched to a halt, while a pick-up heading in the opposite direction swerved around and pulled over up the street.

Beyond, the Corolla moved into the empty lane, nearly sideswiping the parked cars just as the man disconnected, rolled, lurched up and disappeared into an alleyway. The Corolla came to a stop a hundred yards ahead.

The bum ran toward the intersection. An older couple climbed out of the pick-up. The three of them met by the Sedan. The bum knocked on the driver's window. The silver haired old lady slumped inside did not respond. Her head lolled on her shoulder, eyes closed. The car was running in park.

§ § §

Gabrielle zipped up her jacket and pulled on her hood. She picked up her attacker's gun from the floor and got out of the Corolla.

Three pairs of eyes at the intersection followed her every move. "Hey!" The bum yelled, "You okay?"

She didn't answer or turn as she reached the alley.

"Stay put, lady! Let the police figure it out," the other man called.

And the bum again, "Don't go there! He might be armed!"

"Is that a gun?" That was the woman from the pick-up. "She has a gun!"

Gabrielle stepped on the threshold of a passage between the buildings. The alley seemed to cut through the block and continue beyond the courtyard where she stood. She scrutinized the lay of the land, the corners and bushes behind which her attacker could hide. A few seconds, and she backed out and hurried to the car. She noticed the missing right side-mirror—rubbed off together with her would-be kidnapper—so she went back and retrieved it from the road.

The bum at the intersection called again, "Hey, lady?"

She didn't respond on her way back to her car.

50

"You oughta talk to police!" the other man joined.

His worried mate chimed in, "We need your insurance information!" and to the others, incredulous, "She's running off! Write down her license plate!"

"I can't see jack at this distance," her husband answered.

§ § §

Gabrielle revved the engine and took off. "You're dead, fucker," she muttered, tears rolling. She looped around the block, peering at the pedestrians on both sides of the streets. Then she headed straight North, staring ahead, her face grim. After a while, she pulled a cell phone from her purse and pressed a number on her speed-dial.

"I was about to call you," a man's voice came. "We need to talk. In person. Come to the ranch as soon as—"

"The Doll-maker is back," Gabrielle cut him short. "He is in Dallas. Do you know how I know? The fuck shit just tried to abduct me."

Silence on the other end. She waited as she navigated her car toward the highway.

"Are you coming?" The man sounded shaken.

"Yes."

"When?"

"Two hours." Gabrielle hung up.

Later, the three witnesses describing her contradicted each other on what she wore, how she looked, and whether there really was a gun. The biggest stir the incident produced were calls to the Deep Ellum police department from the witnesses' insurance companies and from the distraught son of the old lady, the driver of the white Sedan, whose stroke proved to be fatal.

Chapter 9

At the Ranch

As dusk enveloped the day, Senator Damien Sheppard stood on the stone-and-wooden-beam porch of his remodeled old ranch house watching Gabrielle's car approach. He was almost as presentable as in the photographs from the apartment on Garden Lane, except for the worry-painted haggard shadows on his face. A black Doberman Pinscher at his feet perked up from his slumber. The massive iron gate swung open, the Corolla rolled in, and the dog took off, barking joyfully.

The car, its windshield freshly repaired, slid into one of the guest parking spots, next to an old, well-maintained Buick. Gabrielle emerged, checked the Buick, knelt, and seized the ecstatic dog in a strong embrace to thwart his clawing at her clothes. She cooed to him as a mother to a small child, and he covered her with slobbery kisses. Finally, she got up to hug the older man. He took her by the shoulders and looked her up and down.

"No damage," she assured him.

He examined her bruised and swollen right hand.

"He tried to hold onto his gun," she said. "I took some Arnica already." At Damien's alert stare, she added, "He was wearing gloves. You know how careful he is about fingerprints."

She looked up and stopped, and the little color she had drained from her face. A young face watched her from the dark second floor window. Then, the slight figure moved away, ghost-like.

"I didn't tell you. I am not alone this summer," Sheppard said. "Tom is Artie's nephew. He interns for me. His parents are traveling in Europe, so I thought he can stay here for now. He drives to Dallas every morning, brings me my office mail."

"Working for a brilliant future," Gabrielle said. "Good for him."

§ § §

Sheppard's housekeeper gone for the coming weekend, Gabrielle fixed a salad and fried chicken sausages in the ranch house's enormous kitchen. The

Senator's young protégé, eighteen year old Tom Fletcher, had disobedient blond hair sleeked for success around his still adolescent face. During dinner Tom ogled her, averting his eyes every time she looked at him, and then volunteered to clean up.

Gabrielle and Sheppard secluded themselves in the cavernous study lined by cherry-wood shelves overflowing with dark volumes. The day was dead, and the metal shutters of the windows, operated from the inside and protected by the best glass break sensors, were now closed. Gabrielle paced restlessly, touching things. Sheppard reclined in one of the two roomy leather chairs. Ranger, the Doberman, lay at his feet watching Gabrielle with complete devotion.

"I've got Weizlan's signature," she said. "No need to apply pressure."

"Good."

"I forced his hand…sort of." She squatted to pet Ranger.

"It's your own fault that he hates your guts. You could have done without that experiment. Not everyone can put a condom on their heart."

"I mistook his venom for passion. You know I'm a sucker for intense men." Gabrielle got up from her hunches. "Always hope they'll infect me and I'll feel something, too."

"You'll find someone, Gabrielle."

"You can lie to yourself but not to me, Damien. I can't be with anyone. I can only pretend." Sheppard's face fell more, and she hurried to ameliorate the harshness of her words. "Instead of worrying about me, you should get some love life yourself, old fella."

"I was fortunate to have had one great love."

She raised her brows ironically.

"That's different," Sheppard said. "You and Bobby were kids. But back to your incident. I've told you many times you should never form a pattern. Whenever your life is predictable, you are vulnerable to attack."

"This is the one anniversary I keep. Didn't you always say that traditions are important for someone like me?"

"Obviously, the degenerate knows about your tradition. In any case, we've received a warning, and he has learned you are not some damsel." His voice cracked. "But he may be better prepared next time."

Gabrielle strolled to Sheppard's desk, touching things on it restlessly. "I've practiced that move in my mind a thousand times all these years, imagined I was Bobby saving myself."

"Did you see his face?"

"Not much of it, because of the ski mask. And it was too fast. I believe he has very light eyes." She thought a little, scanning the crowded walnut surface. "Grey or blue. I'm not sure. The fuck is in pretty good shape. He must be at least in his mid-forties…more likely, early fifties."

She lifted a photograph. In it, Sheppard's son Bobby was the same age and build as Tom, but with the dark and beautiful eyes of his mother, whose portrait graced the wall Gabrielle was facing. She opened the frame and took the photo out.

Hidden underneath was another.

Gabrielle shook her head accusingly at Sheppard and gave the second photo to him. A bittersweet smile appeared on his face as he gazed at the picture, Bobby with a girl a few years younger than him, his arm around her shoulders.

"I can't bring myself to destroy it," Sheppard said,

Gabrielle took it from him. "How remarkable," she said, with a vaudeville exaggeration. "Doesn't this girl look like the celebrated Doctor Lubovich? Don't our records indicate that she was still rotting in Romania at that tender age, and didn't leave her motherland until much later?" She abandoned her mocking tone. "If the wrong person comes across it, Damien, my immigration record will be fucked, and more importantly, they'll wonder what I have to cover up…"

She stopped sharply and turned to Sheppard. "Speaking of which, Weizlan dropped some hairy hints today." She watched Sheppard's expression. "Aha… So, he does know something. How does he know…and how much?"

"Not enough. You don't need to concern yourself with it."

"Are you sure?"

Sheppard returned her gaze without flinching. Gabrielle sighed and restored the secret photo under Bobby's picture, and the latter to its frame, then dropped into the second chair.

"Don't worry," Sheppard said. "As long as I am alive, no one will see it. If I die of natural causes, it will do no harm because you will inherit everything I own. And if the causes are not natural…the odds the killer finds the photo and uses it against you are nil."

"Don't talk death. I want you to stick around while I do. When I'm gone, you can go up in flames."

"If you go before me, I'll have no need to stick around." Sheppard took his glasses off and rubbed his eyes. When he moved his hands, he seemed worn, threadbare.

"Okay," Gabrielle said. "First, Doll-maker blackmails us. Then, he decides to go on the offensive. We made no move in between. What gives?"

Sheppard got up, opened a laptop on his desk, and navigated. "He may think we did make a move," he said. "Artie called. Apparently, someone's requested my records in Washington. Mr. Berryhill, a DEA Assistant Administrator."

"DEA! Why?"

"It's not the DEA interested in me. Berryhill was acting on behalf of a friend. An agent in L.A., Joe Vasquez, of the CID." He paused. "Vasquez owns the Blake Johnson case now."

"It went to the FBI? Wasn't the case dead?"

"The new guy resurrected it. And managed to make progress, believe it or not. He found the Doll-maker's lair and almost caught him. Doll-maker escaped. Shot and killed Vasquez' partner in the process. After that, Vasquez sent some photos of me in the company of a certain woman," he paused, "to D.C. for identification. They made me out."

Gabrielle leaned forward, her eyes bright. "How did he find the place?"

"I don't know. Artie emailed me his rap sheet and asked around. Appears to be a talented guy, tenacious too. Nicknamed 'Hound,' whatever that's worth. Hasn't advanced in the ranks much for his age, though. His ethnicity is likely not helpful. But there is something else—an unfortunate family history. It's all here." He gave her the laptop. "Also, Vasquez and his slain partner were very close."

Gabrielle studied Joe's picture on the screen. "So we must thank the intrepid agent for this attack today. Doll-maker must think Vasquez is working with us."

"That would be logical since his place was discovered soon after he tried to blackmail us."

"What else did the Feds find?"

"Who knows? If they had everything Doll-maker sent to us, the FBI would already be on my doorstep."

She stared at him, biting her lower lip, then hunched over the screen, reading.

"He lost a son recently," she muttered. "And his mother died a few years ago…" Her eyes jumped from paragraph to paragraph. "Great," she said, "an underachieving depressive haunted by the sins of his father. Now out for revenge. Who does this remind you of?" Her crooked smile wasn't humorous. She continued studying the information on the screen.

"He could be on our backs at any moment. And Doll-maker already is." Sheppard sunk heavily into his chair.

Gabrielle closed the laptop. "Let me sleep on it." She got up. "I think I'll go for a walk."

"It's too late. You need to be especially careful from now on, Gabrielle."

"I'm comfortable in the dark, you know that. And I need a little exercise after what happened; I had no time to let steam out at the gym."

Sheppard made a start as if to protest but apparently thought better of it. "Take my gun with you, at least," he said, resigned.

"I've got Doll-maker's." She leaned and kissed his cheek. "Don't worry… Dad. I can take care of myself. Plus Ranger is coming with me, right boy?" The dog got up and wagged his tail.

Sheppard's eyes watered. "I love it when you call me dad," he said. "I wish you'd listen to me like a good daughter. Stay close to the house, at least. The fence is electrified and the alarms along the perimeter are on at all times now."

§ § §

Ranger ran ahead and disappeared, distracted by some nocturnal vermin. She didn't call the dog back as she walked away from the house and its two lighted windows. Her work-out outfit was black, and her face was veiled in shadows.

Her sneakers stepped lightly on the sandy path slithering between the shrubs and fruit trees covering the one and a half acre enclosure of Sheppard's sprawling brick house. A bird cried over her head once; otherwise, it was eerily quiet, a strange occurrence for that time of year. Not a frog croaked, and the crickets kept to themselves.

She slowed down, alert, and slipped off the path.

After half a minute, a male figure emerged from the cover of the trees and crossed into the shadows of the tall bushes. He hesitated, looking around. A hand fell on his shoulder, and he cried out and turned with a jump.

"Shhh…" Gabrielle pressed her finger to his lips. "You have been following me, Tom Fletcher."

He stared at her. Slowly, his breathing calmed. "Gosh, you scared me," he stammered. "I am sorry. Can I…walk with you? I brought a flashlight from the hall."

She stopped him from turning it on. "Let's stay in the dark for a while." She was gazing into his face. "You remind me of someone I knew, long ago."

Tom moved toward her. Their faces were very close and her eyes were searching. He was about to kiss her, but she pulled away.

"I thought you liked me," he said in a pained voice.

"Oh, I do." Gabrielle touched his arm gently. "I just remembered that I'm the older woman and must behave myself." She called Ranger and they waited for the dog to return from his secret mission. "Walk me back to the house," she said. "Wanna smoke?"

§ § §

She brought the laptop to her austere bedroom on the second floor, reread Joe's file, turned the light off and sat staring at the night sky in the open window. "A kindred spirit," she murmured to the stars and smiled. After an hour or so of thinking, she took a sleeping pill and went to bed.

Chapter 10

Viper

Less than ten days after Gonzales was established in USP Tucson, Joe received a call that his plan worked. He was relieved they could bring 'GD Martinez' back. Joe and Dante came to see him in the same waiting room at the county jail where the arts-and-crafts session with Lee took place. The first thing Joe noticed when he entered was Gonzales' once again sickly complexion. But the Mexican's eyes were sane and bright.

"How was it?" Joe asked.

Gonzales shrugged. "I'm glad to be out of there. And I've got some news."

Joe wondered if they really got lucky.

"I met a couple hombres there," Gonzales continued. "Ten years a pop for reckless homicide. Cut-throats but trustworthy. They called Conrad a rat, said someone from outside helped him escape. The killer couldn't get inside the prison to get Conrad so he got the rat on the outside, almost. The brothers didn't say anything to the authorities—no one said anything. Nobody cared about the rat, and nobody wants to yap about it with a rabid dog on the loose, understand? But the shit goes down the grapevine fast. Conrad wasn't the first to get iced. It happened before—to lifers, too, even some on the row in other states. All killed gruesomely." Likely seeing the doubt in Joe's face, Gonzales insisted, "You better believe it! They know of some wacky shit happenin' for some years."

There was a satisfied excitement in Gonzales' voice. Joe wasn't surprised the young Mexican fell for an urban legend brewing among the prison populace. "Are you wasting my time, Manuel?"

"No way!"

"You can learn more from the grapevine than from the news sometimes," Dante piped in.

"Are the inmates afraid?" Joe asked Gonzales.

"Only a little. Viper doesn't go after simple skooch, only after the real sickos. The brothers said mind your own business and you'll be okay."

"Viper?"

59

"That's what they call him. He's a myth. They say all kinda shit, like he's got no flesh."

"Right." Joe stood up. He didn't look at Gonzales anymore.

His informant stared at him with a wounded expression. "I'm not saying that part is true. Just what I heard. They say no one seen Viper but some heard his voice. Hissing like a snake. I wish I could find out more…Maybe I need to go back an' stay longer…Want me to go back?"

"No." Joe saw instant relief on Gonzales' face. He stopped in his tracks and turned to Dante. "Wasn't there something about hissing coming from James McKee's cell on the night he was murdered?"

"There was!" Dante's eyes lit up.

Joe remembered the transcript. The hissing was attributed to McKee's killer whispering to his victim before strangling him, but the Florence inmate who contributed that information did say 'hissing,' not 'whispering.' The whole ghost side of it was hokey, but were there, as the brothers in USP told Gonzales, other cases in other prisons of other sickos killed in ways matching their own method?

§ § §

"Kinda cool," Dante said, looking at Gabrielle's picture.

They were holed up in Joe's office. Joe told Dante what he had learned from Don Selvage. "Seems iffy," Joe suggested. "Can't a subject fake it?"

"Not if she monitors his brainwaves and the perp reaches the right state. But there is a bigger problem. I originally majored in psychology, and hypnosis fascinated me. Ah. I was young and idealistic then."

Joe barely hid his smirk.

"To be a hypnotist sounded so glamorous. But they told me no one can be hypnotized unwillingly, so I lost my interest. You can see the problem— why would a criminal want to divulge his secrets?"

"You saying she can't be for real?"

"There are some historical anecdotes of a few skilled performers, but my professor claimed they were con artists. If she *is* for real, I'd love to chat with her. I've another interesting tidbit. I called both prisons, Arizona and Colorado. The strangled and the drowned victims had something in common after all. Can you guess?"

"No."

"Lubovich interviewed them both, prior to their trials. I had no idea she hypnotized them. Creepy cool."

Joe got up. Nervous energy surged through him. "Good digging, Dante. We should give you a chance to ask her about her hypnosis method pretty soon." One of his rare smiles played on his lips. "I've got another task for you. I found no similar prison killings in the NSIS database. Even the two we know about should be recorded, but they aren't. You'll need to make contact state by state, the same way you are dealing with the dismemberment cases. That will be time consuming. Start again by sending inquiries to all the maximum security prisons about any unsolved killings."

Dante made a note in his notebook. "Is that all?"

"Yeah. And do me a favor. Don't discuss this case with anyone until I tell you otherwise." As his new partner got up, Joe had a strange déjà vu moment—it was just like the old times, with Steve, and the comforting familiarity of it made him feel like a traitor.

Dante halted at the door. "Can I ask you something? If Cowell finds out how critical the case is, he's not going to let us handle it, right? I don't understand why. I was told you've solved every one of your cases. But…," he hesitated, unsure how to proceed, "…they throw fish heads at you, never any real meat."

He waited for an answer, but Joe's face closed as if saying, 'don't go there,' and Dante left.

Chapter II

Gabrielle's 'Skill'

Coloqueen Maximum Security Prison, TX – beginning of November

Upon her arrival, Head Warden Portman assigned Deputy McDonald, a dry, fatherly man in his seventies, to escort Gabrielle to Block B, which also hosted Death Row. It was Gabrielle's first visit to Coloqueen, and the antiqued interior and worn concrete walls worked their grim magic on her. McDonald glanced amiably at his charge, liking her calm confidence and her sensible pant suit. They left Block A, where Portman's office was, and hiked across yellow, crushed grass to the barbed wire gate.

"I heard you saved some poor SOB from the fryer," McDonald said. "Had him transferred to a mental facility. Sullivan, wasn't it?"

"Brin James. I recommended his case be reopened."

"What was the guy like?" McDonald pushed.

Gabrielle gave him an askance glance, as if deciding whether he was worth talking to. Her face warmed up. "Brin was wrongly accused because he confessed. In fact, they could have hung all the dogs on him and he would have pleaded guilty. The man is easily confused, dissociated, and has zero confidence in himself. It's an illness. The evidence against him was insufficient; some even pointed away. Unfortunately, after being battered by the cops and…a certain forensic psychiatrist, he started to believe in his guilt."

"Well bless your heart for saving a life," McDonald said. "Only the guilty belong in here."

§ § §

In Block B, they stopped at the bullet-proof glass partition, the guard's fishbowl. A crudely handsome man came out, leered at Gabrielle, and flipped through her papers.

McDonald gave him a severe stare to impart the status and untouchability of their guest. "This is Doctor Lubovich. As you already know, she's here to interview Baca." He turned to Gabrielle, his voice signaling disdain for the 'pig,'

63

as Mitchell was called behind his back. "Dr. Lubovich, this is our MSU Supervisor, Jeff Mitchell."

"Don't forget to sign for the key," Mitchell said.

The older man went into the fishbowl, reluctant to leave Gabrielle with Mitchell, whose oily eyes were basting her like a turkey. In turn, Gabrielle's incisive eyes peered at the Supervisor's face, as if measuring and weighting.

"You the gal hoping to get our newest scumbag off the hook with your shrinky mumbo-jumbo?" Mitchell asked.

She smiled. McDonald wouldn't expect a smile as unguardedly frank and cynical from her, the kind he considered dirty. "Only if the scumbag is innocent," she said.

Mitchell's eyes slid down her body. "There's a lot to like about you, Dr. Lubovich, but I hope you're not one of those bleeding hearts cuckoos trying to end capital punishment. Trust me, we've no victims of injustice here."

"I don't trust the judgment of people who like me so fast," she said, her freaky eyes never leaving Mitchell's.

Little greasy moths fluttered at the pit of his belly. "Is that so?" He smirked. "You such a bad girl?"

The smile slipped off her face. She moved close, too close for Mitchell's comfort, only pride stopping him from stepping back, and her eyes overtook his will. "You've no idea," she said in a low voice.

The macho-wolf-turned-hopeful-puppy Mitchell held his breath. Here was a real woman, a true bitch able to appreciate him…command him. *How did she guess?*

Gabrielle relaxed back and turned to McDonald who reappeared with the card-key and one of the younger guards. Mitchell watched them lead her down the corridor.

When they were out of earshot, McDonald glanced at Gabrielle apologetically. "Did the pig misbehave? He has that tendency with ladies."

"Nothing I couldn't handle," Gabrielle said.

Such a no-nonsense girl, McDonald thought, *she must have shown Mitchell his place.* He discretely checked her hand for a ring and thought with parental concern that Dr. Lubovich's life was probably all work and no fun, just like his daughter's.

§ § §

McDonald and the guard stayed in the monitoring space on the other side of a one-way, see-through mirror commanding nearly an entire wall in the gray interrogation room. Per Gabrielle's request, the cameras on the ceiling were turned off. She always stipulated that she and her subjects were alone during her sessions and that her interviews were not filmed.

She studied the man in prison overalls, leg chains, and arm restraints, who occupied the metal chair. John Baca was outright ugly, with deep-set eyes and the forehead of a hedgehog framed by a brush of gray hair. Thin wires ran from his head to an EEG machine she sent in earlier. The machine rested on a stainless-steel stand that at other times held syringes for lethal injections. Since she hadn't begun working on Baca yet, the EEG's sensor screen read 30 Hz. For now, she simply observed him.

He was watching her too. Her neither concerned nor hostile eyes unmindful of his humanity unsettled him. She reminded him of a cold-blooded crocodile.

"I heard about you," he said, to break the swelling silence. "You hypnotize guys and make 'em sing, the chicken shits." He wanted to make her angry, or to like him—something that might suggest to him how to deal with her. But her face was blank, as if she had no reason to play any roles for him.

Why wasn't she questioning him? Was she going to write him up, to invent his answers? She wasn't here to help him, as they explained—in case he was innocent, as he insisted. He couldn't stand the silence any more. "Your thing won't work with me," he said.

No reaction.

He decided to hold her gaze. Oh, but it was hard. He felt like a naughty cat trying to establish the upper hand with its owner and failed the stare-down contest. Except he couldn't look away. It was like his eyeballs were glued. And then he knew. She saw him, saw through him, because she was different. Because something was wrong with her. He knew shrinks were crazy, but this one was something else.

His heart missed a beat, shuddered, and skipped another one. *Snap out of it!* he wanted to shout. "Aren't ya' getting tired?" he asked, his tongue thick and unyielding.

No answer.

"What the fuck ever," he said. "I won't look at you no more." But his eyes remained fixed even as his brain turned into a lazy slug wanting to give up.

Gabrielle pulled over a second chair and sat down, never breaking their weird connection.

Baca's breath grew shallow. He sagged in his seat. The EEG monitor indicated rapidly decreasing brain activity, down to 25 Hz…20 Hz…In a few minutes, the frequency froze at 9 hertz.

She turned the recorder on. Another minute passed.

"Mommy's here, Johnny," she whispered. "Are you comfortable, my boy?"

She waited. Baca's glazed eyes stared into hers. He tried to say something, but couldn't—yet.

"Snug and warm?" She waited.

"Yes," Baca moaned in a small voice.

She exhaled and smiled to him. Some light, inconsequential banter, a soft touch on Baca's hand, and soon, he was in a world far away from the grey prison walls. A good, simple world, worry and fear free, where his mommy would help him, would never let them catch him—his mommy who was always on his side.

Gabrielle paused. "You did something, Johnny. Something bad."

"Yes." His face screwed up like a kid ready to cry. "I'm sorry, mommy."

"It's okay. You can tell me." The 'mommy' voice glided like a snake in sand. "Tell me everything. I won't judge. You are my child."

Baca's eyes stared fixedly. He could relieve himself of his secret. At long last, he could stop denying and tell what happened. And mommy would understand. Wasn't that why she always covered for him? A sly smile appeared on his face.

"She was very small," he said, tentative. "I like 'em small."

"I know," Gabrielle said with responsive playfulness. "She had a little voice too, didn't she?"

"Like a mouse!" Baca tittered. And then he spoke fast, with the slurred speech of a gossiping girl intimating her first sexual encounter to a trusted friend. He told it all, relishing each moment, recalling his exploits with a vividness he wouldn't master without this special help.

§ § §

…His stubby finger dials the number. He is playing hide-and-seek. The small, Mexican woman he stalked for the last month and half doesn't expect to receive his call at this new place.

In the descending dusk, Baca crouches behind the thick base of a tree, one of many lining the quiet street. The pair of binoculars in his hand is trained on the window of the fancy house across the road. He can see her as she comes to the phone—not very young but petite and slim, the housekeeper of this grand place while its inhabitants are away. The sound of her meek 'Hello?' arouses him, as always.

"*Hello? Hello?*" *he mocks cheerfully.* "*This is a house call.*"

"*You again!*" *The woman recognizes his voice. The fear in hers excites him even farther. The best part, she is an illegal and can't go to the police.* "*Stop calling here!*" *she says.* "*I tell Mr. Fabry! Mr. Fabry!*" *she calls out to the master of the house, as if the old fart was home.* "*It's that* cabrón *I told you about!*"

But Baca knows she is alone tonight. "*I'll see you soon!*" *he coos to her, as he did a few times before. She has no idea that this time, soon is a matter of minutes.*

He hangs up.

§ § §

The smallest details were woven delicately into Gabrielle's prodding, designed to conjure the truth from Baca's memory, to make sure he knew all the facts only the killer would know. To make sure he was guilty, without a doubt…

§ § §

…Screaming, the woman flees through the long hall, her voice no match for the thick walls and the aloof spaces between the affluent dwellings. The air stinks of her fear and the pine scented cleaner she recently used. He moves right behind her but, with the blood beating in her ears, the stupid cunt has no way of knowing how close he is. She glances back, stumbles and falls…

There is a doomed horror in her eyes, and she is exhausted by her terror even before she puts up a hopeless fight.

She scratches at him as his knee pins her pelvis to the floor, and he swears and closes his hands on her neck. He shivers with excitement when her face turn purple and her eyes roll up in her head. But don't die yet, that is not all…

§ § §

An hour later, Baca was asleep and taken to his cell on the gurney. Gabrielle asked for some water and sat back with her eyes closed. McDonald waited, sympathetic, until she got up—in good form, he thought, considering—and he took her to the Head Warden's office.

"What do you think?" he asked as they crossed the dry lawn once again.

Her eyes were distant. "He deserves whatever is coming to him," she said.

Chapter 12

Blondie

Ironwood Medium Security Prison, CA

The tall beefy guard had enough time to thoroughly check out the young blonde's slight ass and weak spine as she hooker-swaggered all the way to Ironwood's visiting room. He led her into the small, square space where she stood, wringing her hands. She seemed to wait for permission to sit down, but he ignored her. Her eyes, furtive under her frizzy hair, were drowned in mascara, and he wondered what she looked like under all the grease.

She made him sick. Who but a down-trodden, spineless skunk would pursue a romance with a murderer of prepubescent boys? The guard could only speculate what favors Craig wanted from her. Whatever the spell he cast on her, the attraction would be hard to maintain once he was transferred. Much stricter rules on death row. The guard spoke a few words on his radio. Soon, the opposite door opened, and an older guard brought in a man in his early forties clad in a prison jumpsuit and leg chains.

Terrence Craig, with his dyed black hair and sharp features, resembled a confident rat. A florid mole on his right cheek had long outgrown its charm. He smiled at the woman. She shrieked and, before the guards could stop her, threw herself on Craig's neck.

"Hey!" The younger guard pulled her away, surprised to notice that she had managed to slip her hand down the front of Craig's trousers. *A fast worker,* he thought. Who would think these two love birds met just once before?

"It's my last handful of ass. Have some consideration, mate," Craig appealed to him.

"This is it," the older man said. "Next time, follow the rules."

The woman whimpered.

"See you soon, honey-bun," Craig told her as he was led away, as sweetly as if he had never harmed a soul.

§ § §

Not long after, Terrence Craig entered the prison's upholstery shop, alone. He was allowed to work there with a few other inmates during his trial. The trial ended, and today was the last day of his meager freedoms.

The shop was deserted.

Craig flipped over one of the chairs, ripped the gauze from the bottom, and pulled out the jeans, sweater, and pair of sneakers hidden inside. It took a lot of scheming to smuggle them in, all thanks to the amazingly resourceful Las Vegas hooker that wrote to him through Inmatesdating.com. As his crazy luck had it, she was eager to meet a month after they became pen-pals. And once they met, she fell passionately in love with him.

He groped where she fondled him and fished out the small card she deposited in the band of his underwear. He admired his mug on the card. It was the prison ID for a 'James Wilson,' the kind that allows lawyers in and out of Ironwood to consult with their incarcerated clients.

Chapter 13

'You always called them first…'

Los Angeles

The receipt faxed from Adam Johnson's new school in Canada was another contribution to the case from Mike Berryhill. Steve's old friend and mentor kept proving to be indispensable whenever Joe needed to speed things up or go around official channels. Joe stared at the numbers. Sixty percent of Adam's tuition was paid by an undisclosed contributor, which traced to a private entity Phoenix Enterprises. The company belonged, as Berryhill's more in-depth digging revealed, to the much lately mentioned Dr. Lubovich.

Joe had no intention of questioning Asia Johnson about this if he could help it. He trusted she honestly believed Dr. Lubovich's support was strictly non-pecuniary, and he respected the latter's obvious effort to keep Adam's mother in the dark about her full involvement. Sixty percent of the tuition totaled nine thousand dollars—a decent chunk of money for someone who, like Dr. Lubovich, made, according to her IRS records, around seventy five thousands last year in her consulting practice. Not unbearable, but certainly not a reasonable amount one would shell out whenever a charitable urge came over.

Flabbergasted, Joe took out and studied the second photo from the Garden Lane apartment. He imagined he could sense more than average capacity for empathy in the lovely features of Gabrielle Lubovich's face. Then he caught himself and became embarrassed, as if someone watched him. He put the photos away and started pacing in the tight space again. Why did Gabrielle Lubovich pay for Adam Johnson's tuition? Why did she try so hard to ship him off to a school in another country? The compassion for a family that had lost a son she got to know briefly may have played a good part. But what else? Was there more than incidental connection between her and the Johnsons? Or more concrete, between her and Blake?

He stopped to write another note to himself. *Talk to the counselor Bosko and Blake's classmates.* He thought a bit and then added, *See how Gayle handles the questioning.* He suspected the glib rookie was amply suited to the task.

71

Another thought struck him. The discarded photo of Blake's severed, bloodless thigh…How serious was the threat the blackmail package contained? Obviously serious enough to prevent Gabrielle from going to the authorities. Did she know the killer blackmailing her personally? Did he menace her and the Senator's lives, or threatened more killings of the innocent?

Was Lubovich eager to remove Adam Johnson from harm's way, the only remaining child of the woman she met and in whose life she became involved? And, come to think of it, did she have any reason to feel guilty for what happened to Blake Johnson and to atone for it with her charity? Would the boy still be alive, even if he ended up with an undeserved juvenile sentence, if Dr. Lubovich had never crossed his path? Was she afraid the killer would go after the victim's brother to prove a point, whatever it was? Did Gabrielle Lubovich hide her sponsorship of Adam to reduce the boy's risk of attracting the killer's interest? A reasonable explanation if the blackmailer, as it appeared from the photos, kept close tabs on her and Sheppard.

Earlier, Joe called the number Asia gave him of a private research institution in New York. After a few redirections, he managed to reach someone in the know. The lady told him that Dr. Lubovich was on travel and couldn't be contacted. She did not elaborate on Lubovich's plans and timeline, but invited Joe to leave his information. Now he wondered if Dr. Lubovich was making herself scarce and unreachable for a reason.

He worked till seven p.m., when he normally left work and grabbed something to eat. But he wasn't hungry. One more thing, he thought, and called Berryhill's private cell. A couple rings and the answering machine came on.

"Hey," he said into the receiver. "It's concerning Lubovich again. I'm faxing you the official request for her Immigration record. If you can forward this to the lab personally and fast-track it, I'd greatly appreciate it. Also, can you check with Interpol, see if they have anything on her? And Mike, thanks for all the help so far."

He hung up, went to the window, leaned his forehead on the cool glass, and stood absorbing the view of the brightening night street and moving car lights beyond the boundaries of the treed lawn. His cell rung in its belt holder. He pulled it out and checked the caller ID. The chief hobgoblin was still in his lair.

§ § §

The first thing Joe noted when he entered Cowell's office was that O'Neal was not present.

"I want you to take a few of yours and Marcus' best men and go to Ponderosa to pick someone up quietly and discretely," Cowell said. His pudgy face looked redder than usual.

Such an arrangement meant good odds for a screw-up. Cowell preferred Vasquez' experience and, more importantly, Vasquez' neck on the line rather than one of his favorites. The SAC turned his flat screen toward Joe. It displayed an FBI mug shot of a weasely-looking man in his forties.

"This is Terrence Craig. He escaped from the Medium Security Unit at the Ironwood facility yesterday. Fifteen minutes ago an anonymous tip came in. Craig was seen entering this house."

An aerial map on the screen indicated a cluster of decrepit-looking residential buildings, one marked with a red cross.

"It's the first escape from Ironwood since it was built," Cowell said.

"What was he in for?"

"Craig's a homosexual sadist. Liked doing wimpy she-boys. He's not a real muscle. But the associates that helped him may be with him, and they may be armed. Scoop him up and whoever is with him with as little noise as possible. But look around first and, if any complications arise, report to me before you do anything."

Joe ignored the SAC's patronizing tone. "If he's a serial, why medium security?"

"He was there for the duration of his trial because of some holes in his case. His sentencing came a week ago."

Craig's liberators' boldness impressed Joe. They were prompt too. Once Craig had been packed off into Ironwood's maximum-security unit to pluck him out would have been impossible.

"We didn't publicize his escape. The last thing we need is people questioning the safeguards of our federal institutions and our procedures," Cowell continued. "It's important that it stays quiet, Hound. All I want you to do is pick the asshole up and return him to where he belongs."

§ § §

Coloqueen Maximum Security Prison, TX/ Los Angeles County, Ponderosa

It was four nights since Baca's session with Gabrielle. The details of it had vacated his memory, but its uneasy aftertaste required regular masturbation to placate. The lights had been out for over two hours and, after beating off, he finally become drowsy. He used to sleep like a baby on the outside. His only other neighbor wasn't a snorer. Once the place went dim at nine p.m., the hush ruled within the thick walls.

Baca's eyes closed and his body relaxed. He was ready to drift-off when he discerned… breathing.

It wasn't his own.

Baca's brain tried to spin it into a dream, and then he put brakes on the shutdown. Eyes still shut, Baca listened, alert, and then realized…the maker of the sound was located right next to his cot. His heart jumped as he readied to fight for his life to the last scream. His eyelids popped open and eyes groped the dark. The walls, small desk, sink and toilet were murky in the darkness and familiar.

Baca lifted his head from the pillow. He was alone in his cell. The section of the corridor visible beyond the bars appeared to be deserted. But the alien breathing continued…

"Missster…Ba-ca…" The hoarse hiss was otherworldly, reptilian.

Baca sat up, his skin crawling. "Who are you?" he whispered, infected by the voice's secretive quality. "Where are you?"

"You always called them firssst…I'm returning the favor…"

§ § §

Dante drove, being the newest member of the team, and Joe rode shotgun. Five more Feds behind them passed time teasing the rookie about the balaclava he had chosen over the Neoprene masks favored by the rest, too tight for his big face.

As Joe scrutinized the satellite view on the screen of his laptop of the small dying town on the edge of Los Angeles County, a fugitive's paradise overrun by tangled streets with the highest percentage of abandoned dwellings in California and easy access to two freeways, his thoughts turned to the anonymous tipster. Joe wondered how he or she found out about Craig's escape if it had been, according to Cowell, kept quiet.

§ § §

Over a thousand miles away, Baca huddled on his cot, clammy with sweat. There were two unseen beings in his cell now. A voice groaned, as if struggling against a gag.

74

"Let me introduccce you to Missster Craig," the hissing voice said. "A few days ago, he received sssome unexsspected help and escaped from prissson."

Baca's stomach convulsed and he tasted his dinner, but from the sound of it, "Mister Craig" fared much worse.

"Don't fight, Missster Craig, there'sss really no point," the hissing voice mocked, solicitous. There was the sound of a tight struggle, then a gagged, voiceless pleading.

"What did you sssay, Missster Craig?" the voice hissed eagerly. The moans turned into a muffled, agonized scream.

"You ssstill with usss, Missster Baca?" the voice inquired when the scream ceased. "My appointment with Missster Craig isss almost over."

A howl of pain followed, snapping Baca's nerves. He drew himself into a ball, trying to cover his ears, wanting to disappear, to melt into his mattress. But he could still hear it all, up to the last mortal shriek and a nasty crunch.

And then he knew it was over.

"Nothing like thisss to make a fella feel alive, isssn't it?" the voice intimated.

Baca's breathing came out short, shallow, and rapid.

"Thisss was your houssse call, Missster Baca. I'll sssee you sssoon!"

§ § §

A dilapidated building, Craig's suspected hideout, stood on a quiet street, as yet untouched by a big conglomerate that recently bought the area wholesale to gut and convert into a business district. The musty, blighted neighborhood consisted of falling apart Tudor, Victorian, and Spanish Colonial dwellings, many featuring Department of Health warning signs on their fronts.

The darkened FBI van parked discreetly on the other side of the street. Six men emerged. Not a sliver of light and no sound came from the house. Three men went to the back. Two others followed Joe and mounted the creaky, disintegrating front porch.

Joe shone a flashlight at the fresh scratches around the recently picked lock, lighter than the rest of the wood. Al Goodman got on one knee, worked for a bare few seconds with his tool, and pushed the door open. The men slipped into a dank, dark vestibule.

Joe followed the convoluted hall with his flashlight, while Goodman covered the rear. Between them, Mike Olsher darted in and out of the claustrophobic chambers sprouting to the left and to the right.

A little light seeped from ahead. "Don't get spooked," came a voice in Joe's earpiece. The silhouette of Pete Brewer, one of the three agents who entered the house through the back window, stepped into the passage from the kitchen. The other two crowded behind him. Brewer pointed to the right.

They turned the corner and Joe killed the flashlight. They halted before a door, slightly ajar, with the light filtering through. Joe took out a small, double mirror and stuck it into the crack. The reflection didn't gather much, except for some old paint cans and a pile of rotting planks close to the entrance.

He pushed the door open and entered. The men followed, guns drawn. A dusty bulb illuminated a rubbish-littered floor. A man lay on a mattress in the far corner sprawled on his stomach. The top of his dark head stuck from under the blanket, as well as his left hand, palm up, relaxed. Joe stepped toward the man. A sharp popping sound made the agents' guns swing sharply in its direction. A wisp of grayish smoke oozed out of a canister sitting upright next to the door. Joe registered the OSHA's Skull-and-Bones label. The smoke quickly thickened and spread.

"Out! Out!" he commanded, pushing the men to the exit. They fled through the fogging room, some gagging. The man on the mattress didn't move.

Joe pulled his mask over his nose, took out a pair of handcuffs, squatted by the mattress and slapped them on the man's exposed wrist. "Up! Get up!" he barked, coughing himself now, and got up.

He almost tumbled backward as the hand yielded without resistance. As if in a bad dream, it hung in the loop of the handcuff a moment and fell out. Joe gawked at the splintered bone and torn flesh, dropped the handcuffs, and yanked the blanket aside.

A naked corpse in a pool of blood sprawled across the mattress. The skull was smashed, but a large mole on the exposed cheek was clearly visible. *Will make it easy to identify.* The customary thought sobered him up, and then a wave of nausea hit with no air to breathe in and ease it.

Joe's sinuses and eyes burned like acid now. His makeshift mask proved useless. He struggled in the direction of where he remembered the door was, ran into the wall, and tried to feel his way along it. He fell to his knees…The primordial panic constricted his chest.

A hand gripped his shoulder. In the grey haze, he caught a glimpse of an air purifying mask worn over the balaclava before its owner deftly thrust another double cartridge gas mask on his face. A few long, suffocating seconds of dim-mindedness and Joe hungrily sucked in the bad-tasting but no longer harmful air, with a deep gratitude to the rookie who left his post to save him.

He was helped to his feet, and then pushed out of the room and along the topsy-turvy hall. Another turn and his guide let go of him. Joe walked through the thinning smoke to the end of the passage toward the van's headlights blazing in the aperture of the open front door. He stepped out on the porch and ripped the gas mask off. His men sat on the scraggy lawn, wheezing. Joe staggered among them. They were all present—except one.

Joe ran back to the porch. "Dante!" he called. His heart beat thunderous against the walls of his chest. His young partner, his savior, had not emerged from the house. "Dammit, Gayle!" Steve's eyes stared into his and then went blank, again.

Joe jumped to the door. A beep from his radio stopped him. He pulled it from his belt, "Dante! Where are you?!"

"Don't be a fool, Agent Vasquezss," the radio hissed. "I've helped you enough. From hhhere on, you're on your own."

Later, he would figure out that this unnatural voice of a make-believe snake from a cheap Sunday school play belonged to someone watching from some safe hiding place nearby. At the moment he could only stare at the radio, dumb-struck, as inertia carried him another step and into the open front door.

"Didn't you hear me? You and your men have five ssseconds. Ssscram!" The radio went dead.

Joe peered into the dark interior. Was Dante still there? A moment of indecision. He didn't have a choice but to turn back. He dashed from the porch to the five dazed men on the ground. "Get up! Get up!" He pulled the slow ones roughly to their feet. "It's gonna blow!"

In less than three seconds, the Feds were scrambling away from the house. As Joe ran toward the van, Gonzales' words came to him. '*…no one saw him, but some heard his voice. Hissing like a snake.*' He made out a shape inside the van slumped in the driver's seat. His heart leaped with hope. He threw the door open and nearly screamed in triumph at the sight of his young partner—gagged, apparently unconscious, duct-taped to the seat, bareheaded, and missing his vest. Al appeared by the van panting, then an explosion propelled Joe onto Dante's lap and knocked Al to the pavement, the reverberation cracking their eardrums.

Joe gawked back at the orange flush and flying debris.

A hissing voice in his head belonging, his gut told him, to the man the prisoners in Arizona's Super Max called Viper, said, *I've helped you enough already…*

Joe looked at the gas mask in his hand, saw what should have been obvious to him as soon as he came out on the porch, and, without thinking, hid the mask under his vest.

Chapter 14

The Blood, the Muck, and the Grind

Los Angeles

J oe is at the breakfast table in his childhood home. His parents argue, as they've been for weeks. Sitting across from him in his pajamas, unshaven since he lost his job, Rafa is thinner than he used to be, dark circles marring his formerly bright eyes. The bitterness of Isabel's heated Spanish, Joe fears, will poison the beans she piles on their tortillas.

"What are we going to do?" she is saying. "What are we going to eat tomorrow? Nobody will hire you now!"

Joe jumps from his seat, runs around the table and ends at his father's lap. Rafa hugs him.

"We'll spend more time together now, boy," he whispers. "I was away from you too much."

A screech of tires outside. Isabel gasps. Rafa's face fills with a madness that scares Joe.

"Hide in the cellar!" Joe's mother says to Rafa, white-faced.

"Don't order me around!" Rafa rises, his strong hands move Joe out of the way.

"Rafa! Go to the cellar!" Isabel pleads.

"I'm not hiding anymore!"

He reaches for something behind the fridge and heads to the door as Isabel screams hysterically, "Don't go! Please!"

Joe's father swings the door open and slams it shut behind. Joe runs to the window.

Behind him, his mother, trying to dial a phone, screams, "Go to your room! Don't look! Get away from the window!"

But Joe can't help it.

Rafa stands in the yard, barefoot, his hand aiming his police gun at a long car slowing down past their fence. Joe sees its tinted windows. The back one lowers, and his father fires as another shot crackles at the same time.

Isabel screams.

In the yard, Rafa falls as the long car peels away.

79

§ § §

Hiding from the morning light, Joe pulled the blanket over his head and lay still for a while, tears soaking the sheet. They were the tears of bitterness, of knowing that the questions he ached to ask his father would always go unanswered. Why did he step out into the yard? Why did he let himself be dishonored, to get killed? Why did he abandon his son? Joe heard voices on the street and cars driving by. It was time to start the day.

§ § §

Cowell had been emitting steam for the full twenty-minutes since Joe and Dante's arrival. But the questions crowding Joe's mind made it easy to tune the SAC out. He wondered what moved Craig's killer to warn him and to spare his team. The most plausible explanation, of course, was that killing a bunch of Feds would attract too much attention and manpower to hunt the bastard down.

Or could it be because, in Viper's book, Joe and his team were not guilty of anything justifying Viper's style of punishment. Which could mean Blake, and possibly Sheppard's son, had done something…On the other hand, assigning a psychopath such complicated moral reasoning seemed too farfetched.

Cowell's rising voice brought Joe back.

"How much more could you screw up, Vasquez? I don't care what you have written in your report!" The SAC's watery eyes drilled small holes into Joe. "I told you *specifically* to pick him up quietly! And what did I get? The fire department and the whole town's police force involved, and the hood's old zombies calling and demanding answers. Harris Construction wants compensation for the three houses destroyed—the houses they were going to demolish anyway! Now, we must lie to the residents and the reporters. They are all over us. And your raw partner didn't even see who whacked him! So much for watching his team's back."

Joe read mortification on Dante's face. The poor rookie was new to Cowell's nerve-racking tantrums.

"Craig is dead, and good riddance," Cowell continued. "We could have him written off with a heart attack, and no one would be any wiser or care. But no, no! Someone on your team has loose lips. I've received a call all the way from Washington. Their panties are all bunched up and they demand we catch the culprit." Cowell sat down, looking like a flustered pig.

"Nothing indicated a trap," Joe said trying to keep his voice even. "The perp put on an excessive act, theatricals. He used tear gas, not poison. He didn't want to kill us. If you want to find out who he is, interrogate the inmates who knew Craig in Ironwood, question the friends and families of his victims. One of them might be your man."

"Well, I'm relieved you think it's such an easy case, Vasquez, since you'll be working it. Only fair you should clean up your own mess, don'cha think? That's what Washington advised, and I am in complete agreement."

Yes. Joe's heart leaped in his chest, but he kept his face neutral. "I'd prefer to stay with the Johnson case," he said.

The SAC cringed, about to do something against his puffed-up alpha-dog's nature. "The man who called me, the man up the chain Hound, advised me to assign the case to you," the SAC said through his teeth. "Apparently someone praised you to him. I must admit, you've got a track record of a rapport with offenders that facilitates interrogations." Cowell forced himself to smile. "It's a big opportunity. Important people want answers soon. Craig's body doesn't look pretty. I wish it had burned with the house but there it is, in the evidence freezer. Someone had too much fun killing the son-of-a-bitch. We need to solve this before all the gory details get out. We need to find out what to cover up— and to get the perp, of course."

In that order, Joe thought.

"Can you imagine if the anti-death penalty bleeding hearts find out? They would say we hire sadists to work in our Federal prisons. It's not enough we keep people for life or kill them on death row, but we torture them as well." Cowell regarded his polished nails and smirked. "That actually sounds good, don't you think?" His face became somber again. "This is not a high profile case, Vasquez—no profile at all, if we can help it. No case, in fact, as far as outsiders are concerned. I want you to give it your all. Marcus can take up the Johnson case. If not for Steve, I'd give it back to the cops. But if you crack this bone, there will be some marrow for you, an opportunity for moving up. You've waited long enough."

Joe knew better than to buy Cowell's altruism. The reason for the assignment was the SAC's need for a fall guy in case the operation failed. He sneered. "No kidding. So long that I'm not sure I care anymore." Joe rose from his chair without looking at the SAC, to let him sweat a bit.

"Look, Vasquez," Cowell started, "given your personal history, you can't expect…"

Joe stopped. *"My history?"* he said quietly, daring Cowell to spill it.

"Okay. Not yours. Your father's. It lends a certain…color…to your profile, as you know."

"Ah." Joe turned to the door, and Dante rose too, looking alarmed.

"If you refuse to help, there will be no chance for you!" Cowell growled at Joe's back.

Joe's hand rested on the brass doorknob. "Okay." He turned back to Cowell. "But I'm not giving up the Johnson case. You want me to work on this new one, fine. I'll work on both. I'll need the department's full support. And I don't want O'Neal breathing down my neck." Joe had almost said 'your lap dog.'

He and the SAC glared at each other, until Cowell eased into a trained smile. "Fine. Keep the Johnson case. But the Craig case comes first."

Joe pretended to hesitate, noting a warning expression on Dante's face. His partner didn't know him well enough yet. Joe nodded to the boss. "Okay," he said, and Dante exhaled.

"I've always believed in you, Hound." Cowell's relief was obvious. "You're one of the best here. Bring in the goods and no one will doubt you anymore."

"Thank you, Don," Joe said, and walked out, Dante trailing.

§ § §

"Wow," Dante said as soon as the door closed behind them. They walked through the hall toward Joe's office. "I can't believe how he went at you. I mean, if not for your lucky guess, six people would be dead. Why didn't you bring that up?"

"A, because he knows that," Joe answered. "B, because it wasn't a guess, but I'm not sharing that with him." They passed a maze of low-walled cubicles. Through the corner of his eye, Joe caught sight of someone watching them.

"It wasn't?" he heard Dante say but didn't answer right away. He glanced back. A slight man standing by the entrance of the copy room hunched over and rolled a mail cart down the corridor. Before the mailman turned, Joe glimpsed thick nerdy glasses and a shaggy, colorless mane. Then it was just the guy's scrawny back—teenage-sized, in baggy Dockers and a wrinkled, long-sleeved shirt at least a size too big. Joe didn't think he saw the guy before. Must have been a new hire.

Joe resumed walking. "I need to show you something," he said to Dante. They reached Joe's office, got in, and Dante closed the door. Joe opened one of the drawers of his desk, took out the respirator and handed it to Dante.

Dante inspected it. "It's not standard issue. Where did you get it?"

"From the same guy who knocked you out. He wore a similar one over *your* mask." Dante's mask, radio, and balaclava were never recovered. "I mistook him for you. I couldn't see much else of him. He pushed this mask on me when I was about to keel over. He led me so I could find my way out. And when I got outside, he called me using your walkie-talkie and told me the house was about to blow up." Joe paused. "Except, he didn't talk. He *hissed.*"

Dante stared at him, round-eyed and round-mouthed, the cool suaveness replaced by a child-like wonderment. "Wow…Then he must be the killer! The one Gonzales told us about! And he spied on us…" Dante plopped into his chair, eyeing Joe as Joe sat down too.

"I think his hissing voice is an artifact of some sort," Joe said. He let Dante work on it a bit.

"And he spoke to Gonzales in his real, normal voice when Gonzales sold him crack?" Dante spelled.

"These two cases are one and the same. Craig was cut on the wrists and near the groin. The conclusions are still preliminary, but Reichman, our big forensic anthropology expert, said he believes Craig lost a great deal of blood through those cuts before Viper went about killing him in earnest. What hard to digest is the bastard murdered my best friend, and yesterday he saved my life. Of course, I don't believe mine or the team's safety was the reason. But still…" Joe grimaced and sat silent for a while. "It's like he took notice of me after Steve and I almost got him…like he is following me, preening for me. He is too smart to bring attention to himself, but all these psychopaths are narcissists. I might be his audience now." Joe gazed at Dante, morose. "I'd like you to be very careful about what you say to anyone, especially Cowell."

"I told you," Dante said, "don't worry about me."

Joe wished he could believe that. If it were Steve, Joe wouldn't doubt. He wouldn't even need to tell his friend to keep this to himself. The loneliness bit Joe anew.

"Don't feel bad, Joe. If you saw him, face to face like Steve did, you would be dead too. And by the way, I didn't have a chance to tell you last night, but I've dug something out for you." Dante took a flash drive out of his pocket and waved it at Joe's laptop.

§ § §

"It's damn strange," Dante said. "Remember the absence of records about the Arizona and Colorado killings? You thought Corrections was sloppy entering the data? Well, this one was not in NSIS either. Which comes across like too much sloppiness to me. More like it was intentional."

Joe studied a mug-shot of a sneering young male with glassy eyes on the screen.

"You can say," Dante conceded, "he doesn't quite fit the profile. The guy was killed outside the bars. But it's still the same crime and punishment scenario. James Carson. Alaska. Animal cruelty case. He hung his ex-girlfriend's husky by the neck in his garage and, while the dog struggled, beat it to death with a bat. They fined and jailed him briefly. He got off by volunteering to go through the state's anger management course."

Dante prompted the next image, a shapeless, bloody sack hanging from a sturdy hook. "This is Carson, dead, about a year after his big brush with the law. By the way, he committed a few infractions before the animal cruelty charge. Mostly domestic violence calls. He never served any time."

"Was he bled before being beaten to death?"

"They didn't check. The cause of his death was too obvious. But there were some prominent cuts on his wrists, along with more superficial cuts on the rest of his body. His ex was questioned to no end but professed she had nothing to do with his murder. They found no links to her, and she was out of town when he was offed. So I would chalk up the murder as very probably Viper's handiwork. All three cases—Bacholski, McKee, and Carson—occurred within the last year-and-a-half. In spite of all the blood and muck, they were all sterile jobs— no prints, no tracks, and no witnesses. Same as with Craig's execution and the Ponderosa place. Surfaces were wiped clean, or so slimy the prints were either partial or disintegrated."

"Or too numerous," Joe muttered. He closed his eyes for a moment and then peered at Dante. "But we always have the grind."

§ § §

Joe called Sheryl Silverman, the Los Angeles County Sheriff's secretary, and mentioned Cowell's name. A few hours later, at seven p.m., he and Dante were installed in a small, stuffy room on a deserted floor in the Department of Corrections building with Joe's trusted laptop, two six-packs of soda, and a large meat-heavy pizza.

Joe searched online for over three hours while Dante combed through the paper maze of visitation requests, schedules, and the Craig case documents. They took a break to exchange notes, finish the pizza and watched, on Joe's laptop, the footage recorded by Ironwood's surveillance cameras.

The first segment showed Craig at the gate. The security guards checked his fake ID, exchanged a few words with him, and he exited. In the second, the woman that came to visit Craig was led by a tall, muscular guard down the prison's hallway. She kept her eyes down, bleached-blond bangs hanging over them. Joe froze the frame on the clearest shot of her face.

"She gave her social on the visitation application as Chandra Morris, a registered Vegas prostitute," he said. "According to the Vegas database, Chandra died from an overdose two months ago. Blondie here used Chandra's driver's license as her ID."

He pulled the next frame onto the screen for Dante. Side by side with the prison image of the so-called Chandra were two mug shots of a young blond woman, her features ravaged by drugs.

"Well, that visiting gal is clearly not Chandra," Dante said at last. "But she made herself look kinda like her." He frowned. "She was smart to keep her face down. And the shot is too grainy, no way to ID her."

"They process all visitor requests," Joe said, "check their socials, the usual. Everything should have been kosher when her app was processed."

"Meaning we'll probably find that Chandra's death wasn't registered, same as Bacholski, McKee, and Garson's."

"The fake Chandra couldn't get in otherwise. So before Corrections checked, either the record was removed or someone on the inside deliberately over-looked it."

Dante whistled. "The perps would need to have a fairly long reach."

"And they are at least two people, that much we know," Joe said. "The fake Chandra took Craig to the house, where her accomplice or accomplices killed him." *Agent Vasquezss…*the voice hissed playfully in Joe's head. He willed the memory away. "You sure you don't remember how you were jumped?"

Dante's face darkened. The doc hadn't found any markings on Dante's skull, no signs of concussion, and no traces of inhaled substances in his blood. "I re-member nothing," he said.

Chapter 15

The Eye of a Viper

Sullivan Maximum Security Facility for the Criminally Insane, TX

Baca was reading the Bible, meaning he bowed his head over the black book laid open in front of him while his eyes glazed over. His back was to the door, in plain view of anyone who cared to check through the security window. His goal was to convince the Sullivan staff that the incident in Coloqueen had sparked in him an interest in religion and impress them as a model inmate. He bet that between maintaining an image of a repentant 'born-again' and his nutcase diagnosis, they would keep him here.

It was another good evening, and he liked his new surroundings a lot. The grounds they allowed him to walk twice a day, the wholesome food, his well-ventilated, clean cell, and no bullies to intimidate or hurt him. They treated him like a person here, a sick person not quite responsible for what he'd done outside. Baca enjoyed his dinner, and the sheets on a real twin bed, not a narrow prison cot, were freshly changed. Only the peep-through window of tempered glass on the door reminded of his incarceration.

He would miss the rush. The pills a mild-mannered male psychiatric nurse brought him twice a day made him sluggish. But if he stayed nice n' low for a few years, the suckers might even let him out as long as he took his meds. He prepared to do that as long as necessary. He'd probably go on disability and never have to work again. Who knows, maybe his urge *would* go away for good.

But then again, what would he do with his free time? Stalking his prey, playing with her, was the best entertainment he had ever known.

Damn, just thinking about it gave him a rise, with the meds in his system and the holy words blurring in front of his eyes—although he didn't get as hot and bothered as he used to. They may even have better meds to snuff the craving completely. He'd hate to give it up—what else was there to savor in life? But he ought to save his hide. He wished he had the affliction, acute paranoid schizophrenia, the shrinks disagreed about. He almost believed he had it. Why would he have heard what he did otherwise?

If Weizlan starts doubting, Baca would fake it better. But Baca suspected Weizlan didn't want to doubt Baca's diagnosis because that would make Weizlan wrong and the young bitch right. The bitch was everything Baca deplored in a woman. He would never enjoy putting his hands on her throat. Maybe, if he took her eyes out…Not his style, but some variety wouldn't hurt. He remembered her unblinking, paralyzing stare, the heaviest ever set on him.

The second time he saw her, after the first interview in Coloqueen, she grilled him about the voice. A good thing Weizlan was there. When she called Baca a lying son of a bitch and said he should rot in maximum security, Weizlan reprimanded her with pleasure. Baca got a hunch that Weizlan hated her, just like Baca did.

Baca had a plan. He talked to the priest working here, as well as to the staff shrink. He told them how the hissing voice still comes back sometimes, how he had heard it before when it told him to kill those women. Baca's lies were getting better and better. The voice that scared him to shit when he dreamt it up had become a blessing in disguise…

A sound brought him back. A hissing breath.

Baca turned on his stool and stared at the peep-through window. He could see no one behind it.

"Missster…Baca…"

He got up, his knees soft, and stole to the door. It was thick and impregnable. He pressed his ear to the crack…Nothing…

He looked out. The small portion of the corridor to the right and to the left visible to him was deserted. Maybe his hearing betrayed him…Maybe the voice was in his head after all…He exhaled, holding back as his breath came out, trying to be as quiet as he could, and pressed his face to the glass, to make sure… Nothing. The relief swept through him…And then he cried out in terror.

An eye stared at him from the other side.

Baca plopped to the floor, plastered his back to the door and drew in his knees. In his mind, the horrible eye loomed dark, huge, and inhuman. Out of sight, it still peered into Baca's very soul—the squirming, self-preserving, wormy thing within him.

It was a long time before he ventured to get off his cold, wet with urine ass and peek out again through the peep-through window.

The corridor beyond was empty.

Chapter 16

Takeoff

Los Angeles – third week of November

Considering the relative rarity of Dr. Lubovich's name, Joe could safely assume that the dossier on her, cross-referenced with her approximate age group, compiled by Choice Point and available to him through the FBI access website would not contain much misinformation. He printed it out and sifted through all sixty pages.

Her immigration records section absorbed his attention, and when the bright light fell on the page, he looked up and found himself standing in front of his office's narrow window. He wasn't aware of getting up. He went back to his desk and made a note about asking Berryhill to request her Interpol file, if one existed.

According to Immigration, she grew up as an orphan after her family had been executed by the local mafia. She fled Romania when she was twenty-two years old. Once in the U.S., she applied for a student visa. She obtained her green card while in graduate school. By now, she was a full-fledged American citizen. Dr. Lubovich's over-reactive compassion found an explanation of a sort. She knew enough loss herself. Joe's heart lurched as his thoughts, inescapably, turned to Alberto and Isabel.

He wanted to call Dr. Lubovich. He had her unlisted number and a good reason; she was a potential witness in his case. But the real motivation was his queer wonder—a vague comradeship for this strange woman whose actions and history seemed akin to his.

He was about to make the call when the phone on his desk rang. He took the receiver. "Vasquez speaking."

"Hello, I am a forensic psychiatrist presently with the Dallas FBI," he heard. The low female voice had a Slavic accent, easy on his ear. He sat back in his chair, sure of who she was even before she said, "My name is Gabrielle Lubovich."

§ § §

"I thought he faked the whole thing," Gabrielle said. "But the details were too specific. I couldn't believe he had fabricated such a story. James Baca is not a clever man. Sly, but not clever. Since he said the ghostly voice mentioned California, I decided to check."

"How did you find out about the Craig case and that I am working on it?"

She chortled softly. "My sources don't matter. What I'm trying to understand is how someone confined in a maximum security prison in Texas could have information about the death of an escaped convict in another state. And such a recent death. I thought you might be curious too. Right now, Baca claims he had a vision. He pretends to have suffered a breakdown. He passed a polygraph conclusively. The local expert, Professor Weizlan, insisted on transferring him to Sullivan, a mental facility. I have protested the transfer. I interviewed Baca and, although he is a classic psychopath, he is not a mental patient. But I wanted to talk to you, to confirm that Baca's tale came from real life."

Joe's thoughts hurried. How was that possible? The auditory "hallucination" Baca, her "research subject," allegedly had followed the likely scenario of Craig's last hour all too accurately. "Tell me," he asked, "when exactly did Baca have this vision of his?"

She told him and then proceeded, quite clinically, to retell Baca's account. He held his breath, his mind racing at the implication that her subject had listened to Craig's murder in real time. "Could there be a speaker in his cell?" he asked when she finished. "Some wireless models are very small and easy to conceal under a piece of plaster on the wall, for example."

She was quiet for a moment, thinking, connected to him invisibly through radio waves. "Yes," she said. "In fact, it's the only explanation."

"Gabrielle," Joe tested her name in his mouth. "Can you check this for me?"

"I think so…" She hesitated. "Yes, although if someone placed a speaker in Baca's cell they would try to remove it as soon as possible. And if they didn't, Baca was transferred almost two weeks ago. His cell must have been examined and cleaned. I'll call Warden Portman in Coloqueen anyway and get back to you."

She sounded earnest. Still, Joe's habits had no intentions of dying. There was no way around the hiccup. Since Gabrielle had been blackmailed by the killer, she may have something to hide and thus not be forthcoming. Joe needed to figure out if that was the case, even if she had an appearance of being truthful.

"What do you know about Craig?" he ventured.

She was quiet, but this time Joe sensed the tension in her silence. "As a matter of fact, I know quite a bit," she said. "I interviewed Terence Craig a few months ago, at the request of the prosecution team."

He hoped she couldn't hear him catching his breath again. He waited for more, but she didn't volunteer. "Tell me about Baca," he said while his hand scribbled on the yellow pad.

"I would rather email you his file. Or would you prefer a fax, Agent?"

"You can call me Joe."

He couldn't help smiling at the lilt in her voice. "Okay, Joe, I will."

He gave her his email, his fax, and his cell number.

"I have a request too," she said. "Would you mind not mentioning my call to anyone so it doesn't get passed on to Professor Weizlan? Our professional relationship is rather contentious, and he hates to be proven wrong."

"You can count on me," Joe said.

Then she hung up, and so did he. He sat for a while, his hectic mind stilled and uncertain, noticing for the first time the sun's rays falling from the narrow glass. He always thought them meager on his side of the building, but today they seemed bright and abundant. Then his fax came to life and spat a number of printed pages.

§ § §

Once the Department's secretary, Ms. McCollum, did her bit as Joe asked her, he called Dante. They met at LAX an hour later and were hurried through the check point, the head of LAX security himself waiting for them, their guns checked along with their permits to carry them. By 6:30 p.m., thanks to McCollum's powers, they took their seats in the first class cabin of the plane destined for Dallas.

"So, again, why the hurry?" Dante asked as soon as they fastened their seat belts, while the cheery female voice from the speakers recited a script on the placement of carry-ons.

Joe took the stack of Baca's case papers from his backpack, pushed the backpack under his seat, and dropped the papers on Dante's lap. Dante perused them while the voice instructed on the use of emergency exits and electronic devices, and reminded them that they were on a non-smoking flight.

As soon as the voice took a break, Dante started to read in a short-hand mutter that, Joe reckoned, was helping him to digest the material in a hurry.

"Sentenced to life…Recently moved to Sullivan, a facility for the criminally insane… Change of status following the insanity plea…"

"We request your full attention as the flight attendants demonstrate the safety features of this aircraft," the voice continued.

"Oh, bite me," Dante said and then read in silence.

By the time the stewardess was done miming the usage of the oxygen mask popping from overhead, Dante had gone through most of the papers. The kid could really speed-read.

"What do you think of Baca's vision?" Dante tapped his ear.

"Hidden speaker."

"Neat. Same here."

Another minute passed before Dante lifted his eyes from the page and gazed before him. "So, he liked to call his victims first…And then he paid them a visit."

"Ahah."

"And that's why we're in a hurry."

"Correct."

"Cool. But we are not going to Sullivan right away, are we? Because it will be way too late. And I hate to miss my dinner."

"What do you think?"

Dante's face drooped.

"…The flight attendants will be offering you hot and cold drinks, as well as a light snack. Alcoholic beverages are also available with our compliments," the congenial disembodied voice assured.

"I can use one," Dante sighed. "You know, they shouldn't call you 'Hound.' You're more of a bulldog."

Chapter 17

Viper's Style

Sullivan Maximum Security Facility for the Criminally Insane, TX

By about nine p.m. they reached the sprawling facility, a cross between a hospital and a penitentiary, surrounded by gray fields drizzled upon by the pitch-black skies. A concrete sign worthy of a small town's entrance spelled, *Sullivan Maximum Security Institution for the Criminally Insane.* Joe rolled down the window of the rental car and gave the guard in a slicker their papers. The man read and called the Head Warden. While they waited, Viper invaded Joe's thoughts again. *Agent Vasquezss…*he hissed to the foreboding lull of rain.

§ § §

Warned about the purpose of their visit, the congenial and ripe-for-retirement Head Warden Hershman personally walked to the West wing with Joe, Dante, and two guards in institutional orderlies' scrubs. The finish on the walls at Sullivan was a dove gray. The metal doors of the cells were of the same color, inset with small, Lexan windows. The light from the bulbs overhead, not barred but recessed, was softer and the overall environment not as depressing as in most prisons.

"Dr. Lubovich doesn't believe Baca was hallucinating. Dr. Weizlan, Dr. Ackerman, our staff psychiatrist, and I disagree with her. Baca is hardly what you would call a smooth operator."

"Why was Dr. Lubovich called to profile Baca?" Joe asked.

"She came to conduct her research. We got a request from above to assist her in any way we could." The irritation in Hershman's voice was unmistakable.

"What kind of research?" Joe asked.

"Something to the effect of weeding out the innocent. Dr. Weizlan doesn't think much of her methods. He's more traditional in his approach."

As you are, Joe thought.

They entered another well-lit corridor where each small window in the doors marching on both sides oversaw a bare, opposite wall. "Neat setup," Joe commented.

"Our inmates are more like patients. They have their privacy."

Joe didn't say the obvious—that so would a murderer.

Yet another set of heavy steel gates let them into the West Wing. They stopped by a guard station. The place stunk of hot quesadillas and burned coffee. While Hershman exchanged a few words with the sleepy-looking individual on duty, Joe observed, behind the break-room's big window overlooking the corridor, four more deputies chatting around a small table. Another man waited by the microwave. None of them turned to glance at Hershman and his companions. Joe wondered how easy it was for someone to pass the window unnoticed by those inside.

They walked on. The long corridor soon exhausted the polite topics of conversation. Their small group moved in silence, Hershman in front, Dante following Joe. Joe's perception of their monotonous progression became dreamlike. The back of Hershman's head bobbed ahead; the curly hair, still pretty dark, reminded Joe of his father. He thought about the letters from Isabel's trunk, now stored on a shelf in his office at work, and wanted to look at them. To ground himself in the present, he shifted his gaze and forced his surroundings back into focus.

And then he saw it—a janitor cart coming from the opposite direction. A garbage bin on the lower shelf, pushed by a teenage-sized guy in a numbing, even rhythm across the corded carpet. Thick-framed glasses and an unkempt beard. There was something familiar about this. An ill-built man with a cart, unremarkable, merging into the background, face lowered as if to appear even more inconspicuous.

As they drew near and passed each other, the guy's dark, surprised, and buglike eyes behind thick, nerdy glasses met Joe's. Another step and the janitor and his cart slipped behind them and temporarily out of Joe's mind.

§ § §

He was the first to react. Amidst the uniform row of doors in the geometrical perspective of the blind-end hall they just entered, the crack delineating one of the doors was etched thicker than the rest.

"Wait!" In one bound, Joe caught up with the orderly ahead and grabbed the man's sleeve. They halted. Joe pointed at the door that was meant to appear shut, but wasn't. He and Dante drew their weapons and advanced.

"Freeze!" Joe barked as he kicked the door ajar and froze at the sight.

Hershman pushed in past Dante and Joe and wavered. The contorted body lay on the cot, a gaping hole in place of genitalia. Baca's eyes protruded above his duct-taped mouth, his face swollen, a rope cutting into his neck and stretching taut from the end tied to a bar of the window. A pool of blood spread beneath the corpse, the steady drip on the linoleum floor resounding in the quiet. Red untidy lines, starting from the deep slash on the cut left wrist, the one visible, painted Baca's open palm. The stink of iron and fresh excrement…

Joe buried his nose into the nook of his elbow to overcome the nausea. The image momentarily blurred, as if he were under water, then he focused and remembered. "The janitor!" he said.

The others gawked at him.

"In the hall! He passed us!" Joe reminded them, urgent.

"I'm not sure," Dante stammered, "if I saw anybody…"

"Call the dispatcher, seal all the passages," Joe told Hershman.

The Head Warden pulled out his radio.

"Stay here! Search the other wards!" Joe said to the others and hurried down the corridor.

§ § §

The sirens wailed. By Joe's estimate, if the janitor had abandoned his cart and ran, he could have reached the station at the gates separating the west wing from the admin building before it was sealed even if Hershman's orders were followed promptly. But by moving too fast the sneak would draw attention to himself.

"Has a man passed through after us?" Joe asked the deputy by the gate to the wing, read the answer in his eyes, and turned back before the guy said a word.

Joe backtracked. A passage branched from the main corridor and he followed it. An unattended cart was parked by a door inscribed with 'Utility Access, Authorized Personnel Only.' The door didn't budge. Joe pulled his TRP out of his belt holster, flicked-off the safety, fired at the automatic lock, and threw the door open.

A narrow staircase stretched behind. Amidst the shrieks of the sirens, he thought he heard the sound of metal slam overhead. He grabbed the railing and rushed up, lifting himself with his arms as much as pushing with his feet. One flight up, he found another door marked 'HVAC' unlocked.

He entered, groped the wall for a switch and didn't find one. The little light from the bottom of the stairwell behind him expired within a dozen feet. A heat-breathing tangle of ventilation ducts and pipes melted into the darkness. The alarms were muffled here.

Joe raised his gun. A few near blind steps and he stifled a groan at a sharp pain in his shin struck by a low pipe. He regrouped and moved on. Cautious, led more by his instinct than his senses, he dodged his way in the obstruction course of columns and protrusions that presented too many hiding places for his enemy.

He detected movement, a silhouette dashed ahead. Joe ducked; his shot reverberated, ricocheting, and went unanswered.

Stepping from behind a supporting beam of some sort, he found himself in what seemed to be a short open passage. His spine prickled. The deeper darkness slithered on the outskirts of his view. A breeze kissed his face…Without thinking he shifted to the left, but not quite soon enough, heeding, as in a slow-motion dream, a bar falling at him from the right.

Everything went blank.

§ § §

He came to, his head buzzing with dull pain, and scrambled to his knees. His gun lay a few feet away. He grabbed it and got up. The sirens still screamed, muffled, so he hadn't been unconscious for long. But how much time did he lose? Seconds, minutes? He hurried ahead, no longer cautious. He reached an iron ladder leading to an opening overhead spilling cold drops on his upturned face. Once again he climbed, but not as swiftly, his head swimming.

He emerged on the top of the building. Yellow tape delineated roofing materials glistening in the rain, evidence of the repairs under way. Under the wash from the flood lights on the towers, the stacks created deep shadows. Next to one such pocket of darkness, at the edge of the roof, a dark figure crouched, busy with something and seemingly wearing a small backpack.

"Hands up!" Joe took aim.

The man raised his head but didn't bother to get up. Joe recognized the outlines of the beard. The guy appeared to nod, although in the lousy light Joe couldn't be sure, and then continued with whatever he was doing as if Joe wasn't a threat.

A strange uncertainty came over Joe. The man squatting before him did not want him dead. He had his chance in the HVAC room but used it only to slow Joe down, leaving him unharmed except for some ringing in his head. Joe's instinct and logic insisted that this man, this fake janitor was Viper, the same man who executed Craig and saved Joe's life in Ponderosa. But Joe also remembered that this degenerate murdered an innocent boy and Steve.

From the corner of his eye, he caught movements on the towers. He stood bathed in light, while his opponent stayed enveloped in darkness.

He aimed above the man and pressed the trigger—

An impotent click. He checked his gun to find the magazine was gone. He was too out of it to notice the Springfield's lighter weight when he recovered it in the HVAC room.

The janitor got up and turned toward him. Joe recognized his slight, weasel-like shape, even though he shed his baggy janitorial garb and wore a more fitting one as well as a cap on his head—a knitted beanie, Joe guessed. The man raised his hand theatrically and dropped something with a loud clunk. The Springfield's magazine.

The janitor waved farewell and stepped off the roof, dropping from sight…

Heart pounding, Joe raced to the edge and stared down into a construction disposal chute attached to the wall.

"Don't move or you'll be shot!" boomed over the speakers from the tower.

Joe dropped into the chute's yawning mouth. His involuntary scream choked as his body crashed against the metal sides. He slammed into a pile of rubbish within a huge collection bin and scrambled to his feet, fully expecting his quarry would assault him.

But nobody did. He was alone.

He fought his way past a discarded tarp, rough-edged particle board, empty tar cans, and fiberglass insulation and pulled himself up to look out of the bin. He was behind the West wing. A tall, chain-link fence enclosed the yard on all sides, and beyond, deserted road ran between the second chain-link and the brick perimeter wall.

At one end, the yard stretched to the gate beneath one of the guard towers. At the other end, from the low building housing the Head Warden's office, a group of armed, uniformed men ran toward him, screaming he-didn't-care-what. No sight of the weasely man, and no place for him to hide, except in the bin.

As soon as the feverish, absurd thought shot through Joe's mind he attacked the debris, digging and throwing, as the whistles and the shouts quickly neared. Too frustrated, he couldn't stop, even as the futility of his efforts became apparent.

The guards surrounded the bin and, when one of them gave a warning shot into the air, Joe finally whipped out his badge, raised his hands, and rasped, "FBI!"

The guy Joe recognized from the checkpoint called to the rest, "It's okay. He's a Fed from L.A."

"I followed the perp. He is a small man with a beard wearing a backpack. He went down the chute before me!"

The guards exchanged words and spread out to hunt. Joe tried to tell himself that the game couldn't be lost yet. Sullivan was sealed. But a feeling of failure gripped him.

§ § §

The local Sheriff's Office combed the three-mile radius area adjacent to the prison throughout the night. Joe and Dante stayed for the search, although their cooperation didn't go as far as to divulge the details of their case.

At first, Joe's story roused the county's Sheriff and the Dallas Homicide Unit Commander. Hershman, who feared Baca's execution might be viewed as an inside job, supported Joe's theory of a janitor. The mysterious imposter was, beyond a doubt, an intruder, since his description didn't match any of Sullivan's employees. But by the morning light, after the Dallas detectives talked to the Head Warden, questioned the guards who accompanied the visitors to Baca's cell, and spoke to Dante who was too honest to hide his confusion, all involved came to quietly regard the janitor a product of Joe's imagination in the aftermath of a gruesome murder.

The presence of the cart not far from Baca's cell vouched somewhat against their conclusion, but could be reasonably explained. The cart appeared to be clean, though forensics would check for blood traces later. Head throbbing, Joe was too tired to care by the time Hershman's secretary brought him and Dante some coffee and donuts. After downing them, Dante accompanied Joe down the corridor. A middle-aged, black, female forensic scientist squatted on her haunches, photographing the floor near the door Joe destroyed.

They both leaned in, and she pointed to a few small, dark spots. "Don't get your hopes too high," she said. "Might be some rat had diarrhea. But blood or not, it's organic and it's fresh. Filmed, but not hardened."

She scratched the coagulated matter off with a razor blade and deposited the blade with a residue into a zip-lock bag, the same kind Joe carried around. Then, she examined the concrete surface with the magnifier and picked up something with tweezers. "You might have gotten lucky!" She held up her prize, a hair.

Dante perked up. It was obvious he wanted to believe Joe's story but had trouble doing so in good faith.

Looking at the precious evidence being deposited into the forensic scientist's roomy pocket, Joe suddenly itched to hear Viper again. Their first face-to-face was urgently unsatisfactory. Joe played a mere spectator to the Viper's teasing, arrogant performance. The urge to shake out of the crafty bastard the trick he used to turn himself into a ghost was natural, but Joe recognized that there was also something else, less savory to his itch—no, yearning—some perverted curiosity Joe didn't care for in himself.

"Can I borrow your flashlight?" he asked the woman.

"Don't hog it," she warned, and unstrapped the flashlight from her belt.

Joe took it and went through the busted door, with Dante following.

§ § §

On the roof, Joe marveled at how good Viper's timing was. The downpour still pelted, washing away any traces the events of the night could leave. They hunkered down at the edge. Joe directed the flashlight at the space behind the chute. The rain had trouble reaching it. The concrete wall was damp but not thoroughly wet.

"Hey!" Dante pointed. "Look!"

The rookie's eyesight was sharp. Joe barely made out vertical scratches a few yards below. *Scuff marks,* he thought.

He sat on the edge, held onto the rim of the tube, and eased off until his foot touched one of the metal brackets attaching it to the wall. In his mind, he pictured himself raging in the waste bin below while a black figure, wedged behind the chute above watched him and then stole back to the roof, unnoticed.

Loosened by this vision, a memory surfaced. The scrawny mailman watching Joe in the Wilshire building. The same under-developed, adolescent body, the same smooth, fluid gait repelling attention, same glasses, but no beard. Was Joe's recall accurate or bent by his harassed imagination? These two being one would imply Viper's pointed interest in Joe, a possibility that the twisted son-of-a-bitch infiltrated the L.A. FBI or had an insider's access to information, and, most sobering, had anticipated Joe's every recent step before Joe made it. Like this visit to Sullivan.

Weighted by the drenched clothes and his suspicions, Joe climbed back. He hoped he had been mistaken. But his instinct knew better.

§ § §

The forensic scientist photographed the wall behind the chute. She didn't sound optimistic about the outcome, and voiced a doubt that the scuff marks were recent. Joe and Dante left the facility close to five a.m.; the state investigators stayed a couple hours longer.

By 7:30, Hershman returned to his office, feeling twenty-years older—too old, in any case, to stay up all night and worry so much. *To hell with it,* he thought, *if they want me to take a hike after this one, I'll gladly oblige.* He already put his three kids through college and had earned an ample retirement. For the last ten years or so he had been a certified double dipper. But all good things must come to an end, especially when they start rotting. His mind so made up, wife notified and calmed, he took out his pillow and a blanket from the old paperwork closet and settled on his couch for a nap.

As soon as he did the phone on his desk rang.

Cursing, Hershman got up and picked up the receiver. "Yeah?"

"Hello, Dr. Hershman," an ingratiating female voice greeted. "This is Dr. Lubovich. I heard of the commotion last night. I worry about the effect it may have on Brin James. I need to see him."

How the hell did she find out so fast? Hershman thought. Clearly, she had an informant inside Sullivan.

"Well, your timing is lousy," he said. "Call tomorrow."

"I am at the main gate, Dr. Hershman." Gabrielle's words were firm, no longer breathy. "I *must* see my patient."

Damn you, Hershman thought. "Wait a bit." He hung up and groaned. Then he radioed her in.

Less than five minutes later she stood in his office, her breath reeking of strong coffee. Hershman assumed that her tired look expressed her worry for Brin James' welfare.

"Thank you, Dr. Hershman. I know how hard this night must have been on you," she said solemnly. "I'll keep everything I see and hear this morning confidential. You can absolutely count on that." Her eyes stared into Hershman's with utmost sympathy, and he felt lulled. Her source was likely the Dallas SAC, Logan, himself. As soon as this comforting thought came to the exhausted Head Warden he became convinced of it.

Without any preliminaries, he summoned a deputy and told him to escort her. After all, she was a person with unmentioned but heavy clout behind her.

100

§ § §

In his cell in the East wing, the area allotted for the least violent offenders, Brin James sat on his bed. He was of less than average height, thin, balding, in his mid-forties, unremarkable but for anxious, guilty dark eyes that inspired automatic mistrust in many he met throughout his life.

"She said I am good," he muttered, as if trying to convince himself. "It's all in my head…" he trailed, cringing, and his face assumed a furtive, mortified expression.

He got up, tiptoed to the door, took a peek through the small window, and then pressed his ear to the crack. The footfalls were approaching. Two people, one in soft-soled institutional shoes, and an outsider, the heels clicking. Apprehension on his face, Brin circled his cell, went to his bed, and curled on it. A few seconds later his door was unlocked. He sat up, his eyes round.

Gabrielle entered. "I brought you some breakfast," she said.

She held out a tray covered with a big napkin. As a part of her arrangement, she could have a meal with her patient whenever she visited him as long as she paid for the extra fare. She set the tray on a small table and pulled up a chair. "Thank you," she said to the deputy.

The young man, unsure how to behave with someone who made Hershman forget the rules, hesitated. She leveled her unwavering gaze at him.

She turned it, softened, at Brin as soon as the deputy left. "I heard about last night."

Brin grabbed her hand and pressed it to his chest, causing her to lean in.

"I did it!" he whispered, desperate.

"Shhh. What did you do?"

"I killed a man! I killed him badly!"

"What makes you think you did it?"

"I know!"

She took her hand away. Her eyes narrowed at him. "How do you know about the murder? Did they question you?"

A confused expression was all she got. "Don't be angry, please!"

"I am not angry at *you*, Brin."

"Don't be angry at them. I am the bad one, the responsible one!" He shook his head. "I know…because…because I can do things in my sleep! I think I even remember something…"

"What do you remember? Tell me."

He looked more and more at a loss under her hard stare.

"You see?" she said. "You don't remember because there is nothing to remember." She walked and touched the lock. "This door is always locked. You had no way to get out."

"I don't know how I got out," Brin stammered. "But I did somehow…"

"And then you went where, Brin? You haven't been anywhere but to the garden here. You don't even know where things are."

"I can see a lot from the garden," Brin whispered. "I know where the West wing is, where the man was killed last night…The other doctor told me the truth sets a man free. I'd be better free, even if they kill me."

She sat in the chair in front of his bed again. "Do you know you are my most difficult case?" Her voice was weary.

"I'm sorry."

"Look at me."

He lifted his head to meet her unrelenting gaze, and she held his for a few long seconds.

"You did nothing," she said, and a certainty in her voice smoothed out his face, lifting the despair. "You couldn't have. Your mind plays tricks on you. Always remember that. Don't trust it."

"I won't. I don't want to," he said, peering back at her, desperate. "I won't!" he repeated, more sure.

"Trust only me."

Brin nodded fast a few times and smiled, and she nodded back, satisfied.

"Chicken enchiladas, your favorite," she said, uncovering the tray and arranging the plates on the small table. "Let's eat. I am starving."

Chapter 18

Joe Watches

Coloqueen Maximum Security Prison

As they walked, the worn concrete walls and the barred, shabby cells along the passage at Coloqueen were in stark contrast to the comforts and neatness of Sullivan. Joe wondered if, before his demise, Baca thought he cheated the system. Did he forget he had been warned? The preliminary forensics report stated he was approached from the back and blasted with a Taser. The shock to his neck would render him helpless long enough for Viper, a man of slight statue, to bound and gag him. Interestingly, Gonzales described his buyer in Garden Lane as a man of medium build. But his memory could have been impaired by his mental state at the time and the long period since the encounter.

"We have more of them caged here than in most states. Interesting specimens, too. Gabrielle even decided to settle here for a while. Good material for her research, she said." There was pride in the warden's voice, the source of which wasn't clear to Joe. Was McDonald bragging about the state of Texas containing the highest number of serial killers or about esteemed Dr. Lubovich finding the locale suitable for her work?

"So you and Doctor Lubovich are on first name terms," Joe commented.

"We're friendly. Not as friendly as some say she is with MSU Supervisor Mitchell." McDonald pursued his lips. "But I'd say *he* is the source of that rumor. She's way too classy for the likes of him."

It occurred to Joe even false rumors often had something behind them.

They reached the guards' fishbowl. McDonald went inside and talked to a swarthy deputy he pointed out to Joe as the aforementioned C.S. Mitchell. The big man, once athletic but now growing a gut, reclined in a chair. He glanced through the glass and sneered dismissively at Dante.

Joe read him as a racist prick, among other things. He remembered the rumor McDonald mentioned. Was Dr. Lubovich involved with this guy? The idea irked him, and he hurried to find an explanation for his reaction. It would be pity, he thought. No woman of intelligence should take an interest in a Cro-Magnon douche playing the alpha dog. McDonald exited and led his charges further into the prison.

"Does Dr. Lubovich work closely with Professor Weizlan?" Joe asked.

"The state profiler? Nah. Between us boys, the old jalopy suffers from professional jealousy. The way that girl works, it's really something. But you'll see for yourself." McDonald winked like a showman to kids at a circus. Joe understood his strutting. The interview they headed to witness was of Matt Salmon, accused of kidnapping and cannibalism, the case that rattled Texas less than a year ago.

They passed through a heavy gate and another corridor, made a few turns, and finally arrived at their destination, a dead end with two metal doors at an angle to each other.

They entered one of them.

§ § §

"This is Tony." McDonald introduced them to the sullen, husky guard in a small, stuffy observation room.

Joe didn't listen. Beyond the window, a dark-haired woman leaned toward a sixty-year old dumpy, watery-eyed man in prison overalls. Joe had an understandable male curiosity of what Gabrielle was like in person, but he didn't expect her to so vastly exceed his expectations. Her photos didn't do her justice. Her grey suit fitted her tight body like a glove, her thick hair was collected in a low ponytail, and even though her face appeared more tired than in the photos, the force of it struck him afresh.

Joe realized Dante was saying something. "…amazing that she can hypnotize without looking." The tactless rookie smirked at him.

"Where's the sound?" Joe asked the other two men.

"You wanna hear?" Tony glared, incredulous. "Have a shovel-full." He turned the volume on and walked out.

"Hey! Where do you think you're going?" McDonald protested.

"Let him go," Joe said.

A male voice droned from the speakers, "…and with boys, you must keep 'em a while and beat 'em to make their meat good and tender."

Salmon nearly salivated as he confided oh-so-intimately to Dr. Lubovich, who was listening with an absorbed attention, nodding approvingly. The grandfatherly cannibal seemed unaware of the microphone before him or the recorder on the small table as she held him on course with her steady gaze. Joe imagined being the recipient of that gaze and shivered.

"First, I killed the older boy, 'cause he had the fattest ass. I ate every part of him 'cept his head, bones and guts. I roasted his ass; that was yummy. The rest I boiled, broiled, fried, stewed—"

"Did he have any birth marks?" she asked, in the same low and soothing voice he heard over the phone. He hungered for this voice ever since, he realized. Hearing it again almost made him forget the unfolding interview. Almost.

"Oh. Yeah. Dime-sized. On his back," Salmon nodded.

"You have a good memory!" Her tone of approval made Joe queasy.

Salmon chuckled like a kid who passed the test.

"Christ…" Dante whispered.

Joe snapped the sound off. "Well," he said, "that's her job, isn't it?" After, they watched idly.

"Jamaicans call the women like her 'obeah,'" Dante said.

Joe half-turned his head, inviting more.

"Remember how I told you no one can be put into a hypnotic state unwillingly? And here she is, proving all the experts wrong."

"Obeah…" Joe repeated.

Gabrielle leaned back in her chair and Salmon stopped mumbling, blinking sleepily, lost and disoriented. Dr. Lubovich appeared…satiated, as if she got all she wanted from her subject and the experience. Another minute and Salmon started to snore.

Look at me, Joe willed, irrationally, and his stomach clenched with concentration. *Look at me!*

Gabrielle's eyes left Salmon and drifted to the mirror. Although not seeing through, her gaze met Joe's.

§ § §

As Gabrielle and Joe exited at the same time from their respective doors, they nearly crashed into each other. She swayed back and recouped, but her expression remained unfazed. He assumed the session left her too depleted to be startled.

"Sorry, I didn't mean to run you over," he said. "I'm Agent Vasquez… Joe…we talked on the phone. This is Dante Gayle." He nodded at Dante, behind his shoulder. "I believe the Head Warden mentioned to you that we would be observing your interview."

Her eyes found McDonald. "I need coffee real bad."

"Of course, dear. This way." He and Gabrielle headed down the corridor, Joe and Dante in tow.

Tony was already drinking coffee in the guard's lounge. Gabrielle poured some into a paper cup and plopped into a seat. Joe took another across from her. She appeared hardly able to keep her head up. Either that, Joe thought, or she avoided looking at him on purpose. If so, was it because her eyes were her tool, too powerful to use indiscriminately?

After a few sips, she said, "They didn't find anything in Baca's old cell."

"I need to discuss a few things with you," Joe said.

"I'm too trashed to discuss anything." She rubbed her eyes. "I must lie down for a while before I drive myself out of here."

"Would you like me to give you a lift? Dante can drive the car we came in," Joe said without thinking, and felt embarrassed.

Her surprised stare was soft, almost child-like, not a tool of any sort. "Thank you, but I'll manage." She lowered her eyes again and downed the rest of her coffee.

"We can talk later. Meanwhile, I wanted to ask you a favor. Would you send me the list of people you have interviewed? That is, if there is no confidentiality conflict."

Gabrielle stared at her cup and nodded.

"You better go to the Warden's office and rest, girl," McDonald said to her, shaking his head at Joe.

They all got up and walked to the end of Block B. Near the guard's fish-bowl, Mitchell stood talking with one of his subordinates. He peered at Gabrielle beseechingly, without his usual sneer—to Joe's watchful eye, like an obvious admirer. Gabrielle didn't reciprocate with any awareness, but Joe's sixth sense gnawed at him. Or maybe it was jealousy. He needed to snap out of it, Joe decided. After all, he didn't know her, even if irrationally he felt like he did.

In the medium security area their group divided. McDonald took Gabrielle to Portman's office, and Tony accompanied Joe and Dante to the parking lot. The bright sun greeted them outside, the autumn air smelled of spring. Gabrielle's face stood before him, her big, almond-shaped eyes regarding him above the coffee cup.

"Keep in mind," Dante said, watching Joe keenly, "even pretty ladies are blackmailed for a reason."

Chapter 19

Squaring Off

Dallas

To justify relocating the investigation to Texas required a partial reveal, so Joe asked Cowell to fly to Dallas on the fourth morning after Baca's sail into the great unknown to hear their report on the Craig case's latest discoveries. Gabrielle came through and emailed Joe the list of all the inmates she had ever interviewed by the end of the same day they met in Coloqueen.

Joe handled the interactions with the Dallas FBI Office and police concerning his and Dante's adventures in Sullivan. Dante holed-up with the laptop, a dozen cans of soda, about as many sandwiches from the nearby deli, and a take-out spread from a Cantonese restaurant recommended by Logan's secretary. After a day of researching the names on Gabrielle's list and diligent nourishment, he unearthed two more cases.

The morning before their meeting with Cowell, they decided what to reveal and what to conceal from their unreliable boss, and to which degree to bend the truth.

§ § §

The lights in the windowless conference room were off. Joe and Cowell sat at the big table across from each other. Professor Weizlan was also invited, since he recommended Baca's transfer and oversaw his treatment, and took the chair next to Cowell. Dante presided over the laptop and the projector on the short side of the table.

"After Ponderosa, we had a hunch to look for certain types of prison killings. That's how we found out about McKee and Bacholski, whose autopsies we emailed you earlier. And just yesterday, these two came to light."

Dante brought up a photo of a hawky man on the screen. "Robert Jenkins, convicted of six killings in Maine, suspected in a dozen more, sentenced to life without parole fourteen years ago. Modus operandi, a sadistic rapist. The victims included youths of both sexes. Jenkins' battered body was discovered in the

107

prison's carpentry shop. The immediate cause of death was a slow, intermittent strangulation. This matches three of his killings where he strangled the victims into unconsciousness and then revived them repeatedly. He was also beaten with a steel bar and raped with a claw hammer, replicating another of his exploits."

Cowell grumbled. Weizlan shrunk in his seat.

Dante displayed another mug shot of a swarthy man in his late twenties. "Allen Fawn. He was accused of murdering three boys in Montana. The prosecution couldn't present a convincing case. He was found in his apartment a week after his release. His punishment was rape with a foreign object, following by strangulation, although Fawn was strangled outright, unlike Jenkins, to match his style. The main difference here is Fawn was actually officially acquitted of his crime."

Cowell's lids were half-closed as if Dante's report was tiring him, and his stubby whiskers seemed to twitch in distaste. Joe imagined the SAC's reaction if he was told that Johnson case tied up into this new one. Cowell would laugh and say Joe and Dante were delusional—or, worse, take them off both cases. Joe glanced at Weizlan, who was covering his mouth with his hand, his face alight with attention.

"So, what we have here, so far," Dante went on, "are six instances where the killers, four incarcerated, one escaped and one released for the lack of solid evidence, were executed the way they killed their victims. We believe it was done by the same executioner, or the same group of persons."

"Wait, wait!" Cowell didn't hide his irritation. "Don't you think you're overreaching here?" The tactless swine glared at Joe. "Trying to make a big deal out of it, Vasquez, aren't you? People are often disappointed with our lenient justice system. They want a killer to reap what he sows. Relatives and loved ones of the victims. What proof do you have these cases are connected?"

Joe groaned internally. Cowell couldn't be as obtuse as he pretended to be, but apparently decided to resist the obvious to the last.

"For one, all of them were drained of blood while still alive," Dante protested.

"That's your conjecture. Bacholski's report says his cuts were accidental, and I bet the other reports made no allusion to these assholes being bled on purpose," Cowell pointed.

"I'd like to know," Weizlan pitched in, "how and when exactly did you find out about Baca? And how did it happen, so conveniently, that you arrived to Sullivan minutes after he was murdered?"

"You beat me to that one," Cowell told Weizlan.

"We received a lead on Baca from an informant who is presently awaiting trial in L.A.," Joe lied. He had prepared the answer to keep his promise to Gabrielle. "After Craig's killing, we found out about a similar case in Arizona and placed Manuel Gonzales in the unit that previously housed McKee. There, he heard an interesting rumor about a vigilante called Viper. The man supposedly penetrates prisons and kills the most heinous offenders in the same manner they had murdered their victims." Gonzales' stint at the Super Max predated Craig's execution by about two weeks, but Joe gambled that his boss wouldn't care to compare the dates, at least long enough not to interfere with the investigation.

"And you trust that informant, a criminal trying to score points to reduce his sentence!" Cowell snorted. "He could have invented or exaggerated that tale to appear useful."

"Another rumor he reported was about a man in Dallas who had a vision of Craig being killed by Viper." Joe was ready to prove this outright lie, if needed, with Gonzales' corroboration. "That's how we came across Baca. Our arrival coincided with his killing by accident," he finished, under the Weizlan's probing stare.

Cowell covered his eyes with his fat paw and just shook his head, so Dante jumped in again, "Another remarkable circumstance is that Colorado and Arizona claim they registered both the McKee and Bacholski cases, but the records disappeared. We believe they were removed by someone else, the same as Chandra's information in the Craig case."

"Chandra Morris is the name used by the woman who visited Craig in prison and presumably helped him escape," Joe clarified for Weizlan's sake. "The real Chandra had been dead for months."

"We believe someone hacked into the NCIC system," Dante stated. "It's also possible they work with, or are connected to, someone higher up, possibly even at the Bureau."

Cowell got up, turned the lights on and stared at Joe, his lips tight. "What the hell are you angling at? I expected a solid investigation to close Craig's case, good and fast, not conspiracy theories to ruin the Agency's reputation!"

Joe glanced at Weizlan. The Professor's eyes were sly slits and averted.

Cowell's stubby fingers tapped nervously on the polished surface. "You disappointed me, Vasquez. I shouldn't have given you the case. Dallas SAC Logan thinks you're a nutcase, a ghost chaser!"

"That so-called ghost killed Baca!" Dante protested.

"No one saw anyone, except for *him*!" Cowell snarled, pointing at Joe. "The only one happy with *his* theory was Sullivan's Head Warden. But even he doesn't honk this horn anymore!"

Joe envisioned grabbing Cowell's pointing finger and breaking it.

"How do you explain that, Vasquez? I'll tell you how. The killers were gone before you found the body. They didn't need to wear a disguise or play hide-and-seek because it was an inside job! Baca's murder has no connection to those others your partner wasted his time digging up!"

How much lamer could Cowell get? The Advil Joe took earlier was wearing off.

"Don't you glower at me! Precious man-hours were squandered, thanks to your lead. Where could your janitor have gone?" Cowell threw his palms in the air for a dramatic effect. "And why didn't he shoot you?"

"Maybe if he had you and Logan would be forced to believe me." The simple explanation almost made Joe smile. He didn't owe Steve's killer anything, not for Ponderosa, not for Sullivan.

Cowell's cell phone rang. "Yeah?" he said into the receiver. When he finished listening, his face was morose. "The lab called," he spoke through his teeth. "The samples taken from the floor by the HVAC door in the corridor were Baca's blood."

"What about the hair?" Joe asked.

"What about it? It's nothing. A synthetic fiber."

"Fake beard," Joe said.

Dante grinned.

Cowell got a grip on himself. "Okay, Vasquez. Maybe you saw someone. It's still doesn't make it the work of an outsider."

"You're probably right," Joe said. "But to avoid the possibility of any *outside inquiries* regarding these other cases in the future…" he nodded at Dante, "…we should investigate any possible connection just the same."

Joe remembered the 'new hire' he ran into in L.A. Viper didn't wear the beard with the rest of his disguise then. The memory spoiled his nascent triumph. McCollum asked around, and those few who could have encountered the mailman at the Wilshire building on that day didn't recall seeing anyone who matched Joe's description. Raising the issue with Cowell was pointless. Joe, hard-bitten by experience, would never communicate to his boss more than was minimally necessary. Imagine telling him about the killer walking freely through the L.A. field office.

What was the sneak doing there the day after Craig's execution? Gathering information? Checking out his new opponent? Had Joe "sniffed" him out twice by a mere accident? Or did Viper reveal himself to Joe intentionally? The implications of the latter made Joe cringe. No, he decided. Viper's skill to blend into the background was extraordinary. No wonder supernatural stories were told about him. Whoever he impersonated, he aimed to remain inconspicuous. Joe remembered the stunned expression behind the janitor's prop glasses. At the very least in Sullivan Viper was taken by surprise. It was even possible being noticed forced him to alter his escape route.

Cowell pushed away from the table. "If these cases are connected, this is big. Too fucking big," he grumbled. "What do you think, Professor?"

"I think Agents Vasquez and Gayle did an admirable job," Weizlan said. "I, for one, wholeheartedly agree with their theory."

Surprised, Joe met Weizlan's spider eyes. The comradery in them, eager and malicious, filled him with unease.

§ § §

"Most sociopaths mellow with age," Weizlan pontificated, "so this Viper must be relatively young. Early-thirties to mid-forties. He is too resourceful to be any greener. And, of course, still high on testosterone. But he is a scavenging wolf. He attacks those already captured and acts with assistance."

"You think someone is helping him?" Joe asked.

Weizlan lifted his sharp shoulders. "You wouldn't imagine gaining access to any maximum security unit without help, would you? This is not an isolated case; it's several murders in different states. And we already know a woman helped the killer organize Craig's escape. I'd say this is a conspiracy involving someone or *someones* endowed with power.

"Viper is a psychopath, which means he has no sense of right or wrong. He may commit other violent crimes in his spare time."

Joe thought about Blake and nodded to himself.

"But as far as the vigilante angle, he is only doing what he is told; he is no more than a tool. Someone directs him to each victim and provides the means necessary to carry the operations through. They may even, if Agent Gayle's intuition is correct, keep attention away from the crimes by manipulating interagency information systems."

"This is a bit beyond your expertise, don't you think, Professor," Cowell said sourly. "Leave it to us to draw conclusions when all the facts are in."

Weizlan gave Joe a co-conspiratorial wink and Joe's unease deepened. The man sounded good, but he was wrong about Baca. If Weizlan hadn't transferred Baca to Sullivan, Baca could still be alive. Did Joe and Dante run ahead of themselves with their reasoning? Or was this doubt the result of Joe's dislike of Weizlan?

§ § §

The Professor left, done with his bit, after assuring his L.A. hosts that he would keep any information divulged during their meeting confidential.

"We'll continue working on this case just as we've worked so far, just as *you* instructed us from the beginning," Joe said to Cowell as soon as the door closed behind Weizlan. "No need to attract attention with a bigger operation."

Cowell dropped into a chair and considered. "Fine. Report everything to me. Avoid telling Logan's guys any more than required to keep things rolling. And try to resolve this as fast as you can."

"Should Dante and I station in Dallas for now?" Joe asked.

"You should," Cowell snapped, recovering his sense of dictatorship as Joe intended. "How the heck would you work this from L.A.?"

§ § §

The meeting was over at 1:10. As they exited the conference room, satisfied but beat, Joe glanced at the adjoining sitting space and forgot his weariness at once. Gabrielle occupied one of the chairs in the otherwise deserted area, and he knew outright that she had been waiting for him.

Dante apparently noticed her too. "Don," he addressed Cowell. "Can I talk to you?" Joe's perspicacious partner went on with the SAC, telling him about some trick to increase the security of the department's electronic data—or maybe something else.

Joe didn't care. He bee-lined for Gabrielle.

"Hi." He peered at her. Her rested visage was prettier than the one she presented in Coloqueen, her skin glowing and her mouth soft and kissable.

"I was rude last time," she said. "Let's try again."

"You were just tired."

"Well, I can talk now." She got up.

"Let's get lunch. I've heard of some decent places downtown."

She smiled. "I must catch a plane in a few hours. But..." she added, at his disappointed face, "Would you mind the cafeteria?"

He didn't mind. He was going to have her all to himself for the length of a meal.

§ § §

They waited for the elevator to arrive. "My partner has a degree in psychology. He told me no one can be hypnotized unless they want to be. But it appears your method works. How do you explain it?"

"Yes, in the accepted view hypnosis is a collaboration," Gabrielle said. "My method is different. The objective is to rob the subject of his will. The interrogator can be trained, but only if he or she is a well-pronounced dominant."

"A dominant?"

"A small percentage of dominants are always present within the population. In hypnosis, a more dominant personality, if properly trained, can always break through the weaker person's defenses."

The elevator arrived and he followed her inside. "That doesn't sound shrink-friendly," he said, "or politically correct."

Their fingers touched reaching for the button. Neither of them was in a hurry to pull away. Then she let him press the floor. Joe's blood thumped in his ears. The elevator moved.

"Professor Weizlan is not one of your fans. I expect few of your other colleagues are either."

"I would have precious little support for my work if not for Damien Sheppard."

Joe kept on looking at her.

"I mean, Senator Sheppard." Gabrielle gazed at him gravely as if she knew he was much better informed than he pretended to be. "He was my mentor in graduate school."

The elevator stopped. "How can you stand it?" he blurted. To the surprise in her eyes added, a bit embarrassed, "You seem too lovely to look into hell holes." They exited and followed the signs to the cafeteria.

"Statistics say about seven percent of people on death row are wrongly accused," she said. "Until society has a more reliable method for distinguishing between the innocent and the guilty beyond *any* doubt, capital punishment should be abolished. Don't you agree?"

"I'm not a capital punishment fan," Joe said. "But I don't pretend to be equipped to make a moral judgment here. My function is to remove criminals from circulation. What's done to them afterward is out of my hands. My only goal is to do my job as well as I can." They entered the open, light space full of people and the smell of food.

"If you and your colleagues truly did their job well, lovely me wouldn't need to look into hell holes," she said and took off toward one of the counters.

The last bit exposed her as a lover of dramatic exits and last words, which wouldn't be all bad except it rang a false note with Joe. Disconcerted, he joined the shortest queue at another counter and, no longer hungry, got a couple of tacos. He paid the cashier and halted at the entrance surveying the hall filled with the hum of voices and clink of silverware. At a light touch on his forearm, he turned and found her standing next to him with her tray. Their eyes met and stayed together. Her direct, candid gaze generated a warm, invisible capsule around their bodies, and his unease dissipated.

"There," he pointed and led her to the farthest part of the room. They found a table by the window. "Why would you see me as a problem?" he asked as soon as they settled.

"It's not personal," she said, taking her plates from the tray and arranging them in front of her. "Tell me, in your investigations, can you be truly open with your boss or even your partner at all times?"

Joe didn't answer.

"And now if you ask me about anything pertaining to your case and I have something to hide, however small for any reason, I can't really come out and tell you, can I?"

Yes, you can, Joe nearly said. It shouldn't have been so, but there they were. "Do you *have* anything to hide?" he asked, half-serious.

She grinned. "If I had, I wouldn't tell you." She became serious again. "The main purpose of the justice system is to serve the hierarchy. At your job, that hierarchy forces you to jump through hoops to get things done."

"You were clearly brought up in a socialist country."

"My country was much worse than yours where justice was concerned. So, what exactly did you want to talk about?"

"You better eat first," Joe said.

§ § §

She studied the photographs spread between them. Their dishes, piled on the trays, sat on the empty table next to them. "So you believe all these murders were committed by the same person?"

"It seems logical."

She nodded. "I see the motif."

"When you interviewed these people, what conclusions had you made?"

"Guilty, every one of them."

"Almost as if Viper used your research to find his victims."

"This is very troubling." She pushed the photos away.

"Any idea who he could be?"

"Not the slightest, but the guy's obviously interested in my subjects."

Their knees almost touching, Joe was conscious of the heat radiating from her, and then of having a hard-on—which was understandable after so many months of abstinence. He didn't worry about the appearances for as long as they were seated, but he'd need to get up at some point. Joe wondered if she felt something also. He grabbed a photo of dead McKee and focused on the repulsive image. It helped. "If he follows your work, he must trust your method."

"More than most of my colleagues do, for sure."

"I'd like to listen to Baca's interview, the one about his vision."

"You need to ask Weizlan for the recording, but I have the transcript. Would you like me to send it to you?"

"Yes, please," he said. "By the way, how would you profile Viper?"

She became thoughtful.

"Professor Weizlan thinks he is a psychopath," Joe contributed, "and a tool in someone else's hands."

She shook her head slowly. "I'm getting a different image. I'm pretty sure he doesn't answer to anyone. Most likely he works alone. That's why these executions hadn't come to light until now."

She kept her gaze on the table as she spoke. She wasn't a modest type, Joe learned already, so averting her eyes likely served to hide their intensity. He sensed the tension coiling in her body. All this while she appeared perfectly poised. He wondered what provoked her agitation.

"The man loves a challenge," Gabrielle continued, deliberately. "A typical psychopath picks someone weaker than himself and uses the same method of killing time after time. Not this guy. Also, a psychopath is an ultimate consumer. To consume, one way or another, is his main drive. He has no principles or scruples. But this Viper, as you call him, is not a true consumer. Obviously he has a compulsion, a blood lust, but also a sense of justice—even if it's warped. He seeks relief, true, but he needs moral sanction to do so. I believe, in his mind, his victims' crimes give him a…permission." Her fingers drew quotes in the air. "He gets high on revenge. He is a blood redeemer. Which is why it's tit-for-tat executions."

"Can't he be both? An avenger and a consumer?"

"I seriously doubt that."

She drew a way more romantic portrait of Viper than Weizlan had, but it was a wrong one. Of course, her ability was impaired because Joe hadn't given her all the information—couldn't give her since she was blackmailed by the killer and, as Dante said, a part of the case. Plus, her main goal was to correct the prosecution's errors, to try and discover some redeeming qualities in criminals. No wonder she saw Viper as a vigilante, not as a depraved psychopath, and even tried to explain his motives.

"What you are saying is he is not a *typical* psychopath."

"I am saying he is not a psychopath at all!" The forcefulness of her words took him aback. She half-closed her eyes as if to calm herself, and added, in a lighter tone, "He is an explosive sadist."

"Aren't they the same?"

She shook her head. "Psychopaths are born, sadists may have the predisposition but they are made. From what you told me, Viper is consumed by an unresolved rage. I wouldn't be surprised if his real target is outside his reach. So…with each execution, he's killing his enemy over and over again."

That would make perfect sense, except Blake didn't fit in. And neither did Sheppard's son. "You talk with such confidence, as if you know him," Joe said.

"I've spent a lot of time studying and thinking about different types of killers." She stared at her fingers and so did he. Her fingernails were clipped short. No polish on them either. He remembered Lana's long, lacquered claws. Even at Alberto's funeral, his soon-to-be ex was so well put together. The uninvited recollection awakened the old disdain, to which Gabrielle's unadorned hands and simple elegance were a salve. He didn't need to lie to himself. This conversation was not about getting her input but assessing her, being close to her, and hearing her voice.

"What do you make of him bleeding his victims first?" he said to get his mind back on track.

"I thought it was only something not to be ruled out."

"Let's say I believe he bleeds his victims intentionally," Joe said.

"If it's consistent with each victim, it must have some deep meaning for him. It could be related to something traumatic in his past. Or he may see their blood as a symbol of some sort. Possibly of their deprived essence needing to be disposed of." She shrugged. "Making them bleed may also serve as an initiation or an appetizer before the main course."

There were no signs of strain in her anymore. She seemed to be simply solving a brain teaser, removed from the images her words conjured. Joe wondered if he'd imagined her earlier discomfort, but then decided that he hadn't.

There was a moment when something, possibly Professor Weizlan's take on Viper's personality, had unhinged her.

"Hey, why don't you bring me in on the case?" She peered at him mischievously. "I may just help you solve it!"

He nearly choked on his coffee and cleared his throat bargaining for time.

She laughed. "I am joking! But seriously, if you do catch this guy, I'd love to interview him. He sounds fascinating!"

Joe's face burned.

Her eyes caressed him. "I didn't mean to put you on the spot. You saw him in Sullivan. What was he like?"

"It was dark," Joe said. "I can only say he's not a big man and fairly agile." Then he remembered something Sullivan's Head Warden told him. "Tell me about Brin James. He turned out to be innocent, didn't he?"

"He was accused of the kidnapping and murder of a ten year old girl. I interviewed him three years ago, right after the conviction, and he was incapable of recalling some…intimate details of the crime. We barely managed to overturn his death sentence. He has an acute case of a guilt complex. You know, some philosophers say there's no such thing as individual guilt and we are all connected and responsible for one another. Well, it's like Brin is attuned to our collective conscience. You can throw any accusation at him. Apply a little pressure, let him consider, and he'll start believing he's culpable. I spent quite a lot of time with him. It's frustrating. Few people are as decent as Brin James."

"And still, he's locked up," Joe said.

"He would not survive on the outside; he is too fragile. Hopefully, he is safe in Sullivan."

"It wasn't safe enough for Baca."

She shrugged. "Baca was a hyena. From what you've told me, Viper won't hurt someone like Brin."

There was a buzz. Gabrielle pulled her iPhone and checked the incoming text message. "I must get going," she said and got up.

As they walked toward the cafeteria's exit, Joe caught a sight of Weizlan alone at one of the tables watching them. He met Joe's eyes and averted his own.

§ § §

"Where are you heading?"

"Minneapolis. Damien has an appearance. I sometimes assist him, in an unofficial capacity."

They exited through the glass doors. A black Prius was parked in front, a gray-haired driver inside. Joe had seen enough of Sheppard's pictures to recognize the Senator, even from the distance, tucked into a car.

"Introduce me to your friend," he said and started down the steps not waiting for her consent.

Sheppard stepped out and walked around to meet them. Gabrielle laid her hand on the Senator's wrist. "Damien, this is Agent Joe Vasquez…. Joe, Damien Sheppard."

They shook hands. "I watched her work," Joe said. "It's remarkable."

"She is very talented." Sheppard's tone had an unmistakable tinge of pride.

"Damien helped me develop my techniques." Gabrielle glanced at the Senator, and Joe took note of a shadow crossing the old man's face.

"The only thing worse than the unpunished death of an innocent is punishing the innocent with death," Sheppard said, stiffly.

Gabrielle didn't seem the same in the company of her friend. The warm, exclusive capsule no longer enveloped her and Joe.

"I guess once Gabrielle's method goes mainstream we can banish those costly appeals," Joe said, his internal strings humming angrily. Then he remembered Sheppard's dead son and the circumstances of his loss, and the strings relaxed. Joe's irrational jealousy evoked by Gabrielle's warmth toward the older man evaporated. Theirs was a father-child relationship, he thought, natural for two lonely, injured souls that started as a teacher and a student and ended as close friends.

Sheppard smiled thinly. "I wish it was that easy." He turned to Gabrielle. "We need to be going." He ushered her into the car. "Good luck with your investigation, Agent Vasquez."

As the senator walked to the driver's side, Joe looked at Gabrielle, strapped into the passenger seat. She stared back at him. On an impulse, he touched the glass. She smiled and touched it from the other side. His heart beat against his ribcage. The engine started and Joe stepped back. The car took off. He basked in the light of the midday.

"There goes the devil."

Joe turned to the doomsday voice behind him to find Weizlan. The professor stopped next to him and they watched the Prius disappearing beyond the intersection.

"Who is the devil, Professor?"

"Isn't that obvious? The Senator is nothing more than her puppy dog."

Joe's irritation awoke again. He wondered what agenda this slippery character had. "Don't hold back, Professor. Tell me what's on your mind."

"Oh, nothing definite. Just some reflections. For one, he's her *very close* friend; no more, or so they let everyone think. They travel together quite often."

Joe glanced at Weizlan and the probing, hungry expression on the older man's face amused him. He surmised that Weizlan hated Gabrielle like a spurned lover. The concept disgusted Joe, but remained bothersome as a splinter under his skin.

"He was a professor of psychiatry before he went into politics," Weizlan continued. "According to the official version, they met when he was her advisor during graduate school."

"The official version?" Joe asked. "You have an *unofficial one?*"

"Oh, I don't know…They always seemed much closer than their history suggests. I should probably also mention that her interrogation technique is not considered kosher by other professionals in our field. Did you get into discussing capital punishment with her? Don't let the views she claims to have fool you about him. He is a vengeful type. I don't know if you've heard, but he lost his son to murder. Sheppard has his connections and Lubovich has her own powers. She can make about *any* man," he paused significantly and his eyes probed Joe's face again, "even a criminal, do her bidding."

Joe turned and stared directly at Weizlan. "Are you implying that Senator Sheppard is the head of the conspiracy you were talking about at the meeting?"

"Not at all." The shifty bastard slipped into the cracks again, and Joe had to restrain an impulse to slap him. "Everything I said is a purely theoretical possibility."

"Why don't you give me something specific? What can you tell me about the man Dr. Lubovich has helped to clear, Brin James?"

"Clear! More like she's pulled all her strings to get his sentence overturned. Mostly those of her Senator's." Weizlan's spider eyes shone with indignation as his voice grew louder. The hate finally inspired his bravery. "She calls James her patient and visits him regularly at Sullivan, which is strange since they have a highly qualified psychiatrist on staff. She keeps James so confused he no longer knows what he did or didn't do."

"So you don't believe he is innocent?"

"My dear Agent Vasquez, I've no doubt he's crazy. There's also no question that he's a murderer. I'd bet my career on it. And I wanted to tell you something else that should interest you. Brin James is the only inmate in Sullivan who wasn't questioned after Baca's murder. Lubovich vetoed it, as his doctor."

Another lover of a dramatic exit, Weizlan gave Joe a mocking salute and headed toward the parked cars.

Weizlan's performance could be a bluff, Joe thought, but he didn't believe so. A lousy actor, the Professor obviously knew something and itched to bury Gabrielle and Sheppard. But why wasn't he going for the kill?

Chapter 20

'Barbarella'

Crookston, MN

It was a perfect little burg, with the air clear as a bell and mostly educated inhabitants. A comfortable, peaceful place to hide from the past, to live quietly, but with hopes and felicity, maybe even a kick or two. Unlike a big city, say Minneapolis just a couple hundred miles away, Crookston, in spite of its excellent literacy, was communally warm and easy on the nerves. Everything revolved around the tidy, well-appointed college campus.

At night, well past the strictly enforced student curfew, the old rented Nissan found its way into the parking lot behind the main dormitory and inserted itself among the thirty-or-so sleeping cars. The driver exited, dressed in black and carrying a business case. Seen by no one, the lithe creature slipped from the semi-lit area and dissolved into the shadows.

§ § §

The small house Barb Hamlin rented-to-own stood on the edge of a cul-de-sac, close enough to the college to do without the street lights. Starless night wrapped the building in a soft gauze of seclusion, with a dim glow filtering through the curtains.

On the other side of those windows, the living room was vaguely illuminated by the light issuing from the narrow crack of the door to Barb's bedroom. The plush and chintzy lair behind served as Barb's communication port with the world outside of Crookston. It was close to one a.m., and the monitor displayed the Instant Messenger dialog.

Her electronic mailbox was overflowing with new inquiries and pokes from prospective suitors. Barb herself was perched in front of her computer wearing her red teddy and nothing else—her usual Friday night get-up. In the two years since she moved to this hole in the wall, she had established a decent life for herself and a nice routine of screwing.

During week days, she toiled as a secretary at the college, drove an almost-new Toyota, and was on congenial terms with her neighbors. On Saturday nights, she met with a few friends, members of the local sex club, most of them high-standing Crookstonians united by the camaraderie of secrecy and superiority over the rest of the conventional, church-going herd. And Friday nights were dedicated to Barb's Internet adventures.

An instant message popped up on her screen. The ID read 'Love Snake.' The promising moniker had a brooding, handsome face to go with it. Barb stared intently at the picture. If she had checked the last issue of Hustler at the campus' bookstore, she would recognize the man from the magazine's back-page Martini ad. Since Barb rarely visited the place, she felt lucky to attract such a hunk, a rarity among the seekers of carnal delights on the World Wide Web. Most of them were average-looking at best going to seed male specimens with a declining ability for passion, seeking some excitement to stroke life into their flaccid egos.

Something animalistic in the stranger's face reminded her of Ike. But this man was gorgeous, and according to the description he was also 6'4" with big hands and feet. She grinned like a schoolgirl.

The instant message on the screen waited for her response. *He might be like Ike*, she thought. *If not, maybe I could teach him.* The simians from the club were mostly paunchy, plus Barb often had to screw their doughy wives in order to have a piece of their husbands. None of them possessed Ike's hungry, dominant streak. She missed his heavy stare and his voice telling her what to do, but Ike was long dead and in a past of which her friends knew only the Disney version.

She typed: *I'm here, waiting for a real man who knows what he wants, and I can give him whatever he wants.*

Barb pressed send and held her breath. The upper half of her messenger box displayed her decade-old photo, the one that got his attention. Her screen name beneath read Barbie-Doll. She was still almost as hot as her picture, blond, big-breasted, and skillfully made-up for a possible web session tonight.

The response came back as fast as it would take to type it: *I've looked for a woman like you all my life. Where have you been?*

Aflutter, she carefully considered her answer, and didn't stir when the land phone started ringing in the living room. The phone by the couch switched to the answering machine. A female alto came on. "Hi, Barb. This is your parole officer. I'll be in town tomorrow. I'll stop by at ten a.m."

At her desk, Barb typed: *Paying my ex-husband's debts. I'll tell you more when we meet.*

Love Snake's response flashed: *Sorry life wasn't fair. I want to spoil you.*

She swooned.

Another message came: *I want to see the goods. How about a little show?*
You first, she shot back.

He answered: *Do what I say.*

Butterflies in her stomach, she typed: *Hold onto your hat.*

She turned the web cam toward the king-size bed covered with a golden, sand-washed silk quilt she splurged on over the Internet and loaded a CD into a player. Then she slid on the bed, assumed her best all-four pose and pouted to the camera.

Merely twenty-feet away, in the shadows of the living room, dark eyes free of the thick masquerade glasses watched Barb shake it on the notebook laptop's screen. Through the crack in the door, those eyes kept tabs on the real-life performer. Gloved hands danced on the keyboard.

In the bedroom, Barb slid in front of her monitor again, and read Love Snake's new message: *Red becomes you, babe.*

She needed to fan herself as she typed: *Your turn.*

A video window opened.

Barb maximized it, turned the volume on, and pushed back in her chair for a treat. The screen showed a bare, windowless basement room, a teddy bear lying on the cement floor.

Barb winced, uncertain.

A teenage girl appeared on the screen. She was terrified, one eye swollen, with smudges of make-up from crying. Naked, with cuts and bruises on her arms and small breasts, she couldn't stop shaking.

A male voice, its owner pointing the camera down at the girl, said, "Suck it, bitch! You wanna live!"

The girl nodded pitifully.

Ike commanded, "Do what I say!"

The girl's face screwed up. She turned to someone off screen, sobbing. "Please let me go! I won't tell! Please!"

The girl threw herself at female feet in red mules. The feet kicked her off. The camera moved up along a pair of toned legs. They belonged to a younger Barb wearing a red teddy, bitch-faced, a belt in hand ready to strike. The girl cowered as Barb hit her with gusto, just as Ike liked it. Just as she liked it herself.

In front of the computer, Barb choked.

"H-h-hello, Barbarella," a snake voice came from behind her.

She screamed, tried to turn, to rise—

A pungent rag clamped over her mouth. Her terrified eyes took in a face hovering above and then rolled up into the descending blackness.

Chapter 21

A Stench of Soft Blackmail

Dallas, TX

Steve was with him. They stood in the back room of the house in Ponderosa. The floor was flooded up to their ankles with a dark liquid, and Joe knew it was blood. Craig's corpse floated at their feet. With all his strength, Joe struggled to move. He lost his balance and fell on top of the corpse. He cried out and pushed away from the cold flesh, and Steve jerked him to his feet.

Joe looked down at Craig grinning at him, still alive somehow.

"I'm fine," Craig hissed in Viper's voice.

And then Baca was there, the noose on his neck and blood flowing from his reduced crotch. "All's good, no worriesss," he croaked, and he sounded like Viper too.

"They're free now," Steve said. "They've paid their debts."

"Bullshit!" Joe shouted. "What did you have to pay? And Blake, and Bobby Sheppard?"

"We are not the debtors, we are the creditors. Better check your facts, buddy." Steve pointed at Baca. "Dead don't lie!" He started to dissolve.

"Don't go," Joe pleaded. "Please!" He grabbed for his friend's shoulder but seized air.

"I'm alwaysss withss you..." Steve's last words came as Viper's hiss.

§ § §

Joe opened his eyes and lifted his head groggily.

"You awake," Dante said without turning, working diligently at the computer.

Joe propped himself up and waited until his dizziness subsided. "How long did I sleep?"

"A few minutes. You could use more napping."

Joe stared at his partner's back. *Check your facts, buddy...*

It was the second night at their new place in Dallas. They worked in the living room equipped as their office. The overpriced furnished apartment provided for them had a double phone line, a computer connected remotely to the FBI network, a printer and fax machine, a small kitchen nook which they used so far only to brew coffee, and two bedrooms, each with a separate bath.

Joe reactivated the dark screen of his laptop sitting on the coffee table before him. New messages blinked. He checked an email from Dr. Lubovich first. The subject line contained 'As promised.' It had an attachment named 'Baca_lastInterview.' Joe opened the transcript and clicked on the printer icon. The printer on the desk spilled about a dozen pages. Joe scooped them up and read, slowing down where Baca described his vision in Coloqueen. When he finished, he decided he had missed the part he was looking for and scanned the whole thing again. *It must be here somewhere…*

Except it wasn't.

"Hey Dante, do shrinks transcribe their interviews differently?"

"It's like any interrogation. The script follows the wording to the letter. Why?"

"Never mind." Except Joe himself did mind, so much that his hands holding the pages shook. *Can you be truly open with your boss or even your partner at all times?* she had said. Joe couldn't tell Dante, not until he figured out why, but when Gabrielle called him in LA she put words in Baca's mouth he never said. Not precisely a lie, since she sent Joe the transcript. But still, why would she add Baca mentioned California when she knew Joe would see Baca didn't say anything of the sort? She was too smart to be flippant.

Also, how did she really find out it was Craig's execution Baca hallucinated about? From her mysterious sources? Does she keep tabs on all her past subjects? And lastly, what was she hinting at when she told Joe that if she had anything to hide she wouldn't admit it? Did she give Joe the obviously incorrect information as a way to tell him something without saying it directly?

"Okay, man, I'm ready. Take a look," Dante said. The printer came to life again.

§ § §

"They chose Weizlan over all these other candidates?"

The list contained the names, titles, and scientific achievements of the top seven people who had aspired to lead the Forensic Psychology Research Department at the Dallas Graduate Institute. As far as Joe perceived, they all exceeded Weizlan in academic merit—unless publications and accolades did not amount to much.

"That's the deal," Dante said. "Weizlan got tenure, which gives him a fat paycheck, in addition to being gainfully employed by the Feds and as a consultant for the State. Interesting, huh? So I decided to check his new employers' sources of funding." He laid out a few tax reports in front of Joe. "See, they received a sizable contribution from the 'Friends of Mind,' a small but affluent charity. If you compare the dates, the money came shortly before Weizlan's hiring, at about the same time as a government commission on violent crime prevention…" He pointed to another sheet, "…facilitated a grant to the forensic department's research program."

"Is Sheppard somehow connected to these outfits?"

"Sheppard was the head of the Institute for about twelve years, so his interest in his old haunt appears justified. And guess what. Sheppard is on the Board of Trustees for the Friends of Mind, as well as one of the Directors of the commission. Both of the outfits are based in D.C. Of course, there's no way to legally implicate his involvement in Weizlan's hiring."

"So, if Weizlan knows something unsavory about Sheppard," Joe marveled, "he has good reason not to bite the hand feeding him—at least, not openly."

"He must be fed precisely because he knows something."

Which made Weizlan another potential blackmailer. "If we are not misinterpreting," Joe said, "Sheppard must have a lot to hide…" *And Gabrielle may be in a tight spot with him,* he finished in his mind.

They were quiet for a while. Then Joe said, "We have a problem here." Probing a lowly professor was one thing. Dealing with a U.S. senator was a different animal altogether.

Chapter 22

'Agent Parker'

While not state of the art, the pumping station at the Dallas FBI building had all the basics necessary to satisfy any dedicated jock without any of the frivolities. A complete although non-duplicate dumbbell rack, two bars with a full set of Ivanko plates, a bench with an incline option, an old Smith machine, and a power cage.

Joe reentered the gym close to 8:30 a.m., his face flushed with an infusion of nervous energy, to see Gabrielle dressed in jock-casual in the midst of her morning workout. He found out from Logan's secretary that she was here and hoped his new haircut was presentable and his under-eye circles not too scary. He exercised earlier, showered, and then got a large cup of coffee at the cafeteria.

He nodded to her through the mirror and feasted his eyes on her doing lateral raises with two sizable dumbbells. His mood lifted with each repetition, her fluid movements habitual and economic, with her shapely, hard body displayed properly in her tight tank and yoga pants. Her personal fitness gadgets lay on the floor by the cage—gloves, looped ankle straps, and twelve-gauge solid steel hooks. She could sooner pass for a gymnast but clearly knew her way around the weights.

Her exterior spoke of a dogged determination, and Joe wondered what sort of determination it was. *Did you choose me deliberately, or by an accident? Did you count on the effect you would have on me?* he thought, watching her set the dumbbells down and turn toward him. "Morning."

"You worked out already?" She stared at his wet hair. "This place is not too bad, huh? As long as there is no crowd."

"I came at seven."

"An early bird. Do you always get your worm?" She jumped and grabbed the overhead bar, facing him. She pulled herself up, went limp for a little rest, and then pulled up again huffing.

"Need a spot?" He stepped into the cage and took a hold of her knees.

He gave her a gentle push, just enough to supplement her own strength, and she rose above the bar flinching with an effort. Another pull-up, and another. His grip on her legs grew tighter. Gabrielle's body moved against his, her

129

breathing laborious, and his coming out in a sympathetic unison. She made nine reps, six of them almost by herself, the tenth with him heaving her all the way up. Then she went slack.

Joe set her down but didn't let her go. "I want you to hypnotize me," he said.

"Nope." Her eyes smiled.

"Why not?"

Still gazing at him, she said, "I don't like to face my limits."

"I'm readily bewitched. I promise."

"I'll never hypnotize you, Joe Vasquez." Her pupils absorbed him and he held her gaze, roping her in. As their connection grew too intense, she weaseled out by pulling out of his arms, "A girl needs a break from her job."

"I can be your break." His voice came out strained.

Her mouth quivered as if her armor spotted a crack, but she regained composure fast. "Okay then."

"Seven tonight? I'll pick you up."

She thought about it. "I'll text you the directions to my place."

Dante's voice broke the enchanted globe they floated in. "Hey!" They both turned to him, standing in the doorway. He waved to Gabrielle. "Better hurry," he said to Joe. "Cowell's pissing steam." He left.

"I need to go," Joe said.

"See you later, Hound." She went to the rack.

The fact that she had learned his nickname sent butterflies dancing in Joe's stomach. Of course, the bastards had a ball there already. Once outside, the grin slipped off his face after a few steps. He turned, went back on cat's paws, stopped by the door to the gym, and peeked through the glass pane.

Gabrielle put on the weight belt, picked up a twenty-five pound Ivanko barbell and hooked it to the belt. She hoisted the support rungs of the cage, facing the mirror now, seized the overhead bar, grunted and pulled herself up, the weight hanging between her bent knees like a bad case of iron balls. Her head rose above the bar again and again in a slow, steady rhythm with the rippling of her muscles far more serious than when Joe had spotted her. The ease with which she lifted herself, unassisted and weighted down, awed him. She was much stronger physically than she wanted him to believe.

Joe stepped off, baffled, but only for a moment. Her small deception was innocent, he told himself. She simply wanted him to touch her, so why would he mind being deceived to this end? The butterflies rose up anew.

Dante waited at the threshold of the open elevator. Joe followed him inside and attempted to clear his head of Gabrielle's center point sliding up and down his face. The cab took them up.

"What are you going to tell him?" Dante asked, meaning Cowell. "Half-truth or the whole truth?"

"We are not telling him about the blackmail."

Dante raised his brow at Joe in a smart-alecky way.

"At the least because," Joe said, "we didn't bring it up earlier."

"Aha, but mostly because you want to figure how she fits in first. No need to be subtle with me." The elevator stopped.

"Well, I should be more forthcoming with you too," Dante continued. "I didn't mention this before, since we weren't so close, but you might not need to be so afraid of Cowell taking your ponies away."

"Whatever you may think, Psychology Major, I know where I stand with Cowell very well." They exited and walked toward the conference room where the devil spoken of waited.

"I caught a rumor before we left L.A.," Dante said. "Unlike you, I'm a friendly dude and schmooze with people. Guys say someone up the food chain is looking out for you."

"Bullshit," Joe said. "Do the guys mean O'Neal?"

"He doesn't gossip with me. As I understood, that rumor originated with McCollum. She overheard Cowell on the phone with someone from D.C., and your name mentioned."

Dante's voice tightened but Joe was too bothered to care about offending his young partner. "Does it look to you or the guys like I have someone? Like I've ever had someone to look out for me?"

"I am only passing on what I've heard," Dante said. "The rumor has it you got the Craig case because of that call from D.C."

§ § §

Cowell wasn't waiting for them alone.

"Agents Vasquez and Gayle," he introduced in a false congenial voice. "This is my…friend, Special Agent Parker. He came all the way from Washington to show you something."

They sat down across from a dry man in his fifties with a tacit face and glasses. The SAC's hesitation at calling the stranger a friend didn't slip Joe's attention. He apprised Parker. Quietly self-possessed, with a confidence of someone a few leagues above Cowell.

"Your boss has kept me in the loop on your case," Parker said. "When this latest came in yesterday, I thought I'd better let you know right off."

Joe watched the SAC watching Parker. *Friends? Bullshit*, he thought. It was clear that Cowell didn't want Parker at the meeting. And Joe didn't blame him; why would this guy from D.C. need to butt in when he could just send them the information?

Dante turned off the light. The screen on the wall lit up. Soon, they were staring at a dead woman. Naked and covered in ghoulish make up, she was slumped with her back to a plush headboard, her intestines trailing. A fuzzy teddy bear sitting between her sprawling legs provided a shred of sarcastic decorum.

"You may remember Barb Hamlin, Agent Vasquez," Parker said. "It's been ten years."

Joe did. He was still in D.C. at the time. An extradition case. The lovely couple they retrieved from Canada kidnapped, tortured, and killed three teenage girls, including Barb's own little sister. They filmed the torture, too. Barb claimed coercion, being the battered wife. Her husband alleged Barb had done the actual killing.

"She got a plea bargain. They released her two years ago," Parker continued. "She went to live in Crookston, Minnesota."

"When was the body discovered?" Joe asked.

"Yesterday morning, by her parole officer. She could see herself on the webcam as she was dying. No extra fingerprints, hair, or fibers on the scene except for what belonged to the victim."

"What about her computer?" Joe said.

"Internet history had been wiped clean."

"What's with the make-up and the teddy bear?" Dante asked.

"She used to calm the girls by showing them how to put on make-up, giving them a teddy bear for comfort, and making them think they would be spared," Joe said.

Dante murmured under his breath, "I bet this time she knew the drill."

"Was she bled before she was killed?" Joe asked.

Parker looked surprised. "She bled a lot, obviously."

"I meant on purpose, first? Were her veins cut?"

Parker shrugged. "You can check on the details, but I don't recall."

Joe considered his question. The killer didn't need to cut the victim's wrists since she would have bled enough without it. "Where is Crookston?" he asked, keeping his voice off-hand. "How far is it from, say, Minneapolis?"

"About two-hundred miles," Parker answered.

Meaning less than a three hour drive. "What time did the murder occur?"

"Between one and three a.m., by the coroner's estimation."

Had Gabrielle interviewed Barb Hamlin in the past? He would bet she had. The pattern held so far. *Except for Sheppard's son*, Joe reminded himself. She couldn't have met Bobby because she was a child, and not in the U.S. yet, when he had died. He left that inconsistency alone for the time being, letting his mind concentrate on the recent events. Gabrielle and Sheppard rallying two-hundred miles away from and roughly about twelve-hours before Hamlin's execution. He wondered if Viper was following them.

Gabrielle hinted to him that laying her cards on the table would get her in trouble with the law. Joe knew he wasn't imagining or wishful-thinking the wistfulness in her eyes at the gym. Almost desperation, followed by a cover-up smile. Joe wasn't so full of himself to attribute that expression to her lust for him. She needed his help and conveyed about as much without saying it. How dire was her situation? The conference room, with the death portrait of Barb Hamlin projected on the wall, became too stuffy and time too slow-moving.

His gaze shifted and he caught Parker observing him. A funny feeling he first had upon meeting the man returned. Dante's words came back to him. *You got the Craig case because of that call from D.C.* If someone up the food chain hand-picked Joe to find Craig's killer, whatever their reasons, then Joe had some leverage. At once, he came to a decision.

"There has been a development in the case," he said. "We believe it connects to another case we're handling."

§ § §

"Steve and I found some old newspapers in the alleged killer's apartment. Each had an article cut out of it. The missing articles were recently restored and turned out to be reports on the killings of McKee and Bacholski, two of Viper's victims. In our opinion," Joe nodded at Dante, "that connects Blake Johnson's killer to the prison executions. We've also found at least one other connection. All the victims were interviewed, in different prisons and at different times, by the same forensic psychologist, Dr. Gabrielle Lubovich. So was Blake Johnson when he was briefly placed at juvenile hall. Dr. Lubovich is presently located here in Dallas. She is also an ex-student and old friend of Texas Independent Senator Damien Sheppard. Sheppard's son was murdered about twenty years ago in the exact same way as Blake Johnson. We believe both the prison executions and the boys' killings were done by the same man."

"I think your agents deserve a lot of credit. I appreciate your setting a high standard for them, but sometimes it pays to let your boys go out on a limb." Parker's thin-lipped smile was as cold as his tone, no matter the words.

Some diplomat, Joe thought.

"This is quite a theory," Parker continued pleasantly, considering Joe with his smart watery eyes. "It might even end up being a close guess, huh, Don?"

Cowell grunted and rocked back in his chair.

"So, what are you planning to do next?" Parker asked. "What kind of assistance do you think you'll need?"

Time to milk that leverage. "We need a parallel investigation into Senator Sheppard and Gabrielle Lubovich," Joe said. "I wouldn't mind some help with that. It's possible Viper is fascinated with her research and uses it to choose his targets, and it's also possible he's interested in her mentor. The murder of the Senator's son needs to be revisited. Also, I recommend round the clock surveillance of both Lubovich and Sheppard, at least to ensure their safety."

"Leave it to us to talk to Senator Sheppard about the added safety precautions," Parker said. "However, you don't have enough evidence yet to probe such a respected public figure."

"I beg to differ, Agent Parker," Dante spoke up. "On the day Joe talked to Dr. Lubovich, she flew with the Senator to Minneapolis to attend a rally, which puts them at the time in proximity to the murder of Barb Hamlin. So, if Viper executed Hamlin, he could even be following them. There is a good possibility Viper killed Sheppard's son. In any case, we have cause to look into a possible connection between Sheppard and Viper in the past."

Listening to Dante, Joe remembered how he and Steve used to read each other's thoughts. Apparently, he and Dante were becoming a just as well-oiled team. He caught Parker giving Cowell a look. So prompted, the SAC swelled up.

"Let me make this clear," he said. "This meeting is off the books. Senator Sheppard is good people. We don't want to meddle anywhere near him. So you go easy on your hunches. As far as we're concerned, a lone fox has found his way into our maximum security hen houses. He's a smart fox. He may have gotten a hold of Dr. Lubovich's research somehow. And she happens to be a friend of the Senator. Otherwise, there's no connection whatsoever. Leave Senator Sheppard, her, and any of his associates out of this. Kapeesh?"

Parker obviously prepped Cowell in case Joe and Dante brought Sheppard up. Joe kept his poker face. He needed to digest this.

"What about the Johnson killing, and the Senator's son?" Dante asked, incredulous.

"You're connecting too many dots," Cowell said, his confidence visibly growing under Parker's approving silence. "Sheppard's son was murdered long ago. Some perps have rituals, some are copy-cats. Who the heck knows? And I am still not convinced, on the basis of some newspaper trash and some accidental body cuts, that Johnson's killer has anything to do with the prison killings." Cowell waited a moment, narrowed his eyes vengefully, and added, "Of course, you can always hand over the case. O'Neal will gladly take over."

He's bluffing. Or is he? Joe thought.

"Please, Don," Parker interjected patiently, and turned to Joe. "While I advise against any surveillance on Senator Sheppard, you can certainly investigate Dr. Lubovich—as long as you don't infringe on the Senator."

Joe had no doubt now. Parker came to guide the meeting in the *right* direction, and the overfed clown bluffed about giving Joe's case away.

"Overall, you're doing a good job," Parker continued. "Your SAC will keep in touch with me. Our guys in D.C. will provide any support you need."

Thanks, but I prefer to use my own guy, Joe thought, grateful to have Berryhill in his corner.

"That's right," the designated babysitter pitched in. "You keep me informed on a regular basis. And don't get side-tracked. Who knows? This case might turn out to be the best thing that ever happened to you."

§ § §

Joe smooth-talked his way out of lunch with Dante and Cowell, opting for a sandwich from a nearby deli. He went to the apartment, called Berryhill, and then sat down with the Sullivan interrogation transcripts. He accessed them before as worthless but still wanted to sift through in case he noticed something out of the ordinary the second time around before passing them on to Thompson and company in L.A.

There was one transcript he really would like to see, but access to Brin James was restricted due to exacting orders from his mental healthcare provider, Dr. Lubovich.

Later in the afternoon, Berryhill called back with an intriguing piece of information. No Special Agent Parker, or anyone matching the description Joe provided, existed among the D.C. FBI brass. Joe pondered who the guy could really be during his drive to Deep Ellum. CIA? He stunk like one of them, the Slytherines. This possibility spoiled his mood. CIA meant counter-espionage, and Gabrielle was a foreigner with a peculiar history. Parker basically egged Joe on to investigate her.

Chapter 23

The Lovely Date and the Ugly Encounter

Interpol didn't have anything on Gabrielle Lubovich. Joe found her psychological assessment, conducted as a part of the security clearance that enabled her to carry out research and evaluations in federal prisons, in his email one-and-a-half hours before their date, and he spent one hour absorbed in reading it.

'I was twelve. Instead of going straight home from school, I went to the movies with a neighbor. When I did come home, I found my mother, younger brother, grandmother, and grandfather murdered. I hid with some friends of my family. Later, they bought me a new birth certificate and sent me to Bucharest. After six years I procured an invitation from someone in the States. I never met them and it doesn't matter who they are because I don't want them to get into any trouble. I convinced the U.S. embassy to grant me a Visitor's Visa, and then I managed to get some money for the ticket.'

'You had no one to stay with or help you when you came?' The interviewer asked.
'Correct.'
'How did you manage?'
'Odd housekeeping and baby-sitting jobs, where they paid me under the table. The usual. Then I applied for a Student Visa.'

In the U.S., her advisor in graduate school, Damien Sheppard—Senator Sheppard now—sponsored her and helped her to obtain a green card. After a few years, she became an American citizen. Joe reread the transcript. He imagined her saying its words in a dull voice, trying hard not to remember, not to feel as she recited her story. He could almost see her face—absent, eyes averted. To him, the pieces of her character and her past seem to fall into a ready pattern, familiar and dear. As if she were someone he knew long ago for a long time, and then lost and forgot for some tragic reason.

Be careful, caro, his mother's voice said in his head. *This woman is getting under your skin.*

§ § §

"Absolutely." Tom tried to sound cool, his blue eyes wide with excitement as a little unconscious smile played on his lips.

"Have some more," Al whispered. "You got to relax, dude!"

Tom, on the phone, impatiently waved the tall wispy teenager and his bong off. "You'll tell me in person. I'll try to get there as soon as I can."

Al pointed at the clock on the wall and rolled his eyes.

"If you are not here before 6:30," Gabrielle said on the other end of the line, "ask the landlady for the key. I'll let her know."

"No problem." Tom's sunny voice dimmed. With his fallen heart, he expected her to offer to pay him for the favor.

Gabrielle must have sensed that dimming. "Thank you, Tom. How about I buy you dinner sometimes soon."

"Oh…sure, Gabrielle." His voice brightened. "Whenever you want me."

In her dismal apartment in Deep Ellum, Gabrielle hung up and murmured, "Shit."

In the psychedelic room of Tom's old school buddy and dealer, Tom danced in triumph.

"If this keeps going," Al said, "you'll be bonking that milf pretty soon. What's fair is fair."

"Don't call her a milf!"

"Okay, a cougar."

"She is not a cougar!"

"Yeah, she's going out, probably on a date with some other, old, established dude, and asks you to keep her dog's company. You want my advice?"

Tom's face fell. "Nope." He got his coat from the chair.

"Don't run to her now. She'll be in a hurry, and you might miss her anyway. The damn dog can spend a few hours by himself. You're already taking him off her hands and driving him to the ranch tomorrow. That's plenty of pussy credit." He followed Tom to the bathroom. "Instead, go there real late so you can run into her when she is back and tipsy. You can always tell her you got caught up in something. If she is not alone, you can check the competition and maybe spoil her bonking another guy."

Tom, shaping his hair into just a right mess in front of the mirror, considered. He might not have taken his friend's advice if not for the couple of beers they had earlier. With the beer and some weed at work on his young brain, the scheme Al described, especially Tom's favorite version with Gabrielle coming home drunk and alone, was too tempting to resist.

§ § §

Following the British-accented directions of his GPS, Joe reached Deep Ellum in time for the lights above various watering holes and the colorful crowds to spill into the dusk. The small street was right outside the Entertainment district. He parked by a narrow, likely historical building, checked his visage in the rear view mirror, got out, and entered through creaky tall wooden doors. An elevator was absent, but a springy step carried him all the way to the fourth and uppermost floor.

Gabrielle opened the door wearing a sleek red dress, the full waves of lustrous hair falling below her shoulders. She stepped back in her high heels to let him in. Before either of them said a word, a bark boomed, and a large shape rushed at him and almost knocked him down.

"No, Ranger!" Gabrielle grabbed the dog by the collar and brought him to a halt before the paws and slobber caused any damage to Joe's best leather jacket.

"Calm down, big guy," Joe said, feeling grateful for the distraction. He rubbed the dog's head, and Ranger, who Joe recognized as the Doberman Pinscher from the Johnson case photographs, wagged his tail vigorously.

Gabrielle scratched the dog's ears. Their hands touched briefly, and Joe's eyes met hers, shining bright and liquid above her long neck and the youthful hemispheres of her breasts. The gloomy, out-of-date apartment, muted lighting and the red dress turned her into a heroine of an old noir story with a mysterious, dark past he was meant to undress.

"You look beautiful," he said.

"You clean-up well yourself." Gabrielle turned her attention to her dog. "My young friend, Damien's intern, promised to pick him up and take him to Damien's place. He's a nice kid but still a kid. They aren't so reliable, this generation. I wish we could bring this puppy with us."

"Can I use your bathroom?"

"Down the hall," she pointed.

The bathroom door was in a small nook. A short iron ladder was attached to the opposite wall. His eyes went up to a square outline of a trap door on the high ceiling. The ladder rose only one third of the way to it.

Joe stepped into the bathroom, a claustrophobic affair with a pseudo-gothic appeal, same as the rest of the apartment he had seen so far. It was slightly steamy, and Joe guessed she showered recently in the stand-in behind the curtain on the left, across from the sink of yellowing enamel. A toilet was in the right corner, under a drop-latch window open due to the lack of an exhaust fan. A black, new poster hung above the tank, a reproduction of one of Bosch's 'Last Judgment' series.

§ § §

Gabrielle walked into the living room, scanned it with a sharp eye, marched to the desk, lifted her purse, and took her attacker's Bone Collector from underneath. She pulled open one of the drawers to stash it but then changed her mind.

She darted out and hurried to the kitchen, a tight, unwelcoming place showing no signs of use beyond an old Vitamix blender, a coffeemaker, a dehydrator, and a book titled "Raw, pure-protein food preparation for dogs" on the counter. A few gallon sized bags filled with Ranger's home-made chow were stacked next to it. Her movements economic and precise, Gabrielle pulled a roll of plastic wrap from the top of the ancient refrigerator, tore a piece, wrapped the gun, and shoved it into one of the bags of dog food.

§ § §

As he was relieving himself, he thought how the print on the wall reflected and accentuated the atmosphere of the apartment. Gabrielle had a dark sense of humor. He smiled as he washed his hands.

For many women, a bathroom is the most revealing space in a home. Gabrielle's had no added feminine touches, and the hall was Spartan as well. The undersized accommodations were a strange choice. He wondered what kind of appeal this domicile had for her. Surely, she could afford something better, more updated and cheerful. Instead of a hand towel, a new soft paper dispenser was attached to the wall, the hygienic type one may find in some restaurant restrooms. It looked out of place, industrial, and, Joe guessed, was introduced by his date as well.

He dried his hands, stepped to the small window, and saw a deserted alley and a row of dumpsters below. He stuck his head further out. A fire escape ladder clung on the right, ending a dozen feet short of the ground. Someone of Gabrielle's build and as athletic could easily climb through that window and reach the ladder.

He was considering this as he came out and was met by Ranger's bark again. The dog sat in the middle of the hall watching him, its amiable tail beating a rhythmic tap-tap on the linoleum floor.

"He likes you. He has a good instinct for people," Gabrielle said as she came out from the kitchen. "You ready?"

§ § §

The Elephant Pit was an upscale Indian restaurant. Glass barriers divided the airy interior into multilevel areas hosting a few tables each. Human murmur, clinking utensils, and soft ethnic music created a non-obstructive background for intimate conversation.

A young waiter in a turban came. Joe ordered a Masala shrimp appetizer and a bottle of Reveilo Syrah. Gabrielle asked for hot water with lemon.

When the waiter left, she stretched to Joe's collarbone and her fingers flicked from beneath his shirt an old, silver crucifix. She held it delicately and he leaned forward a little so her fingers continued touching his skin. "Are you religious, Joe?"

He wasn't sure of her slight smile's meaning. "It was my mother's. I was raised Catholic. But I'm not what anyone would call religious."

She carefully tucked the pendant back. "In your Catholic theology, what does God do to people like Baca, or that other, Craig? Burn them in hell?"

Joe shrugged. "What God does is God's business. As I said, mine is to remove them from circulation." He noted how her little smile hardened. "But if there is a Higher Power, I can't see it destroying a soul someone cares for."

Some distance away, very light eyes spied at them from above the menu.

The waiter brought the introductory fare and wine to Joe and Gabrielle's table and they ordered their main courses—Lamb Tikka Masala for Joe and Tandoori Chicken for Gabrielle.

"The kind of people we're talking about…Who would care for them?" Gabrielle said when the waiter left.

"I don't know. Their mothers?"

She leaned back, her smile frozen. She no longer looked at him, and he instantly missed the connection. Then, free of it, he sensed something, being watched, and glanced around. Before his eyes reached the unremarkable man's table, the latter got up and left, leaving only an unfinished glass of water and a tip.

Joe offered his appetizer to Gabrielle. She shook her head. "Too much cholesterol."

"Okay, then you should have some dessert afterward."

"I don't do desserts."

"Never?"

"Not since my teens. I've no food vices."

"What about your other vices?" Joe poured them both wine. "How do you get your fix?"

"Perhaps I'm a saint," she said, the outside corners of her eyes crinkling.

Joe remembered Mitchell and his chest felt compressed. "There must be something. You don't want to leave it to my imagination."

"Okay. I smoke. Plus, I'm shallow, and attracted only to beautiful, intriguing men—like you."

Joe's face flushed. "Great. Here's to it." He raised his glass, and they drank. "I've read your immigration papers," he said. "You left Romania when you were twenty years old…I'm very sorry about your family."

She swirled her glass and gulped the rest. "Tell me about yours. Vasquez is a Basque last name, right?"

"Yes. Vasquez was my mother's name. But you know that, don't you?"

"I nosed around a little too, yes."

He liked that she did. "So, we're even. What did you find out?"

"Not much. That your parents were immigrants, and that your father's name was Rafael Salazar. I wonder, there were Conversos by this surname—"

"The first Salazar was a well-off Jew. He took his sponsor's name and married his daughter. They fled from the Inquisition, but their children ended up sticking to the new faith." Joe stopped short, surprised that his memory extracted these facts so easily. "What else have you learned?"

"That your father was a cop," Gabrielle said. "And that he was shot."

"I haven't spoken of my father for many years…"

"Even with your mother?" Her tone was gentle.

He shook his head. "Those were deep waters. We didn't go there." How did he learn of his father's family origins? Not from Isabel. His father must have told him.

Gabrielle laid her hand on his, and the tremor in it subsided. He was afraid to move and scare her touch away.

"You don't need to talk about this if you don't want." The warmth of her eyes engulfed him, and so did his desire to hold her, to tell her things, things he always thought better stay buried.

"My father's younger brother was twenty years old," he said, "and a drug peddler for a local gang. A deal went bad and a buyer got killed. My uncle was the fall guy. My father tampered with evidence to help his brother and got caught. The department covered things up, and my father was discharged. Less than two weeks after he was shot by the gang. That's the story."

She gazed at him. "Your father was a truly brave man. He risked everything for someone he loved."

Joe was taken aback. "I never thought of my father as a hero of any sort."

"You really missed him when you were growing up."

"Putting your shrink hat on?" What else did his father talk to him, a tiny squirt, about? With one flick of her cool fingers, this woman provoked a troubling want to remember.

Her face softened to the degree of tenderness he didn't expect in her. She seemed a different person, not only from Gabrielle in Coloqueen or the one at the gym this morning, but even Gabrielle a few breaths ago. She changed like water's surface under a breeze. Joe thought she could keep his attention for hours.

"Most people are so careful, so…cold," she said. "I would give a lot to have had a father like yours. Mine was gone before I was born. I was raised by my maternal grandfather…Raphael Salazar was the real thing. You are too. I can see it."

Joe removed his hand. "My father lost both his honor and his life. My mother struggled to bring me up. I'll never be like him."

They stared at each other across the table, he resisting the loss of control to his doubt and the rogue butterflies fluttering their wings at the pit of his stomach, she with another of her hard to read smiles.

"Cheers to that!" she said, at last, and lifted her glass.

"I'd love to take a train through Europe and the Eastern Bloc, ride through Mongolia and China, stopping on the way and exploring. I could use a companion. Interested?" He was only half-joking.

"Oh, I don't know…I have an aversion to trains." Her mouth twitched. "Must be something about heavy steel wheels crashing on steel rails. All that inertia makes the stopping so slow and unpredictable."

"I don't like planes. Must be something about my feet not touching the ground," he fenced. "But for the right person, I'd put up with flying."

She took out her cell, dialed, listened, and hung up. "I hope Tom picked up Ranger. Maybe we should cut this short." The regret in her voice made his heart skip.

"So, Senator Sheppard helped you to get your green card. You two seem very close."

"He was my adviser in graduate school. We were both loners. He started as my mentor and became a substitute father."

"Did his son's murder influence his politics?"

Gabrielle stared at him hard. "So, you found out about Bobby. Why? Why would you want to know about Damien's past?"

"It may connect to another case I'm working on," Joe said as their food arrived.

§ § §

They walked the well-lighted, festive central streets of Deep Ellum back to Gabrielle's place and Joe's parked car.

"It's only two cases you know about," Gabrielle said. "But if the same man is involved in both, he'd leave a few more corpses in the span of so many years."

"We're trying to find out if there were more victims. I understood Sheppard claimed his son's death was a work of a serial killer."

"He left it all alone. He didn't have enough to go on." She paused. "Don't bother Damien, Joe. He is too old and has known too much tragedy. Surely, you understand. I know you lost your son, too."

Joe stiffened.

She looked at him sidewise, took a deep breath and started, evenly at first, "I was twelve. Instead of going straight home from school, I went to watch a movie with a neighbor. When I did come home, my grandparents, mother and younger brother had all been shot dead." She ran shorter and shorter of breath. "I was very close to my brother. I loved him more than anyone in the world. I still do. He knew me, really knew me, and he loved me." Her composure broke, and he heard tears in her voice.

Joe stopped her, peered into her face. "I know you, Gabrielle." She winced and he pushed, "I may not know you well yet but I *know* you."

Her tears rolled. He pulled her close. And as he held her, he didn't see her expression turning apprehensive as she stared into nothingness over his shoulder. She freed herself, and her eyes found a bright fluorescent marquee with the name of the club—*Voodoo*. A bunch of yuppies aggregated underneath.

"Let's check it out!" She dragged him there.

§ § §

A heavy-set black man of uncertain age channeled Santana on a small stage, a few old-timers making out with their instruments behind him. The incense smoke softened what little light was in the room and rendered the perimeter of the dance floor indiscernible.

It was a long time since Joe danced. He was good at dancing at some point, and with Gabrielle slithering around him his instincts took over. She moved with her eyes half-closed in a self-inflicted trance he suspected served to elude the reality.

Don't turn your back on me baby, the singer crooned, *Cause you might just wake up my magic stick*. Without any thought or effort, Joe was tripping the light fantastic, lost and found at the same time. *Obeah*…He remembered Dante's word for her. He cupped her face into his hands and gazed into her somber, shadowy, bottomless eyes.

He detected alarm there. He wanted to break through to some naked truth hidden underneath. But she slipped from his scrutiny by kissing him, and for a moment he forgot all about the secrets and half-truths.

§ § §

They turned to her street. The nightlife of the Deep Ellum fizzled out before reaching this outskirt.

"Are you safe now? Are those people who killed your family still searching for you?"

"No worries, Agent." She smiled.

He didn't. "Are you in any other danger?"

"Why would I be?"

"You tell me."

She laughed. "They call you Hound for a reason."

He took her cold hand and pressed it to his burning face. It became warm by the time he kissed it. The street was murky, but not dark enough to hide the bluish bruise on the bottom inside part of her palm and wrist. She tried to pull away, but he held fast to examine her hand. He made out the smudged off remains of the nude makeup covering the bruise.

"Do you have a boyfriend?"

"Are you applying for a position?"

"How did you get this?"

"It's nothing. I pinched it with a dumbbell."

He let go of her hand, sure of her lie.

145

They stopped at her building's entrance. "Want to come up?" she asked. "Check for violent boyfriends?"

Joe's eyes following her gaze to the two dark windows under the roof. The evening air cooled his forehead and his mind muddied up by drink and dancing. "Not tonight," he said.

"Ah." She cocked one brow coolly and turned to go in. Joe took her arm, spun her around, and surprised her with a kiss.

"Sleep tight," he said when it ended.

§ § §

As she climbed the stairs, Gabrielle checked her phone and saw a new text message from Tom. *Running a little late sorry*. She reached the top landing, unlocked her door, and stepped inside the apartment. "Ranger!" she called as she turned on the hall light. "You still here, puppy?"

No usual, ecstatic bark greeted her. Gabrielle froze, the phone still in her hand. Calmly, she lifted the gadget to her ear, waited a bit, and said into the dead receiver, "Hey Tom, thank you for picking up Ranger. I owe you one. See you tomorrow." Her voice was light, pneumatic. She pretended to hang up and whistled to the tune of the Puccini's Toreador while noisily dropping off her shoes. Her feverish, shiny eyes didn't as much as flick toward the watchful aperture of the living room entrance as she moved past it and down the hall.

One step, two…nothing.

The bathroom door swung open with a whine. The whistling stopped, and the echo of the shower came. Then the door shut, dulling the sound.

§ § §

Why did he refuse her invitation? Didn't he wait long enough? Didn't he suffer enough? Sitting in the idling car at the intersection, Joe remembered Alberto. The misery that lifted for a few hours stung him anew but, uncustomary this time, without the guilt for his temporary lapse in grief. Not only that, but he wanted to numb that misery, push it into the background of his mind, so he could stay in the here and now, to continue in the land of living.

He knew the reason for this change. It was Gabrielle. Gabrielle, who carried her own misery and needed his help. To stay in the present, he must be near her again soon. But what he wanted the most, at this moment, was to feel her body pressed to his—wanted it so much that a physical pain burst from his groin to his brain, as if a part of him had been amputated. Just as he told her, he knew her. It was the knowledge that went past and beyond the trivial facts. He felt, in the depth of his soul, that they were the same, she and he, the kind that never forgot, never turned away from their dead beloved. Wasn't that why she had helped Adam Johnson?

Then, in his weakened state, everything fell together. The shiner on her hand…*Check for violent boyfriends*, she said…Gabrielle's reason to seek his company for the night may not have been carnal, Joe realized. And the team he asked Logan to assign for her surveillance wasn't in position yet.

The light finally turned green. Hit by a premonition, he wrung the steering wheel into a U-turn and slammed on the gas.

§ § §

The man hiding in the living room quietly stepped into the hall. He wore his jogging suit and the ski mask, but the gun he held was different, a Berretta in place of the Bone Collector he lost to Gabrielle. He crept to the bathroom door. His hand, gloved in latex, touched the knob.

He imagined her naked under the running water, unaware and helpless. He imagined her shock, her fear, her blood filling the tub. Not as satisfying as bleeding a boy, but oh-so fitting. He remembered her narrow body and the hard grip of her hand wrestling the gun from his own. *Why, she might do just as nicely as a boy!* His light eyes darted to the alcove on his right, noting the short ladder and the outline of the flap above, high enough to require an athletic male's strength to pull up to from the top rung.

He opened the door.

The small space was full of steam and the sound of running water. He aimed his gun at the opaque curtain and ripped the fabric aside.

§ § §

Joe parked his car in front of Gabrielle's building and got out. Her windows were dark. He took out his cell and called her for the second time.

She didn't answer.

§ § §

The man swore. The water fell to the scuffed mosaic tile of the empty stall and pooled above the deficient drain. He turned to the wide-open window. As Joe did a few hours earlier, he stuck his head out, checked the fire escape, and squinted at something gray lying on the ground. It looked like the bitch's coat, dropped as she fled.

His angry fist slammed the wall.

§ § §

The attic space spanned most of Gabrielle's apartment at about a three and a half foot clearance. Meager streaks of illumination from the ventilation grate fell on Gabrielle's face. She crouched on all four above her bathroom. Through the slots, she saw the portion of it and the masked man.

As if feeling her stare, his eyes, unnaturally light in the slits of his mask, went up to the grate. In the darkness of the attic, Gabrielle held her breath and resisted the urge to recoil and create a movement. The man gazed directly, not seeing her, then turned his face toward the bathroom door, listening. Gabrielle heard it too, through the sound of shower—a knock at the front.

"Gabrielle!" Joe's voice came from the landing.

Another knock.

The masked man raised his gun and waited.

§ § §

Joe pressed his ear to the heavy door as the fine hairs on his arm rose of their own accord. He took a hold of the old-fashioned knob and it turned. He stood still for a moment before stepping inside. He paused again in the lighted hallway. The even, unoccupied buzz of running water greeted him, issuing from the open bathroom. Joe's hand groped unconsciously and failed to locate his TRP. For his date, he forfeited his shoulder holster and chose to wear his gun under the belt at the small of his back.

"Gabrielle?" He stepped toward the bathroom. A loud thump ahead, coming from the ceiling, startled him. His legs still carried him forward, but his hand closed on the grip of his TRP.

A masked man jumped out of the bathroom and rushed at him. The silencer glared, and Joe ducked as the man fired. The bullet went above Joe's right shoulder. Knocked off balance and falling, he kicked the shooter's gun hand, redirecting the next bullet into the ceiling. Joe's own gun skid down the hall. As he hit the floor, he grabbed the stranger's shins and pulled, sending his attacker backwards screaming.

Joe leapt on him. They wrestled and rolled ungracefully within the tight accommodations, bumping into things, knocking down the console. Joe seized the man's right wrist, twisted it and jerked the Beretta free. As his opponent tried to wrest from Joe's grip, his latex glove came off in two pieces. The light, empty eyes gaped at Joe through the mask's slits.

Somewhere above them, the front door opened and a young baritone said, "Hey…Shit…"

The man rammed his head into Joe's nose, kneed Joe in the groin, and, as Joe crumbled with a cry, fled, shoving Tom out of the way. It took Joe a couple seconds before he dove for his gun and sprung up with it in his hand, pointing at the deserted landing. A teenage boy swayed, rubbing his shoulder and staring at him, scared. *Gabrielle's young friend*, Joe's brain retrieved, *here to pick up the dog.* He lurched back and to the bathroom, saw the empty shower stall and the open window, then hurried to the living room, past the boy who mumbled, "What the fuck, man?"

Joe's hand found the switch on the wall. The light came on and he took in the ransacked mess. A flat-screen on the glass top corner desk, fireproof filing cabinets, their drawers open and their contents scattered, a flurry of books, papers, CDs, electronics, odds and ends under the emptied shelves, and in front of a couch, on a Turkish carpet—Ranger. From where he stood, Joe could see the exit wound of the bullet that killed the dog.

"Call 911!" he barked at the boy and tore out of the apartment to hear the building's door slam way below. He rushed down stairs.

§ § §

He saw his attacker half way down the block and fired three rounds into the air as he ran. A couple of windows above shops lit up. No passersby. A few dispersed lampposts provided the ghostly illumination. The man vanished before reaching the corner. Joe slowed down and soon halted, eyeing a narrow alley-way between the buildings on his left.

It was darker there than the street, but a ray of light from the lamp outside the alley cut across the two industrial size dumpsters and barely indicated the tall stone barrier about a hundred feet beyond them immersed in the shadows. One dumpster's lid was shut. Another, closer to Joe, thrown almost all the way up to the wall with a gap remaining—too narrow, Joe thought, to hide a man. A musty but mostly aired out stink rose from the container. It appeared the garbage had already been collected. As Joe moved in cautiously, his ears caught the small crunch of glass or gravel under a foot.

"Come out!" He pointed the TRP at the gaping cavity. "FBI!" Keeping his head out of firing range from inside the dumpster, he crept closer. "Up!" he barked. "Get out!"

His bet was wrong. With a screech the lid came down, knocking the TRP out of his grip, and his quarry leaped on him from above. Slammed on the pockmarked asphalt, he saw the glint of a blade as a hand swung at him and caught the masked man's forearm. Struggling to keep the knife away from his face, he twisted sidewise and rolled on top of the man, succeeding at pinning the hand with the knife to the ground. The man writhed underneath; Joe's grip loosened and the knife nipped at him, cutting through his jacket and grazing his skin like a burn. Pushed on the bottom again, he elbowed the man's throat. As his attacker let go, gasped, and lost his balance, Joe kicked him in the chest, slamming him against the dumpster. Joe was up, kicked again and growled in pain. His foot hit the hard metal of the dumpster's front while his target dodged.

They faced each other warily. Joe's opponent had an advantage, the knife— one sharp sucker, as Joe had learned already, and Joe's only weapons were his legs. He needed his TRP. He didn't see it, but by his estimate it should have landed on the side of the dumpster. He started circling in that direction slowly, faking intent of getting closer to his adversary. As the latter inched away, his gawking eyes glinted in the stray glow of the streetlight, and something bothering Joe since he stared into them at Gabrielle's place, too shocked then for it to click, resurfaced.

*Pale eyes…Like a silver fish…*This was not an ordinary mugger or a rapist targeting women who lived alone Joe was facing. He was looking at Steve's murderer. *Viper…*The word formed soundlessly on his lips, and when he found his voice, it came out hoarse, "Take off your mask! Show your face!"

The man's back was turned to the entrance of the alley. An awesome bang exploded behind. Joe dropped down without thinking, and the man, unharmed, ducked as well. Another bullet went right above, sending a vibration through Joe's bones. Pressed to the ground, he peeked to see his enemy racing toward the street and disappearing, missed by the third shot. A second of quiet rang in his ears. Joe raised his head. There was no masked man or a pursuer springing after him.

"Don't turn, Agent Vasquezsss," the hiss came. "It might not be dark enough here for your sharp eyesss. I'd hate to kill you."

Footsteps approached from behind. Too stunned to obey, Joe started to twist his neck. But before he could see the face that came along with the odd, familiar hiss, something hard—the butt of a pistol he figured later—whipped the side of his head, and everything went blank.

§ § §

The janitor's eyes stared from behind the thick lenses…He stood up on the Sullivan's roof, his silhouette outlined…Dark eyes…A lithe, agile frame… The middle-built intruder of Joe's height, face covered with a ski-mask, swung a knife at Joe, his light eyes staring emptily…

Two of them…Two of them!

A distant ring…Closer, closer…

Joe opened his eyes and gasped. His cell phone was ringing in his pocket. He lifted his head, still lying in the alley in the dark. His whole body was sore, but his head ached the most.

Another ring. Joe pulled out his cell. The screen said 'Private Number.' He flipped the phone open and scrambled to his feet.

"You owe me, Vasquezss," Viper hissed. The last word came out with a mechanical whistle at the end. "Or should I call you properly—Sssalazssar? That's the sssecond time I've sssaved your hide."

Joe's knees felt soft, shaky. *Salazar, the bastard called him.* "I owe you nothing," he said. "Thanks to you the perp got away. And I think that's exactly what you wanted."

"I work alone, Sssalazssar. But that'sss not important. It'sss you I worry about. Leave the bitch alone. She is poissson. Plusss, you won't want to get attached anyway."

"You think I'll listen to you after you killed my friend?"

"Who wasss your friend? I sssquash human cockroachesss."

"Cut the crap. I don't care if it's your sidekick who shot Steve Mallow because it's the same to me. I'd kill you for him alone. And for the boys too—Blake Johnson, Bobby Sheppard—remember him?"

Silence on the other end. Then, "You are sharper thssan thssat, Sssalazssar. Thssink harder." A menace entered Viper's condescending hiss. "I like you. But if you keep getting in my way, I'll kill you. And I won't do it nicccely."

Viper hung up.

Joe searched for his gun and found it where he expected. He stumbled into the street, deserted for several blocks, with a band of a few late-night teenage

wanderers at a distance; no one running. He checked the time on his cell—
12:20 p.m., meaning he had been unconscious for only about twenty minutes.

He returned to the alley and walked to the old brick and stone wall cutting across it. Just as he suspected, there was a narrow hole in it, next to one of the buildings, plenty enough for an undersized, human-snake killer to squeeze through. The alley continued on the other side of the barrier. Viper must have known the hood well to be able to sneak up on him.

Joe stumbled to the street once more. The world seemed eerie and alien. Old and new assumptions jumbled his thoughts as he tried to shuffle them into a semblance of order. He became aware of a needling pain in his arm. He touched his sleeve and found it was wet with blood. The warning knock from the ceiling at the apartment likely saved his life. Gabrielle's face stood in his mind, and his longing for her was painful. *You don't want to get attached…*

He hurried back to her place.

Chapter 24

The Bliss of Forgetting

Where did you find it?"

"Right by the wall." County Sheriff Costello pointed next to the entrance into the living room, where a distraught Gabrielle was giving her deposition.

Joe, atypically, didn't notice the second gun on the floor in the open earlier before he ran out after the attacker. Of course, he was in too much of a hurry. It was also not unusual that Pale Eyes would carry a spare Smith and Weston. He must not have secured the weapon well to drop it when he jumped Joe. Joe often carried a second gun himself in an ankle holster. Not tonight though, and too bad.

Baby-faced Costello came to assist the night shift cops. The police were alerted and checking the surrounding area. Joe gave the most nominal account of running into, chasing, and losing the intruder. He already asked for a couple officers to guard the alley's crime scene, and intended to call Logan first thing in the morning to get forensics to comb the area for shells and other evidence, even though he feared the search would not produce anything useful. Viper was one slick bastard. Joe's head still spun from the discovery that the monster he hunted had split into two.

"Okay, Jerry, let's look around," he said to the eager young sheriff. While Costello turned his back, Joe found and discretely pulled out from under the remains of the broken console the pieces of the latex glove. He had deposited them into a zip-lock bag and hid it in his pocket, then peeked toward the living room—and met Gabrielle's eyes. She turned away, talking to a curvy female detective.

"Nothing else here," Costello said as he followed Joe to the alcove at the end of the hall.

Joe climbed the short ladder. He knocked around the trapdoor on the ceiling and produced the same hollow sound as the one that warned him of the attack earlier. The picture of Gabrielle rising effortlessly above the over-head bar in the gym played in his mind. He took out his key-chain flashlight, powerful for its size, held it with his teeth, pushed the flap open, pulled up, and anchored himself with his elbows. The cut on his upper arm burned anew, likely seeping blood.

Someone recently disturbed the thick layer of dust on the floor of the crawl space. The grate was to Joe's left, right above the bathroom sink. He guessed this hiding place, in addition to the accessible fire escape, had dictated Gabrielle's choice of the otherwise unpleasant residence. Who was after her—Steve's killer, Pale Eyes, who blackmailed her and Sheppard, or another, Viper, who advised Joe not to get attached? The bruise on her hand…Joe didn't believe Gabrielle's gym story. What kind of altercation was she in?

She hid up here in the crawl space while Joe and Pale Eyes scraped below. She waited until everyone, including her dog-sitter, departed, came down, and left too, most likely using the fire escape for real this time. When Joe returned from his double encounter in the alley, the cops had already arrived and she was back. The story she told them, with him listening, omitted her hiding in the attic. She said instead that she fled as soon as she realized that someone was in her apartment and lost her phone with her coat while climbing down the fire escape—which conveniently explained why she didn't call 911 before her young friend and the neighbors, in response to Joe's shots, did. She described how she searched the nearby streets for someone to borrow a phone from with no luck in this late hour and then returned to the building to ring up her already sleeping landlady—the only part of her tale that must have been true, since it could be easily confirmed.

"What's there?" Costello called from below.

Joe jumped down. "Just a place to store things."

"For a strong guy, maybe. Not gonna work for a lady with the ladder so short."

"Good observation," Joe said, and Costello brightened.

§ § §

In the living room, kneeling, Gabrielle stroked dead Ranger's head.

"I think we're done here, Miss Lubovich." Detective Rosa Sanchez, young and sympathetic, got up from her companionable squat on the other side of the corpse. "Good thinking with the fire escape." She handed Gabrielle some forms to sign. "We have robberies and rapes reported almost every night in this area. Your FBI friend handled things well."

"Call me Gabrielle." Gabrielle stood up too. "We might run into each other in our lines of work."

154

"Well, you call me Rosa then." The young woman shook Gabrielle's outstretched hand. "You new in town? I am too. A couple of months out of the academy. They give me the graveyard shift a lot. I don't know many people in these parts."

"Me neither." Gabrielle stared at her dog. Her mouth quivered.

"Take my card." Rosa got one out of her breast pocket and scribbled on the blank side. "My personal number, in case you get lonely."

Entering the room, Joe caught Gabrielle's dog-sitter's askance stare. The boy stood by the wall, trying to be out of everybody's way, gazing at Gabrielle with a puppy-love expression. *And you too*, Joe thought, and he felt even more tired. But then his eyes met hers, exhausted but shining at him, and his spirit lifted. He marveled at the different expressions she had for different people— for Detective Sanchez, for the cops, for that young friend of hers…And Joe liked the one she reserved for him the best. He took in the whole of her, disheveled, paler than usual, which was to say ghostly, her bare feet dirty, and her stockings torn. He wanted to hold her, to keep her close and safe.

"I'm so sorry!" Tom seemed ready to cry. "I wish I came earlier—"

"I am very happy you didn't, Tom." Gabrielle's keen eyes rested on the boy, wary, weighing the possibilities. "You better go home."

Tom hung his head and left.

"Do you see anything missing?" Joe asked.

"He didn't seem to be interested in any valuables. But I can't find my laptop's external hard drive. It had my most recent interviews. It might be around somewhere though, in the mess."

Joe gave in to the impulse and hugged Gabrielle, and his chest pressed into something square and flat tucked into her bra—much like the hard drive she claimed was lost. He let her go and studied her face. She gazed back without flinching.

"What kind of research do you do?" Rosa asked.

"That's something I've got no strength to talk about right now. I'd rather give you a call tomorrow if it's okay."

"We must take the computer, I'm afraid, since the perp could've been after your files."

"I can't let you," Joe countered. "Our people will need to check it. I have a reason to believe this was not a random attack, Detective."

Rosa narrowed her eyes at him.

"I can't tell you more. This burglary case will be transferred to our jurisdiction tomorrow."

Rosa hesitated as if considering saying something, then turned and went out of the room.

"You can't remain here tonight," Joe said to Gabrielle.

"I would go to Damien's, but he lives too far out in the country, and I have a morning meeting. I'll try to get a hotel."

"You can stay with my partner and me."

"I don't want to impose."

"We have plenty of room. And you shouldn't be alone. You can take my bedroom. I'm sure Dante won't mind."

Gabrielle stared at her dead dog and nodded. She touched Joe's bleeding elbow. "How bad is it? Do you need stitches?"

It surprised him that she noticed the blood on his dark jacket. Nobody else did. "It's just a scratch," he said.

"I've got a good first aid kit. I'll patch you up."

"I wouldn't mind a little TLC."

"You sure you don't want to show it to them? Isn't there a protocol?"

"Don't you want to get out of here already?"

"Not until you show me your scratch. It's better to clean it before the bleeding stops."

In the hall, Rosa gawked at them as Gabrielle pulled Joe to the bathroom past her and Costello.

"Take off your jacket," she commanded once they were alone inside.

"Yes, Ma'am."

She made him pull his shirt off his shoulder. The jacket took the bulk of the damage, but the blood was still oozing out of the cut. Gabrielle's caressing fingers touched the adjacent skin, and Joe saw yet another, peculiar, almost dreamy expression on her face. She was taking her sweet time examining the wound, and his head started to spin, but in a good way. Then she broke the reverie, met his eyes, gave him one of her evasive smiles and said, "Lean to the sink."

Her touch light, she washed the cut with warm water and soap, then ripped a fresh paper towel and gently patted the water off. The roll on the wall, hidden in its plastic shield, now made sense to Joe. The setup was both convenient and hygienic.

She opened the cabinet behind the mirror above the sink, and he gaped at a medicinal arsenal capable of satisfying an army nurse. She dressed his shoulder with the expertise of one, too, ignoring his silent, wondering, pointed watch, then took a cyanoacrylate tissue adhesive out of a full box and sealed the wound.

§ § §

At Joe's and Dante's rented quarters, after all the blood and muck were washed off, Dante went to his bedroom while Gabrielle finished her shower and retired as well to Joe's. Joe finally settled on the couch made comfortable with some extra bedding. But even as the dark and quiet came at last, sleep didn't.

Viper, Pale Eyes, Gabrielle…Joe worried that triangle like a dog worries a bone. Why would, as his instinct and logic insisted, Pale Eyes follow Viper's bloody exploits and reference them by including those newspaper articles in the blackmail package to Gabrielle and Sheppard? How were Steve's murderer and the executioner of the incarcerated serial killers connected? Were they partners in crime?

Blake's, and likely Bobby Sheppard's, murderer didn't hesitate to shoot Steve and so, given a chance, would kill Joe. But there was no escape from the fact Viper had spared and even saved his life twice now. To what end, beyond a whim? In the alley, did he shoot at Pale Eyes to hit, or to scare him off? Or maybe just to make a show of shooting, for Joe's sake?

How did Gabrielle fit into this? She interviewed all of the known Viper victims, which meant she could be a valuable asset to Viper in planning the executions. Such a possibility repelled Joe, just as lifting a rug to find a cockroach scurrying off would. But the sacrilegious thought, born by Joe's hound habit, was countered by Viper's apparent disdain and nefarious intentions for Gabrielle. And, while theoretically, the key words here were apparent disdain, Joe hung to that contention like a sailor to a mast of a storm-rattled ship.

He recalled how she looked at her teenage dog-sitter and her concern for Adam Johnson. She was a caring person, he thought, and losing her family, including her young brother, likely made her even more so. But could his hunch that the boys' association with her would bring them to the killer's attention be also true?

And why exactly did Pale Eyes break into her apartment? Did he plan to attack Gabrielle on her return, or was he only after Gabrielle's external hard drive she reported missing. Joe strongly suspected it was the hard drive he felt in her bra when she hugged him. If his suspicion was correct, then she must have retrieved it from some hiding place when she came down from the attic. She obviously didn't want Detective Sanchez or Joe to see what was on it.

Gabrielle expected Pale Eye's visit. Was she afraid of Viper as well? She didn't hide her preparedness from Joe; in fact, she demonstrated it to him. More than ever he believed that she wanted—no, needed—his help. But he knew, had he asked her directly, she wouldn't tell him anything. She conducted herself like a savvy card player without showing her hand. That darn woman, in his bed some fifteen feet away, behind the wimpy door she hadn't bothered to lock.

After an hour or so of playing possum with his eyes closed, body tense, and brain turning to mush, he resigned to a long night followed by a bitch of a headache tomorrow. Then he thought that Benadryl might help, and so he got up and went to the kitchen. He turned the stove light on and took a small medicine bag out of a drawer. He poured water into a paper cup on the counter, but then faltered and turned…

Gabrielle stood naked in front of him, her pale body streamlined and seemingly glowing, her bottomless eyes drowning his.

Joe dropped the cup into the sink, stepped to her, and took her into his arms. She pressed her face to his chest.

"Make me forget," she whispered.

He picked her up and carried her to the bedroom.

§ § §

When she pulled him onto her, strong and silky fingers digging into his shoulders, he pushed away. He wanted to look into her eyes and make her look at him. But she wouldn't let him, nipping on his neck with her teeth, and he gave in. When his exhaustion caught up with him at the peak, he collapsed next to her in a near black-out. They both got off, but the pursuit felt empty. And Joe knew why—there was too much unsaid between them.

"Thank you for saving my life back at your place," he murmured into her ear, his face pressed into the pillow and hers facing up, their cheeks touching.

She gave no indication of hearing or understanding him. Instead, she took him into her arms, and, as her tenderness spilled on him, he came undone and sobbed. Later, as he drifted off, his tears spent, he decided that tomorrow morning he'd make her tell him everything. He would promise to keep her secrets, whatever they were, and together they'd find a way out.

And then the sleep came, deeper and more peaceful than he had in years.

§ § §

The morning light streamed between the curtains. Joe lifted his head from the pillow. He was alone in bed. He got up, pulled his trunks on, and wandered into the living room. A shirtless Dante, the significant hulk of his flesh sparsely covered with pajama shorts, sat at the desk.

"She told me she had a meeting," he said without turning. "She used my shower so not to wake you up." He nodded at the laptop. "I want to show you something."

Joe peered at the screen over Dante's shoulder.

"Recognize anyone?" Dante asked.

Another graduation picture. An old one, obviously scanned from a print. A few clean shaven young men in black robes and mortar boards, their hair tight on their temples, crowded on a groomed lawn, smiling to the camera…

"That's Sheppard." Joe pointed at a tall blond youth with an intelligent face.

"Anyone else?"

Joe scanned the faces. He returned to the thin boy on the left, next to the future Senator. Deep set eyes, tacit smile…"That's Parker!"

"Actually, his real name is Arthur Landaw. I didn't find much on him, except a listing with the Eastern Bloc Diplomatic Corps in the seventies, and one A. Landaw among the staff of the Bureau of Diplomatic Security in the eighties. These boys all aimed high, so by now he is likely in the upper echelon in D.C. somewhere, either Defense or CIA, a big enough shot to order Cowell around. Which proves, Hound, some powerful folks want you on this case."

"I am not going to be their bitch, whatever they expect."

"Sheppard may simply be looking for the best man available. Imagine if Cowell didn't give it to you. Who would be handling it?"

O'Neal, Joe thought. *And he would butcher it*. He stretched. "What time is it?" he asked.

"I am glad one of us slept well. First you woke me up and made me play the good host, and then, when I fell asleep again, you shared your ground-breaking sack performance. I am not going to remind you anymore that you are fraternizing with the possible co-conspirator in the case. Or, at least, an important witness that may be withholding information."

"Why would Sheppard go clandestine instead of coming out and helping us?" Joe went to the kitchen to fix coffee.

"He may have overreached a bit when he conducted his own investigation. So his hands are tied now, and he's placed his hope for justice in you."

Joe stared at the Benadryl pills on the counter. *You don't want to get attached*, Viper hissed again in his head.

He went back to the living room, picked up his ruined jacket from the chair, took out his phone and dialed. Her answering machine came on immediately.

Either Gabrielle turned her cell off or it died without a charge. "Call me back as soon as you can," he said into the receiver and added, feeling powerless, "Please, be careful."

§ § §

"I can't believe he called you afterward," Dante said when Joe described the events of the previous night. "That was his second chance to off you, but he didn't. Hey, maybe he has a crush on you. And maybe he's the jealous type."

Joe made another unsuccessful attempt to reach Gabrielle, and then dialed Sheppard's number, ferreted out by Dante. The Senator's gruff voice came after the third ring. He didn't seem surprised nor did he reprimand Joe for invading his privacy. He either didn't know or didn't want to volunteer Gabrielle's whereabouts, and didn't ask any questions after Joe's brief recount about the prior night's events. Which meant he already heard it from Gabrielle.

"How secure is your house?" Joe asked.

"I have a Brink's system; the doors and windows are impregnable."

That the senator lived prepared, just like his ex-student, was telling, Joe thought. But Sheppard's home couldn't be safer than a maximum security prison.

"I also have a vault, a safe-room equipped for short-term emergencies," Sheppard said.

That was better. "I understand Gabrielle plans to stay with you for a couple of days. Can you two camp in the vault?"

Sheppard laughed without humor. "I can ask her many things. But I doubt she will listen."

Joe wanted these two to hunker down in the bunker until Viper and the masked man, and whoever else presented danger to them, were put away—Viper in a special, impregnable loony bin somewhere, and Steve's killer rotting six feet under. "Try, Senator. I'll get the local cops to keep an eye on your place. I hope you don't mind."

Sheppard hesitated answering, and Joe sensed his lack of enthusiasm before he finally said, "Do what you deem right, Agent." Next, Joe contacted Sheriff Montoya of Red Springs County where Sheppard's ranch was situated to make the necessary arrangements.

When he finished talking to the sheriff, he saw a new text message, from an 'Unknown.' Joe opened and stared at it for a few long second: *Ask the bitch how she got rid of her Maine accent.* As a true narcissist, the sender expected Joe to guess his identity right away, as well as who 'she' was. Was Viper spying on them both, and did he know about their night together?

"Did we ever get anything on the location from the Johnson photos?" Joe asked Dante.

"They sent us a fax. It's a needle in a haystack scenario."

Joe dialed the D.C. lab and asked for Jim Crocker, Berryhill's familiar, who had been examining the pictures. After exchanging greetings, he said, "Narrow your search down to Maine. It's urgent." His refreshed mind raced.

"Why Maine?" Dante asked after Joe hung up, and his meaty face mimed a jaw drop when Joe showed him the message.

"So, he communicates with you on a regular basis now. I wonder what category of perverted this belongs to. What do you think he is after?"

Joe took out the zip-lock with the torn glove. "See if you can lift some prints, and then compare them to the collection from the Johnson case."

"Is this from last night?"

"Came off the guy in the scrape."

"Did the cops catalogue it? Or have you decided to save them the effort and us time and paperwork?" Dante got up. "I need to cool it for at least 48 hours." He carried the bag into the kitchen and deposited it in the empty refrigerator.

Joe wondered about Viper's tip. If valid, it could help to zero in on the location of the countryside photo from Pale Eyes' apartment. Viper wasn't likely planning to realize his murderous plans for Gabrielle, if such existed, before Joe had an opportunity to explore his latest clue. But Joe didn't want to take chances. There wasn't much he could do at this point but call Logan and receive an assurance that the team assigned to keep a watch over Gabrielle would be in place by the evening.

He checked his messages. Nothing from her yet. She could still be at her meeting, or just keeping her phone turned off to avoid being hassled about safety precautions.

He called Berryhill. After a few beeps, the answering machine came on. "I've another favor to ask," Joe said into the receiver. "Can you check on a guy in D.C., named Arthur Landaw? L-a-n-d-a-w," he spelled. "He was in the Bureau of Diplomatic Security in the eighties. He is someone important and very interested in the case. He came to our meeting with Cowell under false pretenses and called himself Agent Parker. Find out what you can. Thanks Mike."

Dante reappeared in the living room. "You remember our appointment today, don't you?"

Joe did, and rejoiced at the legitimate distraction from the wait.

Chapter 25

A Flash from the Past Case

"He was very involved at first," Karl Strauss said, "but we didn't progress fast enough for him."

The detective who worked on the Bobby Sheppard case some twenty years ago and long since retired was a potbellied grandfather blissfully going to seed. Joe and Dante occupied plastic chairs on the Strauss' creaky veranda in Oak Cliff overlooking the back yard littered with sliders, bright toys, and a swing set between two old apple trees.

"We struggled and didn't have much to go on," Strauss continued. "The few fingerprints we lifted turned out to be duds. It rattled Sheppard. He got this idea that someone switched them and that the real fingerprints had been destroyed. He stopped helping from then on. He was always a man of ideas." Strauss' wry chuckle told Joe that even now, years later, the memory still ruffled the old detective's ego. "He got it into his head that the killer was serial. Could be true or not; we had no way of knowing. Now you boys remember, we worked in a different time. No real crime database, not much of the Internet either, unlike nowadays. All work was done by hand, call to call, step by little step."

"Do you think Bobby Sheppard's killer also murdered Blake Johnson?" Dante asked.

"Honestly, I wouldn't put my money on either a yes or no. Twenty years difference here. People change, even killers. Most chill-out with age. Unless he started pretty young and is in his mid-bloom now, I'd say it's someone else. The bleeding business can be some sort of ritual with different sickos performing it. By the way, have you talked to Sheppard yet?" Strauss peered slyly at Joe.

"Not yet." Joe decided not to elaborate.

Strauss chuckled again, this time with glee. "And you won't. He won't give you the time."

"What was his input into the investigation? Did he say anything of interest when he bailed out?"

"He called the killer 'Doll-maker.' The bit about him being a serial was only Sheppard's hunch, coming from an academic shrink you understand. He said to me, 'It may be his first kill but sure as hell not his last.' After he decided that

163

our lab lost the fingerprints, I had another conversation with him. He was mighty angry, said he gave up on us and the whole system. I said he shouldn't give up on the search of his son's murderer. And he said, 'I'm not giving up.' So I said, 'You should share with us whatever you find.' And the bastard asked, 'What's gonna happen if you catch him?' I said, 'Whatever the law decides. Could be the chair, or a psychiatric ward.' And you know what he said? He said that's not good enough. That's an easy death. Let's see who catches him first. If you do, you deal with him, and if I do, I'll deal with him, my way. And I must tell you, the look he had when he said this…if you ever saw the face of evil, that was Professor Sheppard, the future Senator."

"Was that the last time you talked to him?"

"Pretty much in person," Strauss said. "I had a strong hunch he was hiding something even when he supposedly cooperated with us. Then I heard about a compound he was building for himself on his ranch. We wanted to look around, but he kept us out. We couldn't even get a warrant to go inside, just walked around the fence. His house is more like a fortress. He still lives there when he comes back to his home state. But he's tough to touch. He's got connections. Do you know he went to school with last term's vice-president? They were both in Skull-and-Bones, a brotherhood of the rich and privileged." Strauss' voice became bitter. "I'll tell you something else. He had an airtight alibi, but I always suspected he played a part in his son's death somehow. Maybe someone wanted to even a score with him so they killed that poor boy. You know the last thing I said to him? You better be sure you understand what you are doing, Professor, because you might get the wrong guy. And how'd you live with that?"

"And what did he say?" Dante asked.

"He said nothing. I hope I gave him something to think good and hard about."

§ § §

Berryhill called close to four p.m. as they drove back. "About Landaw, Joe…" he said. "Don't dig there. You won't get anywhere." He sounded terse and Joe didn't ask any questions.

After they hung up, Joe saw a text from Gabrielle. *I am fine. Take care.* He tried to call her and got 'leave a message' at the opening, as before, which meant she turned her phone on briefly to send him the text then went AWOL again.

Back at the apartment, they drank coffee in the living room, when the fax came to life. It exhibited a satellite image of the barn, with an address beneath. Crocker's guys managed to locate the place—some farm near Mapleton, Maine.

Chapter 26

Gabrielle Gives the Slip

At 9:15 p.m., an hour and a quarter into his surveillance shift, a freckled FBI agent was in the driver's seat of the trigger vehicle, a five-year-old Nissan Altima parked one door down and on the opposite side of Gabrielle's apartment building. The agent raised his head from the headrest and observed a hunched specter emerging from the entrance. The old lady's coat stretched over her sloping shoulders and billowed above her tucked-in butt. A wrinkled handkerchief covered her low-hanging cranium, a roomy old-fashioned purse hung from her elbow, and thick stockings draped loosely over her knobby, bent legs. She waddled, arthritically and unaware, past a small blue Fiat parked along the sidewalk, the outrider, another retrofitted wolf in sheep's clothing.

In the Nissan, a sardonic female voice came over the radio. "Want me to take a stroll and check out Mata Hari? I could use some exercise."

The agent's partner stirred from his stupor in the lowered passenger seat. The freckled one pulled his iPod's buds from his ears. "Stay put," he said into the mic. "It's her neighbor, the old Russian lady from the second floor."

"Kinda late excursion," the female voice pointed out.

"Must be heading for the bus station. Her daughter's family lives in the suburbs. You read the sheet, right?"

The partner stretched back in his seat. The coat and stockings passed the third strategically parked car and then out of the perimeter of the stakeout and the view, melting into the thickening gloom up the street. The freckled agent laid his head back again and continued his heavy-lidded watch of the building's exit.

§ § §

The three cars constituted the FBI's hunting pack, assigned per Joe's request to monitor Gabrielle's movements and surroundings. Every morning, when the subject emerged from her nest, the group transformed into a small floating box, unobtrusively surrounding and following the target.

As she progressed another block, the old lady's posture and gait markedly improved, and apart from her clothing she didn't appear old anymore. At last, Gabrielle turned a corner, dove into the courtyard behind a closed shop, and pulled the handkerchief off her mane. She quickly changed from her coat and stockings into a jacket and pants she brought with her and stuffed her disguise into the purse. Then she went through another connected enclosure and finally came out on the block's other side and into the lights of a big street.

She walked a couple blocks toward the center of the Deep Ellum, dropped a disposable phone in a trash receptacle on the corner, and got into a waiting cab.

§ § §

Coloqueen Maximum Security Prison

At one a.m., while Joe was already asleep at a hotel by the Bangor's airport, Jeff Mitchell walked Gabrielle to a very special and rarely visited area at the back of building B called the 'museum' by the Coloqueen personnel. She was one freaky girl to request seeing it, but everyone knew the freaky ones were the naughtiest. MSUS Mitchell turned off the security cameras along the passage himself. At its end, he opened the heavy lock of a steel-clad door. They stepped into a moldy smelling air and Jeff threw on the switch.

The yellow light lit a concrete corridor in the oldest section of Coloqueen. No cameras were installed here. It was as dead end as the dead ends come, and for an escapee the worst place to go. There was talk about renovating this part and setting up some shops for the prisoners, but the allowance Coloqueen received yearly laughed at such aspirations.

The corridor hadn't changed since the condemned of the past walked it thirty plus years ago. Jeff and Gabrielle retraced those last steps. They entered the execution chamber. Another light switch was turned on. Gabrielle stood before the one article on display: Old Sparky. Although the wood hadn't been conditioned for a long time and the leather straps were visibly brittle, the contraption still looked a formidable monster.

Mitchell checked his watch. They needed to get busy if they were going to get busy at all. His partner Ian would cover for him, but there was an off chance someone from the warden's office would decide to come by and chat with them, or there could be a genuine emergency. Mitchell opened his mouth to say something, but then Gabrielle moved to the chair. She sat down, placed her elbows on the armrests, and aligned her ankles with the ankle straps.

"Whata you doing, baby?" he asked, wondering if she wanted to fuck here. Just something a freaky girl would go for.

She ignored him, staring above the door. He followed her gaze to an imprint of a hand in the wall's plaster. A very creepy vibe came over him.

"I like your thinking." He tried to sound cool. "But I doubt I can get it up here. Come on, we haven't got the whole night."

"Shut up." Her cold, commanding tone turned him on again. He stepped to the useless, no longer powered by the deadly current lever and waited, obedient.

After a while she stood up. "Take me to ward four."

He led her. Ward four of Coloqueen's former death row was just a stretch and a bend away. They had passed it minutes ago on their way to the chamber. The barred door had no lock and she walked right in. Mitchell stayed out, a stiff rod in his pants, longing to be invited.

She sat on the cot, pulled her legs up, hugged her knees, and gazed around, her white face forlorn. Her eyes stopped on the wall next to her shoulder. Mitchell could see the scratches on it, writing etched coarsely, a prisoner's name starting with an 'S.' She traced the letters with her finger. Mitchell waited.

At last, she swung her feet to the ground and beckoned. He approached timidly and, following her nod, kneeled.

"What's up, baby?" he asked just to say something, unable to look away.

"Shhh!" She took a hold of his face. "I need you to answer my questions."

§ § §

At six a.m. next morning, at the end of the shift, Mitchell's partner Ian Curtis found him sitting on the floor by the kitchen. MSUS Mitchell seemed out of it, but when Ian slapped and shook him he came to his senses.

He couldn't remember what happened after he walked Gabrielle down the corridor at the museum. There was a plastic bag containing some weed and a couple pills clenched in his fist. After some annoying hysterics, his bud promised not to breathe a word of Mitchells' misstep to anybody ever, in line with their covering each other's asses before. Afterward, Mitchell was amazed at his nerve to sneak Gabrielle in. He might have gone crazy. No pussy was worth such a risk. But not remembering their date bothered him even more.

Chapter 27

Maine

Joe woke up without an alarm at eight a.m. sharp, washed, dressed quickly, and collected his sparse gear. He grabbed breakfast provided for the hotel's guests downstairs and then drove his rented, foul-with-chemical-smell car out of town and past the autumn hills, orchards, tree-farms, and the rust tabby-colored countryside. By early afternoon, he swerved onto Farmington Lane, a dirt road running through the fields of dead corn. He was close, according to the coordinates faxed to him by John Crocker, so he slowed, on the lookout for a view similar to the photo taped to the dashboard.

Soon, an old barn showed up, about two-hundred yards off the road. Joe was pretty sure it was the one, even though less of the building was visible among the withered crops that rose taller than the spring ones at the time the picture was taken. He inched the car forward, looking for a lane crossing and a post…and there they were.

In the photo, the post had a chipped sign nailed to it saying, according to the experts in D.C., 'Doghole Farm.' The sign was gone but Joe could see the nails that once held it in place. He pulled over and got out, a tractor's rumble reaching him over the whispering gray skeletons of corn. He walked toward the barn.

Joe heard the lazy bark before he saw the dog and the dry, old man in greasy overalls that tended an engine in the shadow of a wall near a derelict pick-up, to which the engine seemed to belong. An ancient Doberman got up heavily to meet Joe. He could have been Gabrielle's dog's less massive grand-father. The farmer glanced up.

"Howdy!" Joe said. He rubbed the dog's big head as the old man straightened and wiped his hands on a dirty rag from his pocket. "I'm Agent Vasquez. Pete Forman, isn't it?"

Pete examined the badge Joe presented with red-rimmed eyes. "FBI, huh?" he said and shook Joe's hand. "What do you want here?"

"Just looking for someone, asking around." Joe nodded at the benevolent creature lying at their feet now, tongue lolling. "You like this breed?"

"I inherited the runt with the farm from my brother." Pete shrugged. "Mike bred Pinschers."

"I thought about getting one." Joe squatted and scratched the dog behind the ear, the way he saw Gabrielle do it.

"Mike quit breeding them years ago after his favorite, prize-winning stud was killed."

"That's too bad."

"I myself don't care 'bout breeding dogs. Used to help around the place now and then, my farm being next door. Then my brother died, and it's too much bother for me. I sold all his dogs except for a couple. Kept 'em till they died off and gave away all their puppies save for Bumpers here. A direct descendant of Ranger, the one that was killed. Now Bumpers is older than me, in dog years. But we're still waddling around."

Joe's hand petting the dog froze. He rose. "Ranger? That's a good name for a dog," he said, an adrenalin-charged emptiness forming in the pit of his stomach. "Tell me more."

Pete raised his white brows. "What more do you want?"

"Tell me about the dog Ranger."

The old man squinted in disbelief. "Is that what you came here for? To talk about dogs? I thought you were looking for someone."

"I'm in no hurry." Joe smiled. "Why don't we go sit down somewhere? There must be a nice, cool place where Uncle Sam can buy you a sandwich and a beer."

"There sure is," Pete beamed back. "What was your name again, son?"

"Joe," Hound answered.

§ § §

They sat on the covered porch of The Hills Tavern, a local mom-and-pop eatery and bar. The hamburgers and fries Joe got for Pete and himself were greasy, but without much competition for miles around Hills enjoyed high traffic. The pitcher of beer he also ordered proved to be money well spent. It worked wonders for Pete's memory and the laxity of his tongue.

"Did your brother have a big family of his own?" Joe asked.

"Nah. Just him and the wife. They used to take in foster kids, orphans, once in a while. But that was years ago."

Joe took Gabrielle's photo out of his pocket and handed to Pete. "Could she be one of the foster children your brother cared for?"

Pete scrutinized the photo. "Hard to say. She's what, thirty-ish? The age might be right. My brother took in mostly boys to help 'round the farm."

"Sure. No girls, then?"

Pete chewed on a toothpick. "There was one, actually. Could've been the right age and coloring, though she was a scrawny slip of a girl." Pete shook his head. "Nah, it can't be. That one died young."

"What was her name?"

Pete thought a bit longer. "Emily…That's right."

"Can you tell me about her?"

"I suppose you want to see if your gal and Emily could be cousins or something, eh?"

"Something like that," Joe said, and poured Pete another tall glass from the pitcher.

"Now, the reason I remember Emily," Pete said, handing the photo back to Joe, "is because Ranger, my brother's dog I mentioned, was killed when she was here. She really liked him, played with him a lot. Then a neighbor kid, Mattis' boy—Chris was his name if I remember correctly—damn kid poured lighter fluid on the dog and set it on fire. I always knew that kid would come to a bad end, and I was right. He ended up with a five-year stretch in Redshanks for breaking and entering. After Ranger died, Emily got funny in the head. They took her to a doctor, some shrink. He told my brother that Emily should go to other foster people, far away. Then I heard, sometime after, that she passed from the flu."

"You said the kids on your brother's farm were orphans. Did Emily have any relatives?"

"Hmm. I don't know about that. Anything is possible. She was a ward of the state, but not exactly an orphan. I heard my brother saying her mother was as crazy as a shit-house mouse. Pour me another glass, son. Oh! I remember the story. Supposedly, Emily's mother laid her out on some train tracks when she was a baby." Pete took another deep sip of beer and set his mug down, wiping his mouth and shaking his head. "Some people are like that; they want to kill, but are too afraid to use their own hands."

§ § §

Dallas, TX

Ranger's body was stored at the Dallas County Medical Examiner on

Southwestern Avenue. When Gabrielle picked him up, she wrapped him in a blanket she brought with her and refused any help carrying him. Once in her car, she laid the dead dog on her lap and across the passenger seat, removed the blanket, and examined the cadaver. A rough, postmortem scar marred the dog's scalp where the bullet was extracted, but a subcutaneous RFID microchip, no bigger than a grain of rice in the scarf of Ranger's neck, was overlooked.

Gabrielle pulled a switch blade knife and a pair of tweezers from her classic black Prada tote, made a small cut and plucked the chip out. With some napkins and antiseptic solution from the tube she kept in the glove compartment, she thoroughly cleaned the chip, the tools, and her hands.

Discarding the napkins into a recyclable grocery bag, she took out her cell phone and found a number. She listened to the beeps while staring at the tiny RFID tag on her left palm. Unlike the current versions read only from up to several yards away, this high-tech experimental tracer was paired with a super-sensitive receiver able to detect it within half a mile. When the answering machine came on, she said, "Hey, Tom, it's Gabrielle. I am depressed and lonely. Let me know if you feel like hanging out."

She put the phone away, kissed the shaggy scarred head on her lap, covered Ranger with the blanket, and drove off.

§ § §

Forty-eight hours of mandatory cooling were up.

Dante cleaned the remnants of Thai take-out from the table, laid out his fingerprint kit, and got the bag with the latex glove from the refrigerator. The tear made his job easier. Carefully, he turned the glove inside out and inserted PVC tubing into the fingers. He rolled each finger 360-degrees six times over a length of black Gellifter, while protecting the rest of the glove with a sheath cut from a Teflon container. Out of five fingers, the thumb, index, and the ring finger yielded clear prints on the strips. He set up the desk lamp and an ALS guide angled to the axis of the digital camera lens and photographed the prints. The whole process took him two hours.

After transferring the pictures to the computer, he snacked on some chips and washed a candy bar down with a bottle of soda. He was impatient for the results. He had a gut feeling he was about to get something. Imagining how impressed Joe would be swept his tiredness away. It was deep into night. Alone, by the lighted desk, Dante waited. At last, the portraits of Joe's attacker's fingers appeared on the screen.

The three prints were nearly perfect.

Now he could compare them to the collection from the suspect's apartment in L.A. He inserted his personal Johnson case CD, opened the file and ran the fingerprint matching software as his heart beat a lovely rhythm. In less than ten minutes, Dante stared at three identical messages. 'Match found.' *Behold and weep*, Dante thought, wishing his partner was back already.

Someone knocked on the front door. Hound returned early and without a warning, but so timely. Dante got up and hurried to let him in. As he unlocked, he guessed Joe must have forgotten the key.

He swung the door open. "It's you!" He said, dumbfounded. "What are you doing here?"

§ § §

Maine

Joe slept fitfully. Among his vague, fragmented dreams, a black lithe figure stood above his bed, gazing down at him. He couldn't see the face, or much of the rest, but there was a strange intimacy in that silent watch in the dark.

At last he jerked out of his sleep and, as he gawked from his pillow, the Viper from his dream vanished and Joe was alone in the bedroom of the bed-and-breakfast he found in Presque with the help of the traveler's guide. The alarm clock on the bed stand showed seven a.m. and, on his cell charging next to the clock, waited a text from Dante: *Call me.*

Joe did so before getting up, and his partner picked up right away.

"The glove is gone," Dante said.

"What do you mean *gone?*"

"I left it by the computer. I remember that much."

"You're not making sense, Dante." Joe sat up.

"Sorry, I've got a killer headache. Here's the deal. I got the fingerprints off the glove yesterday; good, clear ones. They matched a few prints from the Johnson case. I got all that last night, sometime late I think. Then…I don't know what happened. I woke on the couch, maybe two hours ago. Now to the worst part. The glove is gone and the prints are gone from the camera. I think they've been erased. The Johnson print matches I found disappeared from the screen and the software apparently didn't auto-save them. The CD I used, my copy of the Johnson files, gone. I turned the living room upside down and searched both bedrooms. And I feel like I was drugged."

"What did you eat?"

"Thai takeout, delivered here. I also had a soda and a candy bar, but those I bought myself on the way to the apartment. I am going to powder the door and brush through things around here."

Dante sounded hurried, eager to make up somehow for his loss by doing something constructive. But Joe didn't hold a hope for finding any clues. Whoever got inside their place would be smart enough not to leave traces. Joe's mind raced. The thief was someone who knew about the glove, and the number of such people was very limited. But if the thief had an interest in other files related to the case, he was out of luck. Those files were on Joe's laptop, the one he brought with him to Maine.

"Change the lock today," Joe said. "Call Logan's office, make sure they have an alarm system installed right away. Don't say anything about the glove, but ask them to direct you to one of their docs for a checkup." Then added, "Don't fuck with it. You're lucky to be unharmed."

§ § §

Maine

"For something that old we'd have to go to the Vault," said Mr. Andranski, an elderly clerk at the courthouse of Garfield, a small countrified town not far from Pete's farm. There was a conscious dignity in both his voice and his shriveled little face. His decorum sprung full bloom from the moment he laid eyes on Joe's badge.

"The vault?" Joe was impressed.

They stood by Mr. Andranski's craggy desk in Garfield's courthouse records room, a tiny space with old-fashioned file boxes cluttering the walls and one window letting in some of the late afternoon sunshine. Mr. Andranski fished out a set of keys from a neatly organized drawer. "Please, follow me," he said.

He led the way out of the room and down some cement stairs. "Our town started at the beginning of the eighteenth century," he said, "and this building goes all the way back. Our librarian, she's also the courthouse's secretary, scans all the new records into her computer. We don't often check the older ones, but we store them safely."

The lock on a half-rotted wooden door at the back fell open at the first touch. The clerk still made the appearance of a fuss, turning the key and grunting a little, while casting a careful glance at Joe who, having no desire to embarrass

Mr. Andranski, pretended to be oblivious of the performance. His host turned on the murky fluorescent light, and as they stepped into the basement reminiscent of a well-swept root cellar, the smell confirmed that the old records were indeed not disposed of, but left to rot naturally.

Grimy file cabinets stacked on top of each other formed a few rows of low walls. Andranski took Joe to the first of them and explained that it contained Garfield's history of the past six decades. After a short search, they found what they were looking for, a couple of thin, red cardboard folders with black on yellow labels. *'Property of the Garfield Municipal Office: 1960-1985.'*

Andranski opened one. "This must be the year. Look at them, all the dead. Some mean flu season." He pulled out a yellowed paper. "My, my. Not enough being an orphan, but to die at twelve, that's not fair, not fair at all." He passed Joe a death certificate. It had a name at the top: Emily Howard.

Despite the decrepitude of Garfield's antiqued premises, the old man's dedication to keep his shop organized impressed Joe. "What about her foster family, or whoever she stayed with at the time?" he asked. "Do you think we can look them up?"

Mr. Andranski searched the papers at the end of the '1960-1985' drawer, then went through the contents of the one underneath. "Way they did it before," he said, "was they pulled all the deceased papers and put them together. My way is to file those at the bottom, by name. Hers should be here, too."

"If you could find anything about the girl's blood relatives that would be very helpful."

The clerk nodded, peered at the file separators, and pulled out a cardboard folder. It was unpromisingly thin. Mr. Andranski opened it. "Nothing in here," he said, puzzled. "This is not the way it should be. It's been a while since I looked at those records, but they shouldn't be touched..." His brow furrowed.

Joe took the folder from him. "Are you sure this is it?"

"Look." The clerk pointed, agitated, at a tear at the top of the open cardboard skin. "That's where the contents sheet was glued. It was ripped off."

Joe stared at the tear. It seemed fresh.

The clerk's face became pinched. "Another out-of-towner came to me less than a year ago. Said he was searching for his relatives. He nosed in this very row. I took note because not many visitors ask to be taken to the Vault."

Mr. Andranski got to his knees and started hectically checking the other lower drawers. After a few minutes, he struggled to get up and Joe helped him. "Everything else seems in order. But this is bad business—stealing municipal property." Mr. Andranski shook his head, upset. "He seemed decent enough, very polite. I left him here for some time."

"Did you record his name?"

"Unfortunately, no."

"What did he look like?"

"A distinguished gentlemen. Wore a suit."

Joe pulled the envelope with the photos out of his pocket and found Sheppard's photograph. "Is that him?"

Mr. Andranski squinted at the photo. "My memory is not what it used to be, but I'd remember this face. No, the man who came here had dark hair. Tall, thin, and hunched a little."

"Old or young?"

"Not young, not old. Younger than myself. But as I said, I don't remember him that much. Not sure I'd recognize him again."

Who else would be interested in a little orphan Emily Howard enough to come to an armpit of a town in the middle of the boonies to search for her records? According to Andranski, not Sheppard. Not Steve and Blake's killer, quite possibly Doll-maker as Sheppard called his son's killer. He had fish eyes and was likely blond, and to Andranski still young. And not the janitor, the man Joe deemed to be Viper, because he was neither tall nor hunched. Who else?

Then, Joe thought about someone. Someone he met not long ago. An evasive man, hateful of Gabrielle, of insufficient qualifications, but employed recently as a head of the Forensic Psychology Department and Research at the DGI.

"Did he wear glasses?"

"Well…I think yes, he did."

Joe had only one bit of information left to check here. "Where was the girl buried?"

"If she was buried locally…" Mr. Andranski examined Emily's death certificate and nodded in satisfaction. "Just as I thought, she's at Lindbergh Cemetery."

"Where is it?"

"Follow the main road all the way to the end of town."

Joe thought for a moment. "Where can I find the sheriff?" he asked.

§ § §

Joe's anxiety ran high throughout his last day in Maine. The urge to hurry back to Dallas gnawed at him, but he couldn't leave just yet. Arranging for a productive phone interview with the Redshanks' Warden would take more time and explanation than he was in a mood for, so he decided to ambush a medium security facility in person instead.

He entered the Aroostook Corrections Office a little after four p.m. The Parole Officer on duty, a brisk man in his late forties, asked to be called Eddie as soon as they shook hands. He sat Joe down, and after ensuring his secretary brought his guest a half-gallon cup of bad, reheated coffee, literally rolled-up his sleeves and started his electronic and paper pursuit for Chris Mattis, Jr., Redshank's one-time inmate.

In less than half-an-hour an old mug shot of a young thuggish male was faxed to them, along with the related documents from the Redshanks Prison.

"Mattis…Lemme see…" Eddie sounded like a younger version of Pete Forman. He shuffled through the print-outs, brows raised, while Joe waited.

"Tough luck, Agent. The guy managed to burn to death a few months after his release."

So, Joe's only remaining link to the mysterious Emily had been dead for years, burned to death shortly after leaving the safety of the penitentiary. "How'd he died?"

Eddie stabbed his thick finger at the old police report. "Says it happened at night on one of the county roads. Mattis' truck's gas tank was leaking and must've caught a spark when he started the engine. He couldn't get out for some reason; the doors were stuck, or he was too drunk." He handed the sheet to Joe. "They didn't test for alcohol back then, but they put that down as a likely theory. I'd say a correct one. A freak accident. The gas tank exploded and he roasted inside—"

"…like a dog," Joe finished and a crooked smile touched his lips.

Chapter 28

A Late Night 'Cook-out'

Coloqueen Maximum Security Prison, TX, end of November

The late-night assignment was to satisfy the Justice Department's request for the immediate evaluation of Coloqueen's newest addition: Dan Holoway, who stashed at least three female corpses along tired Texas highways. The expert of choice, Dr. Lubovich, met with Holoway at midnight, a few hours after his admission to prison. Holoway's trial was scheduled to start the next day.

Jeff Mitchell and Ian Curtis manned the observation room. They sipped coffee and watched Gabrielle and Holoway through the one-way mirror with the sound off. They had no desire to listen to Holoway's nasty spittle.

"Looky-here!" Ian said and pulled a near-full box of cream donuts out from the shelf under the control panel. "Must be Bob and Ricardo left them for us, bless 'em." He and Jeff each took a pastry. Ian swallowed his in three bites and grabbed another. "Yummy." He nodded at Gabrielle and smirked, his mouth still full. "You never told me, how was that piece of ass?"

Jeff finished his donut without tasting it. Ian's question irritated him. He had no idea how Gabrielle's ass was. Whatever drugs he took during their date erased his memory about it. Pot, Ecstasy, or something else, the weird shrink somehow screwed with his brains in the process of screwing him. And apart from the pharmaceuticals, she could be as capable of making one forget as she was of making one remember. But he sure hoped there was some diddling involved. In the brief moments of believing that, he felt a bit better.

His self-respect demanded another date with her outside the prison walls and without hocus-pocus this time. But whenever he thought about calling her, a nasty voice whispered in his mind, "Danger, sailor!" In addition, he wondered if his manly performance at the museum, the one he had no memory of, wasn't up to snuff and if that's why she acted so official around him tonight. The bitch couldn't expect him to perform after turning him into a zombie!

"All 'em whores are the same," he said through his teeth.

His bud opened his pie hole to make a smart comment, but saw Mitchell's morose expression and shut it. Instead, he nodded at the window. "Ain't she afraid of the psycho?"

"I'd like him to try anything," Mitchell grunted and patted his holster. The familiar weight inside reassured him a little.

In the interrogation room, Holoway's eyes glazed over. Gabrielle checked his EEG then smiled toward the mirrored window.

Seeing her smile, Jeff Mitchell's confidence grew a notch. "Those cunts," he said. "Once you plow 'em, you can't get rid of 'em." He glanced at Ian.

His buddy appeared to be distracted, yawning and rubbing his eyes. Mitchell wanted to say something snide, but instead yawned himself so wide his jaw cracked. He was tired, so tired…

What the heck, he thought, and blinked sleepily.

A loud thump to his right interrupted his descent into slumber, but only briefly. He gaped for an unclear moment at Ian, now sprawled on the floor. "What the…" His tongue lay thick in his mouth. He staggered to his feet, but oblivion caught him before he got up and sent him down on top of his partner like a deadweight sack. He moaned once and was out cold.

§ § §

Gabrielle raised her hand and waved, a signal the session ended that she and Mitchell agreed on beforehand. She waited but nothing happened. She got up, walked to the observation window, pressed her face to the mirrored surface, cupped her hands, and peered through. Mitchell and the guard lay heaped under their chairs.

She knocked hard on the glass. Nothing.

She went back to the snoring Holoway, who was sagging in the chair about to fall, and pulled him down to the floor. She walked out of the interrogation dock. Outside, she rattled the next door's handle. Seen through the small Plexiglas pane, Mitchell and the other deputy still lay unresponsive. For a minute, she listened to the silence as the lights flickered overhead, her face wary and sharp like an animal's. Then she took off her shoes and sprinted down the deserted hallway.

§ § §

On the plane from Bangor

Joe wasn't sure why he brought the letters with him. He planned to read them at some point, which is why he packed them when he went to Dallas. Right before he left for Maine he grabbed them, without thinking, from his suitcase and threw them into his padded backpack, along with a few changes of clothing and his laptop. The latter contained maps and detailed building schematics of Sullivan, and Joe honestly intended to study those on his flight in an attempt to unravel Viper's amazing escape. But he couldn't concentrate on this task. At last, he stashed the laptop into his backpack and took out the letters.

He studied them, attentive to the smallest detail.

The fragile envelopes were well-preserved. The chaffed bends of the flaps and the wear along the sheets' seams indicated many reads throughout the years. Joe wondered when his mother read them—during the day, with him in school or at work, or at night while he slept. How did she manage to keep them out of his sight?

He braced himself and started to peruse. Soon, he was absorbed. Their sunniness and simplicity came from a world different than the one he always inhabited. In some deep way his father's sentences reminded him of that lost world and filled him with inexplicable nostalgia. The letters had passion and warmth, and a hopeful recount of the mostly financial difficulties of his parents' youth. When Rafa wrote to Isabel, he was significantly younger than Joe now. His exuberant Spanish bore witness to the intensity of his hopes and love. The love and intensity Joe's life, so far, lacked.

As Joe read, his hand stole to the side of his neck, and a mark left by Gabrielle's teeth latching onto him a couple nights before. The skin was still raw under his fingers, but somehow touching it felt good. He read further. One of the letters mentioned his then twelve year old uncle; Rafa called him a trouble-maker. The image the words conjured had nothing in common with the one in Joe's memory, the recall of which always brought anger.

Among the letters, a small photo of Rafa showed him at no more than twenty, squatting in wide, white trousers on the grass over a rugby ball. He was not the husky, serious man Joe remembered, but young, thin, and other-worldly handsome, with an open, luminous face. Joe took out his wallet and put the picture in a plastic separator behind the snapshot of his mother. With a pang, he thought how Isabel never carried her husband's photo in her own wallet, so as not to upset him. He stashed his own into his pocket and the letters away into his backpack.

He sat back, took out his phone, and reread the text Gabrielle sent him in the morning: *Can't wait to see you again.*

He smiled. Something brewed in him, wizened and cynical, but happy. His mind broke free, for the time, from trying to fit too many puzzle pieces together. Of all the revelations accomplished, the most important held that, while the concept of dishonor he thought so certain and dear for so long turned a moot one, who Joe was and what he was going to do became clear.

§ § §

Dallas, TX

Dante picked Joe up. The call from Coloqueen came before the airport's lights receded behind them.

"Agent Vasquez?" Coloqueen's Head Warden sounded out of breath. "You need to come immediately!"

§ § §

Coloqueen Maximum Security Prison

Joe and Dante showed their badges to armed men in SWAT gear at the checkpoint, drove in, and parked next to the Emergency Response van. They barely got out of the car when the ambulance arrived, with flashing lights but no sound effects. The intention to avoid publicity was obvious. They marched toward the heavily-cordoned, Maximum Security Block.

"All the way from L.A.!" one of men in charge of the entrance commented after examining their badges. His partner sneered, "This is a lockdown situation," and to Joe, "What are you boys doing here?" Joe told the guards to call Portman, and some minutes later the Head Warden led him and Dante to Block B. The inmates stood by the bars of their cells along their progression. A few called out. Most kept silent.

Joe's party reached the corridor full of guards, cops, and paramedics, and followed a fresh, make-shift walkway of raised wooden planks through the open steel door into the brightly lit big kitchen. He walked past deep sinks and wide chrome counters with unsentimental, institutional utensils laid out near pans for mass cooking. The place stunk of bland meat boiling, an oddly normal smell. Joe's heart raced.

Dante called something after him, but as Joe became aware of an object before him the words failed to reach him. Strapped to a counter covered in blood were the butchered remains of a man. A knife stuck out, driven through the chest. A bloody wellsaw, the kind butchers use to cut bones, lay next to the body. On the gas stove, a huge pot still steamed, thick gray foam floating at the top.

The old cannibal Salmon had been cooked.

§ § §

"I don't think the paramedics can put this Humpty back together again." Dante had the true cop's sense of macabre humor.

They stood in the corridor.

"The medics are here for Dr. Lubovich, not for Salmon," Portman explained. "She's okay. They gave her something to calm down, so she can talk. She's our only witness, of sorts. Found sitting on the floor outside the kitchen in shock. Mitchell and Curtis were supposed to attend to her but someone drugged them. So she went to look for help. All the internal locks were opened; the killers obviously got the codes. She wandered into the kitchen and found…Poor gal. Good thing she didn't run into them." He faltered as Joe took off.

§ § §

As he approached, he detected her shaking beneath the police blanket and the stains of blood on her stockings. Gabrielle sat on the ground by the paramedic's van. Squatting next to her, a bald man wearing the dark uniform of the County Sheriff's department jotted on a notepad.

Joe stopped near a young paramedic. "How is she?"

"She seemed catatonic at first, but when we tried to give her a shot she came around and resisted. The blood isn't hers. Still, they should be taking her to the hospital, not questioning her."

Gabrielle raised her head and their eyes met. At once, he needed to gather her into his arms, to block the horror of Coloqueen's kitchen from her memory. He walked to her.

"Why didn't you stay where you were?" the cop asked her.

"I didn't know what to do. I didn't know what was going on. I didn't want to be a sitting duck. I wanted to get out. I had left my purse, with my cell phone in it, in the Head Warden's office…"

"How did you find the kitchen?"

"I didn't know where I was going. I was trying to find somebody, or the exit."

"When you entered the hallway by the kitchen, did you hear anything? Did you see anyone?"

Gabrielle shook her head and huddled deeper into the blanket.

"That's enough," Joe said. "You can question her more after she gets some rest." He showed the cop his badge. "This is my case. You can confirm that with your supervisors."

The bald man rose from his squatting position, obviously annoyed.

Dante approached, along with the young paramedic. "I told you," the latter said to the cop. "She needs to go to the hospital."

"No hospitals!" Gabrielle seized Joe's wrist. "Get me out of here!"

Joe turned to Dante.

"Go," Dante said. "I'll stay."

Joe helped Gabrielle up. She clung to him as he led her to the car, dropping the blanket on the ground. "We are *not* going to the hospital?"

"No, we are not," he confirmed.

§ § §

Dallas/Maine

They drove in silence through the sleeping city. She reclined on her side, knees drawn up on the seat. Joe kept glancing at her, trying to make out her face as the street lights illuminated her silhouette in evenly-spaced, brief moments. He didn't know if she was awake or slumbering. One time, he thought she watched him. But in the next illumination, she appeared to be dozing off.

Joe wasn't sure how much time had passed. Except for the even hum of the engine, the silence in the car was eerie. And, with a surreal pang, he became aware of Viper's presence—so acutely that, without thinking, he turned and checked the empty back seat.

After a while, Gabrielle sat up, and Joe's uneasiness fell off right away. She picked up her purse, took a pack of cigarettes, and offered it to Joe.

"I quit a long time ago," he said. "You should, too."

She rummaged in her bag for a lighter. Before she found one, Joe reached, plucked the cigarette from her mouth, lowered his window and threw it out. She stared at him.

"What?" He glanced at her.

She didn't say anything, but pulled her knees under her in the seat again and leaned her head against its back, looking at him. The side of his face turned to her felt warm. The lights of Dallas blinked ahead. With one hand on the wheel, he reached out and stroked her face. She held his hand. And everything was alright.

§ § §

Gabrielle didn't stir for the remainder of the trip, and sleep-walked as Joe led her to his apartment. Using a miniature, infrared remote Dante supplied, he disabled their new alarm before entering. Once inside, he reactivated the alarm and half-carried Gabrielle into his bedroom, where she murmured one word, "Clean."

She slumped on his bed and proceeded to peel off her clothing. He turned the bedside lamp on, went into his bathroom and started a tub. She stumbled in with a little bundle, dropping her blood smeared stockings into the waste basket. Technically, they were evidence, but Joe didn't care.

He helped her climb in and sat on the edge while she washed herself and her clothes. When she was done, she pulled the plug, staying folded while water drained, and then rinsed the tub. He undressed, climbed in behind her, pulled the curtain closed and turned on the shower. They lay back together, her head on his chest, and let the hot water cascade over them till the warmth relaxed their internal shaking, and their bodies merged into a perfect fit. They stayed this way until the steam became too hard to bear. Then he got out and brought some towels.

Back in the bedroom, she dropped on his bed and he knelt over her. They gazed at each other. For an instant, he thought it happened—the portal opened. But she closed her eyes and the connection broke. Desperate to regain it, he held her shoulders, but she wrapped her legs around him and kissed him on the mouth, deep, and he forgot everything else. For a while, at least in their flesh, they were one and whole, unconscious of the secrets dividing them.

§ § §

Dante got home at four a.m.

He reactivated the alarm, stepped into the dark living room, and halted. Gabrielle's naked form stood before him. Before he could utter a word, she pressed her finger to his lips. Her eyes locked with his and he remained silent.

She led him to the desk, where she turned on the lamp and gently pushed him into the seat. The desktop's LCD monitor was moved aside to make space for Joe's open laptop.

She took Dante's right hand and put it on the laptop's keyboard. She whispered into his ear as he typed…

§ § §

It was still dark when Joe woke up and found himself alone. The anxiety gripping, he got up. The sound of a flushing toilet stopped him halfway to the door leading to the living room. Exiting the bathroom, Gabrielle walked to him and slipped into his embrace.

§ § §

Early in the morning, Garfield's two reputable alcoholics and intermittent residents of the local single-cell jail pulled a small, dirt-smeared coffin from a freshly-dug grave. They looked at the Sheriff supervising their work. He nodded. One man picked up a crowbar, and pried off the lid. When it fell aside, his friend whistled in surprise. The men crowded around the coffin.

§ § §

The sun peaked into the room between the blades of the shades. In its light, Gabrielle, sleeping on her back with her lips slightly parted, had the rare appearance of vulnerability. Joe wasn't sure if he slept at all after waking up earlier or only lay motionless and exhausted, constantly coming back to the awareness of her body next to his. He gazed at her for a while now. She appeared so serene. She was calm and cool most of the time, he thought, but she never seemed peaceful when awake.

At last, her eyelashes fluttered, her mouth closed, and so did her face.

He shut his eyes without thinking, and felt her turn toward him on her pillow. He wondered if the animal in her, as keen as his own, saw through him. His cell phone rang, breaking the silence. He opened his eyes. Hers were closed now. He turned and took his phone from the night stand.

§ § §

The grave diggers sat on tombstones and smoked while the Sheriff made his call. The empty coffin gaped at their feet.

§ § §

"Thank you, Sheriff. I appreciate it." Propped up on his elbow, Joe hung up and said without turning, "Good morning, Emily." The response was a movement in the bed behind him. He lay back and watched her sit up.

"I haven't been called that name in a long, long time," she said. She dressed, walked into the bathroom where her blouse hung to dry, and pulled it on, yellowish traces of blood still visible.

"You were not truthful with me," he said.

"Goes both ways," she parried.

"You should have been. You can be now." He heard how unconvincing his words sounded.

She glanced at him with her brow cocked ironically. *Neither of us can trust another*, her expression said.

"Your friend who burned Chris Mattis alive to avenge your dog, is he Viper? Did you screen prospective prey for him? Made sure they were guilty enough to qualify?"

She searched for her shoes and found them.

"Did he work with you and Sheppard before, and now you and your untouchable Senator—father, mentor, brother in crime, lover, whoever he is to you—are afraid of him? I didn't want to spy on you. I just followed my case… Emily." He sat up and shook his head. "I don't think I can get the hang of calling you by your real name."

"You don't need to. Emily is long dead."

Sadness overcame Joe. "You've got the Slavic accent down pat, by the way," he said as she opened the door. After so many years, it was likely no longer an accent for her.

"Thanks," she said and walked out. He wanted to call after her, to try and stop her, but didn't.

§ § §

After a shower, Joe went into the living room and found Dante on the couch, dressed in shorts and a tee, a big mug of coffee cooling in his hand. "She

187

had a taxi waiting. Must have called for it earlier. You look like you have been ridden all night."

"You look like shit yourself," Joe said.

"I slept less than three hours, and those were full of strange dreams, hombre."

Joe picked up his traveling backpack from the chair. Finding it unzipped made him stop. He took his laptop out and brought it to the desk. "Oh yeah? What kind of dreams?"

"That's the irritating part. I don't remember, and I've got a bitch of a headache again. I wonder if it's gonna be a recurring thing now."

Joe opened his laptop and pressed the start button.

"Maybe the glove thief caused brain damage with whatever crap he used on me," Dante continued. "Except, the docs can't find any traces of anything."

Joe logged in, left-clicked on one of the folders, right-clicked on the first file of the list, went into the file's properties, and stared at the information. *Accessed at 4:20 a.m....last night.* Even if Joe wanted to lie to himself, the computer couldn't. "So, you don't remember your dream, huh?"

"Not. A. Thing."

Joe looked up. Gayle gulped his coffee, his tired, probing eyes on his senior partner. Joe turned his attention back to the screen. He checked the last access time for the few remaining files—exactly the same, 4:20 in the morning, when he was asleep and Dante, apparently, in Gabrielle's power. She wouldn't have had long enough to read through the contents, only to copy them.

A man can trust no one except his mother, he thought. *A mother who lives for him. And if he is lucky, he might have and trust a friend who is closer than a brother. But beyond that, a man can trust no one.*

"I wonder why Cowell assigned you to me."

"He didn't want to at first. He kept advising me to go with O'Neal. But I insisted."

"Didn't they tell you about my disreputable standing?" His own unfairness irritated Joe further.

"Actually, I heard a lot of good things about you, thought I can learn something. Plus, you are not exactly white. Thought I'd have a better chance not being used if I worked with you."

Joe sighed with remorse. "I am glad we ended up together, Dante. Got anything new?"

"You bet. Your girlfriend pays yearly to an upscale nursing home here in Dallas. Claims it as a charitable donation on her income tax. The beneficiary is a woman named Mary Howard. She is in her seventies now, Alzheimer's, was institutionalized most of her life. She gave birth in her youth and tried to kill the baby by throwing it under a train. Apparently, she believed the child's father was the devil himself."

"Gabrielle's real name is Emily Howard," Joe said. "That's what I found out in Maine. Mary Howard must be her mother. Sheppard could be the psychiatrist who dealt with her as a child when she had a nervous breakdown. He faked her death, took her away, and raised her."

"Woa…" Dante stared at him. "Say again."

Joe picked up his laptop. "I need to check something."

He went back to his bedroom, took his digital camera from under the bed on the side he occupied last night, attached it to his laptop, and started the download. He brought up a shot of Gabrielle sleeping and, in a few clicks, another image, side by side, of Chandra, Terence Craig's visitor and liberator, taken by a security camera in Ironwood prison. He took Gabrielle's picture early in the morning at an angle to match Chandra's. He made one of the images transparent, adjusted the size, and laid it over the other.

He stared at the result for a full minute. Chandra's three-quarter grainy face, with her excessive blond frizz, made the match inadmissible in a court of law, but Joe didn't care about the courts. If he had his way, no court would ever see these two images next to each other. He erased the results of the overlay, exited the software, closed his laptop and went back to the living room.

"Okay…" Dante said. "I got it. Sheppard got her a false identity. But why?"

Joe sat in the chair. "Do you want to know more than you need?" he asked. "The less you know, the less you'll be liable. And if they ever blame anyone, it will be me."

Dante peered at him from the couch. "If you want me to help you, you got to talk to me," he said. "I trust you, Joe. You won't do anything to let bad things happen to good people. I am not going to report to Cowell behind your back and bury the woman you love. Our friendship means more to me than brownie points. Plus," he grinned, "as far as I'm concerned, Cowell can go fuck himself."

§ § §

"So, Gabrielle may have known Viper since she was a kid. At which point did they part ways do you think?"

If they ever parted, Joe thought.

"What if Sheppard isn't aware?" Dante continued. "What if she used him for Viper's sake?" Dante's voice was a velvety as ever but every word cut Joe to the bone.

"Not likely. She was too young," Joe replied.

"A wily teenager?"

"She wouldn't do that."

"Joe, you are in no position to judge what she would or wouldn't do. Imagine a manipulative older boyfriend—or he could be her brother, or even her father—who killed the bastard who killed her dog. She was heavily under his influence. What if the psychiatrist that treated her wasn't Sheppard? At some point, Viper faked her death and got her out of the system. By that time, she probably participated in a number of his crimes. Then he killed Bobby, and Sheppard was on his heels, so Viper planted Gabrielle close to Sheppard to keep a watch. Say, she pretended to be from abroad and became Sheppard's graduate student. She developed her talents and, for a while, supplied Viper with information he needed to get to his victims, to feed his need, you know. Meanwhile, she and Sheppard became close friends and she wanted to switch camps, but Viper and her past held her by the throat."

"There are two killers, remember?" Joe said. "Viper didn't kill Bobby— we can be pretty sure of that."

"No we can't, and you can't trust your gut on this because, whether you want to admit it or not, you established a rapport with him," Dante pointed. "You might be right, but we must consider all possibilities."

"The possibility I would bet on the most is that Sheppard and Gabrielle controlled Viper in the past, and now he is a loose cannon. The question is, how do Bobby Sheppard and Blake Johnson's murders fit into this? How are the two killers connected?"

"You know, whoever murdered those boys fits Viper's victim's profile perfectly," Dante mused.

Joe already played with the idea. Viper and Doll-maker, not connected, but an executioner and his prey. It stood to reason, and was possible to use in Gabrielle's defense if needed, that Viper manipulated her from the start of her life. She was unable to shake the connection off and lived in fear, Viper's target herself. As Joe formulated this, whether for himself or for the theoretical jury, his mood improved a bit. She likely got fed up with assisting the monster and refused to do more scouting for him. It could have happened after Craig's execution.

The more Joe thought about it, the more convincing this theory appeared. He remembered the wistfulness in her eyes fixed on him. He was her chance to get out of the quagmire, but she had a good reason to be reticent. No matter. She relied on him not letting her drown, Joe knew that in his bones, and she was right. He would do his darndest to save her even if she wouldn't, or couldn't, save herself.

Wondering where Gabrielle was now, Joe picked up his jacket and took out his cell phone. It had a new message from the lab. He listened to it and said to Dante, "Ballistics confirmed the gun from the apartment is the same that killed Steve."

"Well, this backs up a good portion of our theory. Of course, the problem remains we now have to chase two psychos instead of one," Dante said. "The most likely scenario, Doll-maker found out about your gal's involvement with Viper, which is why he was able to blackmail her and Sheppard to prevent them from exposing him."

"So both Viper and Doll-maker have good reasons to keep this pair quiet," Joe said, and thought with a pang that there was only one reliable way to ensure that.

"We must corner and question them." Dante shrugged. "We have no choice."

"We don't have any real evidence yet." *And it would need to be a darn good one to corner someone like Gabrielle or Sheppard,* Joe thought. Plus, he needed to know more.

"We can bluff…" But Dante didn't sound certain.

"That won't work with either of them." But there was something Joe could and would do. "We're going to visit her Sullivan patient," he said. "And we won't be asking for her permission this time."

Chapter 29

The Saddest Music in the World

Dallas

You think it was an accident?" Rosa's nose and eyelids were red and swollen.

Gabrielle was sure that the young detective cried shortly before their meeting. "I do, sort of, but you got me here for a forensic post-mortem evaluation. If you catch the killer and let me interrogate him, I'll tell you what I think," she said. "Right now, it's just a hunch. The boy wasn't a junkie, so the perv likely spiked his drink to render him unconscious and used him for sex. The traces in the tissues attest to that. The 'date' got out of hand, so the perv got scared and hacked-up the body to dispose of it. A non-premeditated murder."

"I don't care if it's non-premeditated, the bastard deserves hell." Rosa's face twitched with hatred.

They both tried to avoid looking at the remains of Brandon Mole, aka Dandelion, arranged in their proper places on the table a few feet away. Although Brandon no longer could be called Dandelion. His formerly bright, springy hairs hung matted and colorless. The lower part of his right leg and his right arm were still missing. The located body parts had partially disintegrated after weeks of exposure to the elements.

"You can't let it get to you. You'll burn right out of your job." Gabrielle touched Rosa's elbow.

Rosa nodded and her new friend led her out of the chrome room of death and up the stairs to the corridor.

"I'd rather go now, if you don't mind," Gabrielle said.

"Of course. Thank you for doing this."

"What are friends for, but to give their expert opinions? Keep me abreast of any developments, would you? I'll help you in any way I can."

"Gosh, thanks! You'll be the first to know about anything." Rosa sighed and hugged Gabrielle. "I just…I can't talk about these things to any of my friends back home. Or to my family. And I've got to talk. I guess I'm still unseasoned."

"It's okay." Gabrielle patted Rosa's back and carefully disengaged. Her face paled so much one would think she was ready to faint. But her hard eyes glistened bright. "I'll send you my report."

She walked down the hall past a group of cops talking. At the door, as if feeling something, she stopped and looked back, catching a movement as if one or a few of them turned away quickly. They were six, all similar in their uniforms. Normal, middle-aged men appreciating a pretty woman walking by. Nothing to be concerned about.

Gabrielle turned and exited the building.

Chapter 30

Weizlan Gets His Revenge

In the foggy semidarkness, the place appeared to be a long decommissioned train depot. His hand felt for and gripped his trusty Springfield and his eyes searched the greasy ground under his feet, threading the passage winding among the mounds of rubbish. He suspected he shouldn't look close at those, and immediately the nearest came into focus. Something white stuck out—a human foot, the toes rotting.

Some small, distant sounds snapped him to attention. He strained his ears, and a child's sobs became clear.

"Alberto!" He took off, desperate urgency chasing him over limbs and bones scattered everywhere, some in pools of a dark liquid. He failed his boy once; he couldn't let him die again, alone.

"Alberto!" he called. The fog thickened, and he stumbled, unsure where the crying was coming from. Then a rumble came and covered up the baby sound, sending tendrils of panic down Joe's spine.

The rumble grew into an earsplitting roar, and the enormous shadow of an engine rushed past, the wind blasting. The train flew on, and a tiny bundle could be seen on the tracks. Joe ran to it screaming his son's name, his skin bathing in a cold sweat. As he approached, the bundle turned into a larger shape, someone in a long coat, face down. He rolled the body over.

Gabrielle was dead. Her trunk terminated in a bloody mess of innards, her legs gone. Joe's knees gave in. Sightless, she gazed past him. Her eyes were not dark but blue. Steve's eyes...

Joe touched her and his hand passed through the air. Her body was gone, and only an empty bundle of rags lay before him. A chuckle, unnatural and familiar, coming from nowhere and everywhere, made him raise his head.

"Show yourself!" he shouted.

"Thssey alwaysss die," Viper hissed, somewhere close. "Thssey all do..."

Joe spun around. Invisible, Viper laughed at his folly.

§ § §

Viper's laughter still rung in Joe's ears when he woke up. He didn't move or open his eyes for a while, trying to interpret the nightmare in a rational way. *I've got to get a grip*, he thought. It was his damaged brain, stuck in the loop of despair, which manufactured a dream about her death in place of the old one about Alberto.

He couldn't afford to dwell on dreams.

§ § §

The question of how Viper escaped Sullivan never stopped bugging Joe. He had documented the timing and the positions of the personnel, the detailed schematics of the facility, and studied the transcripts of interviews with the guards, nurses, and some of the inmates. The more he tried to come up with a possible route, the more he believed that Viper didn't flee the grounds right away.

If Viper was back on the roof after Joe went down the chute, with all the pandemonium going on, he had a limited time to retrace his steps or to conceal himself. Viper's stellar record testified that he always prepared extensively, so where did he go?

Joe supposed the hare-footed and agile killer would be able to reach the East Wing before police arrived en masse and while Joe turned somersaults in the refuse box in the yard. Moreover, it was also the only place he could go. But once in the East Wing, where to next? It crossed Joe's mind before that Viper had temporarily cooped-up there, and possibly even permanently, being back home.

The East Wing hosted a few wards, including that of Brin James.

§ § §

Sullivan Maximum Security Facility for the Criminally Insane

"Yes, I would say he has the making of an efficient killer once he is in his manic state. Don't judge him by his appearance. Crazy or not, his IQ is 145, enough to mastermind about anything," Weizlan said to Joe as they stood watching Dante and the two junior agents borrowed from Logan surveying the framing on the barred windows behind the East Wing. The State profiler's presence during the interview with Brin James, endorsed by an enthusiastic Cowell, was the condition from Logan, since James was not just an inmate but a patient of the state's psychiatric institution.

"Hey!" Dante called to them. "Better check this!"

As Joe and Weizlan approached, he pointed at the bolts keeping the heavy, iron bars in place. "Someone tampered with these not long ago." To demonstrate, he pulled one of the bolts by the head, and it lifted out. "This is the laundry-room window."

"The laundry is right across the hall from James' cell!" Weizlan exclaimed. The excitement in the Professor's voice was deplorable. Joe itched to ask Weizlan about his blackmail dealings with Sheppard and to see the look on his face.

Cowell had no inkling yet that James, as Viper, could tie Senator Sheppard to the case. Joe saw all too clearly what a godsend lone whacko James would be to Cowell. The Craig's execution would be forgotten before becoming known to the world as one in a series of gruesome slayings under the very noses of federal authorities, and Hound Vasquez would get a congenial pat on the back, which was no more than Cowell thought Joe deserved.

Dante pulled another bolt, then another…Assisted by the agents, he grabbed the bars and shook the steel structure. It careened, separating from the concrete hold.

§ § §

Beyond the glass window of the interrogation cell Brin paced, glancing anxiously toward the mirror. Joe, Dante, and Weizlan observed him from the other side. His rounded face seemed a bit doughy, but his body was wiry in spite of the good food, supposedly quiet life, and middle-age. Such a physique could be the result of an anxious nature or some serious exercise—the kind one needs to be able to sneak out of one's comfortable confinement and commit grisly murders.

"He was tried and sentenced three years ago." Weizlan stated what Joe already knew. "The evidence was overwhelming if circumstantial, but more importantly he confessed. And a polygraph confirmed his confession. Then she came waltzing in!"

"Three years ago is when the prison killings started," Dante pitched in. "At least those we know of so far."

"Exactly!" Weizlan played one of the guys. "She does her Ouija Board routine, her Senator gets involved, and the case is blown open again. Suddenly, the State Commissioner calls the MHD's secretary, and the whacko is shipped here to enjoy the sunshine and free drugs."

"Are you okay?" Dante asked Joe. "You look ashen."

Joe didn't feel okay, but his instincts bid him to keep quiet. He needed time to access the situation and figure out what to do. The dice was out of his hand and rolling. Rather than answer Dante, he nodded at the man on the other side of the mirror. "I think he's cooked enough," he said.

And in they went.

§ § §

Gruesome images from Coloqueen's kitchen were spread on the table, a part of Weizlan's shock tactic, him being the specialist on the interrogations of the mentally disturbed. Brin stared at them spellbound, rocking in his chair, hugging himself.

"Who let you out of your ward?" Weizlan thundered.

Joe glanced at the two other men hovering close by; Dante's big, dark face was naturally menacing, and Weizlan's, glad and greedy, with Gestapo eyes. Joe was destined to play the good cop on the scale of scariness.

"I don't know," Brin said. "I don't remember…" He seemed anxious and earnest to Joe, although Joe appreciated Viper's acting abilities. Weizlan was questioning Brin for about an hour, confusing him, and springing the same, paraphrased questions on him—a tactic Joe was trained in but always despised as it worked only on exceedingly stupid subjects.

"Do you remember killing John Baca and Terrence Craig?" Weizlan asked, for a hundredth time.

Brin froze. His eyes darted furtively at one of the pictures on the table, then returned and glued to it. He swallowed and quickly nodded a few times.

Joe's heart skipped. "How did you get out?"

Brin shrugged. "I did it!" His eyes were on the photos.

"Did anyone help you?" Dante asked.

Brin broke into sobs. "I don't remember. I did it! She said I am good! But I'm no good!"

Weizlan bore a look of vindicated triumph.

"How can you be sure that you did anything if you don't remember how you got out?" Joe asked Brin.

"He could be made to forget," Weizlan pointed.

It was clear who Weizlan's comment was aimed at. Joe managed to keep his fury out of his voice. "If *I* remember correctly, you don't believe in such things, Professor."

"I never said I don't believe in her method outright. Some deplorable psychological tricks, if you will, work in certain conditions, and can be used on the mentally unstable. I could never lower myself to learn or use them."

Joe glared at him. "I need a word," he grunted through his teeth as he left the room.

Dante and Weizlan followed him out of the room. "We are done here," he said to them. "None of us are equipped to continue this interrogation. We must call in our reprogramming experts from D.C. And until they arrive, this man must stay where he is, isolated and watched over twenty-four seven."

"I agree," Dante said.

Weizlan puffed up. "I don't think Sullivan is the right place for a confessed murderer. He has his ways of getting around the restrains. I'm obliged to make a different recommendation."

Joe and Weizlan stared at each other, a standoff. For a moment, Weizlan's dry, scowling face appeared to Joe as the contorted visage of a corpse. The fleeting image was so vivid he needed to look away. "Suit yourself, Professor," he said. "We'll make our recommendation, and whatever they decide to do with him is their business."

Chapter 31

Doll-maker Unmasked

Dallas

Interesting…So, the boy didn't talk to the cops directly. It was the principal…Oh, Rosa, I almost forgot. You may want to call Joe Vasquez. Remember the guy you met at my place? I believe he had a case similar to this in L.A. Here, I'll give you his number." Gabrielle dictated it, listened, absentmindedly, then said, "Yes, honey, any time," and hung up.

For an unidentifiable while, fallen out of time, she sat on the couch, completely still, watching the dust particles dancing in the stray beam of sunlight. Her bare feet rested on the carpet, next to the large stain left by Ranger's blood. She hadn't steam-cleaned it, and she had no intention to move to another apartment.

Finally, she got up and went to her desk.

§ § §

"How do you know about my case?" Joe listened and started at hearing Gabrielle's name. "Yes, please, recoup it for both of us." He turned on his cell phone's speaker so Dante, at the wheel, could hear Rosa too. In about ten minutes, they learned the gist of the Dandelion case.

"Thank you, Rosa. Yes, I'll send you what I have." Joe hung up.

"So, it's another one," Dante said.

They were quiet, both thinking, until light came into Joe's eyes. "Look what we got so far," he said. "The cops lost evidence in Bobby Sheppard's case, right?"

"Ahah."

"Blake Johnson spent some time in juvie shortly before he was murdered." Dante nodded.

"And now," Joe's voice rose, "this boy in Dallas…Before his abduction, he told on his classmates who vandalized school property, and his principal went to the police."

"You mean Doll-maker may be a cop?"

"It makes sense. He'd go from one department to another covering his tracks

201

in every state. And it would also explain why he'd put up such a good fight—he's got the training."

They exchanged glances, and Dante said, "If he's a cop, we know the department he most likely works at right now, and the approximate time when he got transferred here…"

They stopped at the intersection, veered into the turn lane and, as the light turned green, drove left, changing their course.

§ § §

A beep went off on Gabrielle's laptop, announcing an encrypted message with an ID and password. She navigated to the page 'Deep Ellum Police Department—Personnel' and logged in. The flash drive containing the fruits of Dante's labor was already inserted into one of the laptop's slots.

§ § §

"I didn't expect to see you guys so soon," Rosa said. "What's up?"

Joe glanced toward the desks. A few police officers were checking them out with some curiosity.

"We need to run a query for personnel transferred to Dallas between a month and two and a half months ago, possibly from California," he said. "And we better do that privately."

In a couple of minutes, the query yielded three names. Joe's heart beat a mad fandango. He couldn't believe it could be that easy. *None of them will turn out to be who we are looking for,* he thought.

Dante brought the first man to the screen—dark-haired and dark-eyed. Next, a blond guy with large, intense eyes. Joe shook his head. Dante clicked on the third name…

§ § §

The software found a match to the fingerprint Dante managed to lift off the glove. The ID photo of the fingerprint's owner showed a cop in his 40's, with mousy hair, an easily forgettable face, and the pale eyes of a dead fish. The officer's name, under the photo, was Paul Kosinski.

Gabrielle peered at the screen, etching the commonplace features into her memory.

§ § §

Paul Kosinski, in his dark jogging suit, stood in the awning shadow of a closed magazine kiosk, watching the entrance of the new District office building across the road. It was the end of the day and the employees and volunteers poured out into the quickly darkening street. He waited until the double glass door let out Tom Fletcher. Kosinski trailed the Senator's pet intern before and knew already he would be heading back to the ranch.

The boy slung his back-pack over his shoulder and strolled toward the parking lot two blocks away. Kosinski followed.

§ § §

"Hey Jason, have you seen Paul today?"

"He's out, called in sick," one of the men answered from his desk.

Rosa stepped back into her office.

"We'll need to run a comparison of his fingerprints to the collection from our crime scene," Dante said to Joe. "Though a match can't legally pin him to anything. Damn. I wish we still had the glove."

"I'll send a squad car to his place," Rosa offered.

"Try to locate him without alerting him," Joe said. "We might be mistaken, but if he *is* a killer he'll bolt."

In the next ten minutes or so, Rosa called up orders while her even younger male assistant sent Kosinski's photo to patrolmen around town. Joe listened to a message he received and immediately got on the phone with Logan's secretary. After exchanging a few words with her, he hung up and turned to Dante, his face dark. "Brin James is dead. Slashed his throat with a shank."

"How'd he got hold of it? That's a county jail for you!" Dante's tone rung with disdain. He added, "Bummer for your girlfriend."

Joe remembered Gabrielle's words. *The man who killed Craig and Baca is an explosive sadist, an avenger, a blood redeemer.* An avenger, a blood redeemer wouldn't wallow in guilt, real or imagined, and wouldn't slash his own throat with a shank. Joe's anger at Gabrielle rose; if she wasn't so damn secretive her precious patient would still be alive. What else could Joe do with that un-screwed window in Sullivan?

Chapter 32

Show Me Yours and I'll Show You Mine

Gabrielle woke up to a shrill ring of her phone.

She lifted her head groggily from the couch where she slept half-dressed and grabbed blindly for the gadget on the floor. She checked the ID, scrambled into a sitting position, and took the call. She exchanged a few words and then asked, "Who was watching him?" After hearing the answer, she thanked her informer and hung up. She sat hunched, staring emptily, her skin gray in the grim midday light of her living room.

Her cell beeped with an incoming text message. She pressed 'OK' to view it.

It took her a few seconds to absorb the image, a gagged and bound Tom Fletcher, terrified and looking into the camera, or more precisely at that captured moment into the pale fish eyes behind it. Gabrielle's face contorted. She waited, and the call soon came.

"Lubovich?" the unfamiliar voice said.

Her expression smoothed out, became blank. "Yes, Kosinski."

A brief silence, then a forced laugh. "So you figured me out. But you're too late. Now, listen carefully. I want to see what you have on me. I'm familiar with most of it, so you can't trick me. I also want all the physical evidence you filched, including the glove I dropped in your apartment. The police report didn't mention it, which means you or your Fed friend scooped it up."

"I need time to retrieve the info and the evidence. My friend you mentioned kept it." Her eyes became harder and brighter.

"You have until eight thirty tonight. I'll give you the location to exchange our goods. And don't count on my patience. I might have some fun while I'm waiting. If you're late, this one joins the rest of the lost boys. Now, before we meet, send everything digital to me. I'll text you where to download it. By the way, I sent a letter to your old boyfriend about a year ago with some interesting facts about you to start him up. He's a smart man, able to dig. Done well for himself lately too—I heard he's now the big cheese in your alma mater. If you go to the cops or feds and try to fuck with me, you and your politician will go down with fireworks. If something happens to me, Weizlan will be forced to testify, according to a provision in my will."

Gabrielle heard a muffled whimper on the other end. "You'll be sorry if you touch Tom," she said.

"Oh yeah? What will you do? Set your rabid mutt on me? I'm not sitting in a cage like the losers he likes to off." Kosinski's voice got a hardened edge. "Remember, girlie, if you involve your hissing friend in our transaction, say good-bye to your puppy-boy. You see, I know everything." Kosinski hung up.

"I see you don't," Gabrielle said to the dead receiver.

§ § §

They were driving when Joe's phone rang. The number was restricted. Adrenalin shot through Joe's veins before he answered.

"I've never shared a kill, Agent Vasssquezss. I do not like to share," Viper hissed. "But we have thsse sssame enemy, ssso I want you to partake in the exssecution. Tonight. eight p.m. sharp. Find me. You sssnooze, you loossse." The connection broke.

Dante watched Joe, knowingly.

Joe called Jerry Costello.

§ § §

Gabrielle listened to the rings with calculating care on her face and her finger on the button, ready to end the call. To her relief, the answering machine came on.

"He grabbed Tom," she said into the receiver. "He took the bait, Damien. I am sorry, I had to do that." She inhaled deeply. "If we don't see each other again…you'll need to forgive me all my transgressions anyway…I love you." She hung up.

She sent one last email. By the time the attachments cleared, her phone rang. It was Sheppard, but instead of answering she switched the power off.

She checked the time on the computer screen, logged out, and went to her bedroom. An outfit was spread on her bed—sturdy, stretch, comfortable pants, a long-sleeved, soft shirt, and a zipped jacket with several pockets, all in non-shiny, non-reflective black. Gabrielle changed and laced on her light-weight, rubber-soled boots.

In the bathroom, she opened the mirror cabinet and took out a vial of powdered methamphetamine hiding among the many bottles there. She shook a dash on her forefinger, screwed her face fastidiously and sniffed it all in. Her head flipped back, her eyes shut and her teeth showed, as the drug hit. She shuddered, blinked a few times, and was back again, lively with color. She hid the vial in one of the inner pockets of her jacket, threw on a long overcoat, and went downstairs, leaving the apartment's door unlocked.

§ § §

They saw her smoking at the entrance of her building as soon as they turned the corner.

"Is she coming or going? Look at that get-up…" Dante said.

She is waiting for us, Joe thought.

They pulled to the curb next to her car. Costello, who followed in his county Ford, parked behind them. When Joe got out and marched to her, Gabrielle dropped and stomped her cigarette then went into the building, forcing him to follow her inside. Dante came out and leaned on the car, and Costello waited in his cruiser.

Joe let the door shut and faced Gabrielle. "Keeping secrets is one thing. Stealing evidence is too much, Gabrielle," he said.

"What evidence are you talking about? The one *you* stole? You never reported it, so it's no longer usable. Any lawyer would argue it was planted."

"We need that glove."

"I need Brin James. Alive."

He wondered how she found out about Brin so quickly. Their faces mere inches from each other, he also wondered about her abnormally bright eyes and her skin's unusual lively color.

"He wasn't fit for jail." Her tone, measured and controlled, carried no indignation or anger and chilled Joe. "Are you so desperate to close your case you contented yourself with a scapegoat?"

Joe knew how weak his words sounded even before he let them out of his mouth. "Unfortunately, he confessed."

"He always does. Was it Weizlan who attended to the questioning?"

"Primarily. I protested the transfer."

"I guess the professor insisted?"

Joe didn't answer, which was an answer in itself.

A tic started at the corner of her eye. She overcame it quickly, half-closing her eyes. In a few seconds, the hardness in them dimmed and her face relaxed. She gazes at him perfectly calm, and he marveled at the masterful shifting of her masks.

"One of the windows in his wing was rigged," he said. "It could serve as an access to or from the building. And the question is, who could loosen those bolts, and why? I hate it, Gabrielle, but it doesn't add up well."

"Have you checked the other windows? Maybe they're all loose."

"Only one window was tampered with. The laundry window, near Brin's cell. I know there are two killers, Gabrielle. One your senator called Doll-maker, who killed Bobby, and another—your amigo Viper, who executes prisoners. You lead me to suspect Doll-maker knows something about Viper, and it's easy to guess that he is Viper's target himself. I also know Doll-maker blackmailed you and Sheppard. I know who he is…" Joe waited, and then said, "You don't seem surprised or curious, so I assume you have figured that out too. Every cop in Dallas is looking for him, and once he's caught he will be questioned. He might want to cut a deal and spill the beans about yours and Sheppard's extracurricular activities. Now, I've told you everything. It's your chance to do the same."

"Bravo, Agent, I don't think you need any help from me."

His fury grew, but so did a feeling that, for whatever sick reason, she wanted him to blow up, and so he tried his best not to. "What was Doll-maker really after in your apartment? And why don't you tell me about your connection to Viper?" He paused and added, "How deep is the hole you've dug yourself into, Gabrielle?"

"As I said, you are more than capable of solving this without help. I believe in you, Agent."

Her mockery did it. Joe flung her against the wall. "Three kids were bled to death and chopped up! You have information about their killer! How many more people must die? I am trying to save your fucking life, too."

She smiled, successful in pushing him to lose control. He gave her a furious jerk. She smiled wider. He felt a dreaded squeeze of the familiar icy hand in his chest. Their eyes dueled. Then, hers softened. She no longer smirked but stared steadily at him, and he was certain she wouldn't tell him what he wanted to know. And weird or not, also that she didn't lie to him. Whatever she had chosen to tell him thus far had always been the truth. For the first time, an idea struck him—that her mental settings were unlike his own, alien.

Her eyes moved to his lips…returned to his eyes…"Better do it now," she said. "Might be the last time."

His kiss was of war and frustration. When he started to disengage, she held him by his shirt. He pulled away finally, swaying a bit and hating himself for his weakness and that swaying. He got the handcuffs out and slapped them on her wrists. She didn't resist or say anything. He patted her pockets, took her cell phone and her key ring.

He led her out and to the cruiser, opened the back door, and pushed her inside. "Lock her in detention," he said to Costello. "No contact of any sort until I call. Lock the station from inside. Don't let anyone in. Someone may come for her—or after her, and he is one tricky son-of-a-bitch. So you stay put and wait. And don't talk to her or even look at her, understand?"

Costello nodded, wide-eyed, and took off.

Joe and Dante watched him enter traffic at the end of the block. Then, they went to search Gabrielle's car. A few seconds later, Joe pulled an FN-57 out from under the driver's seat and sniffed it. "Hasn't been fired lately," he said and put the gun back. They groped around the grill, bumpers, and fenders but found nothing else.

"We gotta deal with that suicide," Dante said.

"No. You gotta. But first, I need your premier hacking skills."

§ § §

Joe checked Gabrielle's phone as they walked up the stairs. The key pad was locked.

"Tough titi," Dante said. "You can't get around Blackberry codes."

Joe called and talked briefly to Berryhill. At the top floor, they found Gabrielle's apartment unlocked. Once inside, Dante went immediately to her desk.

Joe pulled out the kitchen drawers. One contained an infrared camera and a box with a simple laser microphone. Both gadgets looked unused. He phoned Rosa Sanchez next, who informed him that her efforts to locate Kosinski so far had been unsuccessful.

"Bingo!" Dante exclaimed in the living room.

Joe went there and waited for his partner to reset the bios and take over Gabrielle's computer's operating system.

After ejecting and returning to his pocket the hacking memory stick he brought with him, Dante pointed to an icon on the screen. "Some sort of tracking software. She used it right before we came. I am sure you can figure out what it's for."

Joe's phone buzzed. He checked the ID and said, "Cowell." Then Dante's phone rung. They waited. This time, Cowell left a message at the end.

Dante listened to it. "The shit has started to fly."

"Call a cab, I'll keep the car." Joe sat down at Gabrielle's desk.

Dante arranged for a taxi and hung up. "I'll tell them I don't know where you are, but they'll start wondering what you're up to soon. You better come up with something peachy, and fast."

Chapter 33

Viper's Justice

The county's tiny police station, halfway between the outskirts of Dallas and Sullivan, was routinely closed on the weekends when the citizens would seek assistance in the city. Being Sunday, the building stood locked until Sheriff Jerry Costello opened it and escorted Gabrielle inside. He took her to the bathroom and then to the holding cell, where she sat on the bench.

About ten minutes passed. Jerry started to whistle, fiddle with the papers on his desk, and otherwise pretended to be cool and preoccupied. Just another day at work, Ma'am.

He was still shy with women. Too aware of Gabrielle, he avoided her eyes in the rear view mirror all the way to the station. Such prudent behavior would have made following Joe's prohibition to interact with her easy, if not for Jerry's inherent kindness. Whenever he braved glancing at his charge, she seemed so sad…Sad good looks are a dangerous combination to a young male's romantic imagination.

Now, she gazed at him from behind the bars. Jerry was torn between her beguiling gaze begging to be met and Joe's explicit warning.

After a few minutes, he heard her sigh. "Jerry…" she whispered.

"How do you know my name?"

"I am scared, Jerry." She ignored his question. "Agent Vasquez doesn't realize what danger I am in."

"Don't be scared, Ma'am. It's pretty safe here. We are locked from the inside. No one can get in, unless they blast through the door, and no one would do that in the middle of a town."

She lowered her face and shook her head, and Jerry thought she was crying. "The man who wants me dead can enter any place," she said. "He will be here soon."

The rational part of Jerry's mind whispered 'beware', but it was too late—his heart, filled with pity and curiosity, hijacked control.

She sighed again, and Jerry despaired at that sigh. "I didn't talk to Agent Vasquez," she lifted her face at Jerry beseechingly. "I was too scared. But I've decided…I'll tell you. I see now I have no choice." Her voice waned at her last words.

Jerry always knew he was easy to talk to. Everybody said that. Agent Vasquez, on the other hand, was an aloof guy and, in Jerry's observation, too hard on this poor woman. If Jerry listened to her, he might even help Joe break his case. Wouldn't that be something? And what harm could come from simply listening? Jerry got up, took his chair, and went to the holding cell. He sat down in front of the bars and stared at Gabrielle, earnest. She smiled, almost shyly, and kept on looking back.

Her gaze, soft and unwavering, enveloped him, caressed him, tickled some tender spot within him…

She was saying something, something good and right…Before he knew it, he was unlocking the cell, and she went on speaking in a soothing voice, taking his hand and leading him…

§ § §

His cell rang while he still searched through the folders on Gabrielle's desktop, a few minutes after he located the file containing the fingerprints Dante had retrieved from the latex glove. Joe glanced at the caller ID: Weizlan, coming from the professor's home, not mobile—which meant the call was unlikely a Cowell's trick to get in touch with his stray agent.

Joe answered. "Yes, Professor."

"Measssure for equal measssure, Vassquezzz," the hiss came. "I always consssidered myself a good balancssser." The line went dead.

Joe punched the defenseless redial button. There was no answer. There couldn't be. Joe was up and moving.

§ § §

Another call came while he drove from a number with a Canadian area code. He took it.

"This is Blackberry's technical support," a baritone introduced himself. "Are you Agent Vasquez?"

A few minutes of juggling driving and following the instructions of the tech recruited by the resourceful Berryhill unlocked Gabrielle's phone. Joe thanked his helper and hung up. Glancing from the road to the gadget and back, he checked her most recent communications. One was marked 'Damien.' The next three, including two messages, came from 'Unknowns.' The last text received, an hour and half ago, presented a grouping of numbers, likely an IP address.

Joe opened the one before it. The image took the wind out of him. Some-one honked and he realized he ran a red light. He prayed that there were no traffic cops close by. His eyes kept returning to the young scared face on the screen. He recognized the dog sitter he met at Gabrielle's place. Frantically, he checked the rest of her communications. It would take a court order to force an ISP to reveal the IP address' physical location, long abandoned by now anyway.

Tom, she called the kid, but Joe didn't know his full name. He needed it to call Rosa and let her know. Rosa would mobilize state-wide resources to search for both Kosinski and the boy.

Joe summarized for himself. Doll-maker broke into Gabrielle's apartment, searched for something and didn't find it. So, he kidnapped Gabrielle's familiar and told her to give up that something or the kid ends up like Bobby and Blake—and that new, recently found boy. Same if Gabrielle contacted the cops. But Joe proved to her she could trust him. Why did she keep her fucking mouth shut?

He placed another call. The rings went on, impotent. Jerry Costello, ordered to guard Gabrielle and wait for Joe's instructions, didn't answer. Joe tried both Costello's cell phone and the station's land line. Nothing.

It was 5:20 p.m. Not much time left to figure out Viper's rendezvous location.

§ § §

A three-story, upper-class condo hosted one unit per landing. Weizlan lived at the top. Joe stopped before Weizlan's door, cold emptiness forming in the pit of his stomach. Taped right beneath the brass knocker to the dark, fake leather was a fresh pair of latex gloves.

Viper was a considerate son of a bitch.

Joe pulled out of his pocket and donned disposable gloves, a few of which he carried along with those all-around useful Ziplocs, and although he knew the ones Viper left for him would be pristine he bagged and pocketed them. He took out his Springfield, released the safety, and pushed the unlocked door.

The sparse foyer didn't bear any signs of intrusion. Joe hesitated. At first, his ears registered nothing but his own heartbeat. Then, a gurgling sound.

"Professor?" he called as he moved into the pristine living room of an old bachelor's pad and into an adjoining home office. Weizlan sat in an armchair pushed to the side of the desk, away from the window. His throat was slit from ear to ear. He looked like a giant Robin with his chest bright red, the last blood still coming out in small gushes. He didn't see Joe and died within seconds.

213

As Joe watched, he thought how Weizlan's throat must have been slashed the same way as Brin James'.

Measssure for equal measssure, Vassquezzz.

Joe turned away from the corpse.

The open, fire-proof safe gaped, empty, in the corner, papers scattered across the floor. On Weizlan's desk lay a number of eight by ten photographs, a display for Joe's benefit. There were nine pictures altogether. One showed Bobby Sheppard, with his name and the year of his death printed beneath. Blake Johnson smiled from another. Brandon Mole looked at him from the next. The other photos were all of young men, each bearing names and dates.

Joe touched the copy machine, still warm. The last of the photos in the printer's output tray, the enlarged pic from Gabrielle's phone, of the Doll-Maker's latest prospective victim, was marked 'Tom Fletcher' and bore a question mark instead of a date.

As Joe stared at the boy's face, he knew what he must do. He couldn't call Logan, Cowell, or the police. He had no time to spare—which Viper, no doubt, counted on. And Tom Fletcher would pay dearly for their clumsy intervention. As for Weizlan, he no longer needed help, anyway.

§ § §

Nearly two hours after Dante broke into Gabrielle's computer and about forty minutes after the foray to Weizlan's, Joe still struggled through the mess of her desktop and internet history. He checked caches, dug into her virtual trash bin, found nothing in the obvious places, and was reduced to searching the system directory. He finally tried an unusual-looking folder, marked with numerals. Another, named 'Joe,' waited for him there.

The folder's properties established that Gabrielle created it a few hours ago, shortly before his and Dante's arrival. He opened the first of the two files in it, a compilation of a few documents with a meager scatter of yellow highlighting. He recognized some of them, undoubtedly copied by Gabrielle during her last 'sleepover,' but not others she added. He wondered if their hookup was all business on her part or pleasure as well. He hoped, for his aching heart's sake, it was the latter.

He scanned quickly through. Manuel Gonzales' deposition (*'I brought some rock to this apartment on the West side, near the train depot,'* highlighted), Dante's report on the Doll-maker's apartment (*'If he was killed by the tenant, it wasn't done there'*), two news reports from long and not too long ago about the killings that never came to his or Dante's attention: *'The body of Matthew Clark was found yesterday near the Smith train park in Maryland…'* and *'The body of a nineteen year-old man was discovered by the Silverthorn train station.'*

Pictures of Matthew Clark and a later identified Ivan Chomko were among the nine he collected at Weizlan's. The last two cases had five years between them. In both, the bodies were found in the vicinity of train depots.

His mind prowled hectically. *Think, think, put yourself in the killer's shoes. He would need a place to bleed them, a 'slaughtering pen.' He would need to hang them upside down, the way you'd hang pigs. Then he would cut their throats. Once they ran clean of blood, his soft, pale, beautiful dolls, and he had every-thing he could have from them, he'd need to dispose of the bodies. He would chop them up to scatter around. But what does he do with the blood? Train depots. Freight trains…. Bleed 'em in a car, collect the blood in a bucket, send the rest of the DNA chug-chugging across the country, and no one would be any wiser.*

Doll-maker used train cars as his operating rooms. That's what Gabrielle discovered and left for him to find—on her timeline.

He closed his eyes, took a few long breaths, and then stared at the last file. A text document again. The first line said Tom Fletcher. A few spaces below was the scan of a license of some sort, issued to Gabrielle's dead dog, Ranger. Underneath an ID and the program's name 'Infra-red long-distance position-ing' was a series of numbers, likely an installation code.

Joe clicked on the desktop icon pointed out to him by Dante and studied the interface, allowing locating anything or anyone tagged with the infrared chip as long as the seeker had a device equipped with the receiver and got within a one mile radius of the object. He scrambled to search Gabrielle's desk. The receiver—a small antenna fitting on a cell phone—was in the top drawer, as well as the cord to copy the program from the computer.

The clock at the bottom of the screen indicated 7:25 p.m.

Joe was pretty sure now about the general area of his search. Once he got there, he had the software to lead him to the chip. But to keep his appoint-ment with Viper, he needed to hurry.

Chapter 34

Chickens Come to Roost

K osinski chose the empty cargo car a day before when he came to the shunting rail yard to get oriented. The area was deserted and unlit, unlike other parts of DIT. Outside the connex the red glow of the dying sunset turned the hulks of the strung together sidecars and a few gentry cranes the color of dried blood. Inside, a lantern illuminated a bag of tools, a new and sturdy plastic bucket set upside-down, a cordless electric chainsaw, and Tom's unconscious body wrapped in a tarp on the car's floor littered with grit and padding hay.

Kosinski took a come-along winch and the battery powered screwdriver out of the bag and climbed on the bucket. Breathing laboriously, he mounted the hook to the holes he predrilled at the center of the ceiling. He was near finishing when a buzz came from his jacket.

He jumped down and took out the source of the sound—a small video camera. The view screen was divided in four sections. Three were blank, but the fourth showed a slight figure approaching from the side of the car, as picked up by one of the infrared button cameras he installed earlier. Kosinski swore.

There was a knock. "May I come in?" Gabrielle's voice inquired.

Light eyes gaping, Kosinski pulled out his Beretta and trained it on the metal door. It opened with a screech.

"How the fuck did you find me?" he spat.

Gabrielle stood waist level with the car's floor, face calm, empty hands raised. "I have my ways," she said. Her eyes found Tom's body.

"You were supposed to wait for my call! Are you a moron? You want me to blow your head off?"

She pointed at the unconscious boy with her chin. "I'll give you the directions to the evidence once I see that he is alright."

"Are you alone?" The suspicion made his voice shrill.

"Naturally. You know I can't bring police into this. What are you afraid of? Your bugs will let you know if someone else comes close."

He stared in disbelief as she climbed inside. He kept her under gun point, stepping backward and turning, crab-like, until his back turned to the open door

217

while she squatted near Tom. She pulled the tarp off the boy's face and checked the pulse on his neck.

"Enough," Kosinski barked. "Get up!"

Gabrielle glanced up then past him, and her eyes widened.

"I'm not falling for your tricks." Kosinski kept the gun trained. "As you've said, I'll know if anyone comes along."

As if not hearing him, she covered the lower part of her face with her hands, staring with terror.

"I said put your fucking hands in the air!" Kosinski jacked up the volume.

A hiss from behind chilled him like a blade's touch to a throat. He spun, his pale eyes white with panic, and fired into the opening…

And gaped into the dark—at nothing.

"What's the…"

"Hhhere…hhhere…" came a hiss from behind him.

Shock-whipped, Kosinski swung around once more and howled as a hard, rough edge slammed into his hand from below, knocking the Beretta out.

Gabrielle faced him, standing now, holding the chainsaw she hit him with. She pressed her chin down, her lips moved, and out came the voice of Viper. "Isssn't it fun, Paul Kosinssski?"

Kosinski's eyes bulged at a small microphone attached to a plastic collar sticking out from under her jacket, a mouth piece transforming her voice. Her face, illuminated and deeply shadowed by the lantern at her feet, lost its cultivated sophistication.

"All the others were warm-ups," she said lifting her chin, her voice no longer distorted. "Cheap thrills. You are the one I've always wanted. The things I have in store for you!"

§ § §

Joe left his car parked by the fence and climbed over. Once on the other side, he took out his cell and waited for the software to find its bearings again. The locator took its sweet time, and that's when he heard the shot. He pushed the phone back into his pocket, drew his TRP, and hurried over the tracks.

He clambered over a coupler connecting two flatbeds and stopped, uncertain. It was quiet. He pulled his cell out once more. Sensing the target close, the interface promptly flashed the directions.

§ § §

Kosinski scowled. "Damn, have you tricked everyone! You're good at sneaking in from behind, I give you that. But coming out like this—Big mistake, girlie."

Gabrielle pressed the switch on the chainsaw. It started with a soft *whoosh*. "I love it when I am underestimated," she said.

"Put that down before you hurt yourself!" Kosinski tried to fake it but didn't sound too sure. He lunged for his gun.

In one swift move, Gabrielle slashed with the buzzing saw. He shrieked and went to his knees, holding his right hand. She operated the saw with remarkable precision. Kosinski was missing the tips of two fingers.

"Fucking bitch!" he screamed through his spit and tears.

"My practice is paying off. Great model, by the way." She raised the saw approvingly. Her hungry eyes, feral like a cat's following a bitten mouse, locked with his as he squirmed on the floor in pain. "Want to go piecemeal? I'm all for it."

He was a measly foot away from the gun, and Gabrielle waited. Breathing shallow, he inched, watching her. She lifted the wheezing saw, ready to strike. Kosinski froze. They peered at each other silently, and Gabrielle's face no longer twitched.

"Crazy bitch," he repeated in a tired croak. Through the link of their stares, her will descended on him. He tried to fight it. His hand trembled, ever so close to the Beretta, and faltered.

A buzz came from below. Gabrielle squinted, in wonder, at the camera at her feet. "We have an early guest," she said.

Disconnected from her gaze, Kosinski blinked, disoriented.

She pressed her chin down and, with her free hand, touched her collar, switching the outlet of the sound. As her lips moved the words came, amplified, from the microphone she left attached right outside the door. "Welcome, Agent Vasssquezss. Nicsse of you to join usss."

§ § §

Joe stepped stealthily, gun extended in both hands—on guard since he made out, from about fifty yards away, the light streaming from the opening of the connex. As he approached, Viper's voice jolted him like an electric whip. Joe's mind grasped right away that he was observed and addressed remotely, but he expected Viper to pop right up, some hideous sight to go along with his creepy hiss. His adrenal gland pumping its flight-or-fight reserves, Joe stopped to the left of the open door, the coupler being in the way, and the car's interior came into his view.

His eyes darted from Kosinski to Gabrielle, to Tom's prostrate, wrapped body, to the corrugated sides and the back wall. Not finding his enemy, Joe imagined him hidden by the entrance, a few feet and a thin sheet of metal away. Then, he became aware of the wheezing sound and gaped wildly at the chainsaw in Gabrielle's hands.

"Where is he?" he rasped. "Where is Viper?"

"Here," came the hiss.

The world wavered. He anchored himself in space with the line connecting his TPR to Gabrielle's chest. "You…All this time…"

"Yes," she said.

Kosinski shook his head groggily and got to his knees. Above him, Gabrielle and Joe were accessing each other anew. "Drop the saw," he said.

He glanced briefly at Kosinski, but from his position couldn't spot the Beretta on the floor, and returned his attention to Gabrielle. The earth seemed to move uncontrollably beneath him, and he fought dizziness by digging in his heels.

Then, Kosinski grabbed his gun.

Gabrielle threw the saw at him, striking his shoulder as he fired, deflecting the bullet above Joe, who staggered backward and went over the rail. Gabrielle ducked to the wall as Kosinski fired at and missed her on his dash out. He leapt over Joe and ran.

§ § §

Joe fired from the ground aiming for Kosinski's feet, the bullets spraying loose gravel short of the target. Gabrielle exploded out of the connex on top of him, knocking him down once more as he struggled to get up, and bolted after Kosinski.

Joe swore, scrambled up, and followed, his cotton legs submitting to his habit. Kosinski fired on the run. Blind shots, but they slowed his pursuers while he swerved and disappeared behind a boxcar. Joe caught up with Gabrielle and ducked next to her, behind the wheels of a flatbed.

"Look what you've done," she said. "Next time I serve justice, you're not invited."

Joe was still finding his breath. He said without looking at her, "You shouldn't have killed Weizlan."

"He was a lousy psychiatrist."

Kosinski shot at them, hitting the edge of a wheel. The metal sparks showered them, forcing them to huddle together. Joe was grateful for the bullets and the lack of time to think or absorb things.

Gabrielle peeked out. "He's getting away!" She tried to shove Joe off as he pulled her back.

"I'll deal with this!" he snarled, pushing her down. Then he was up and moving.

He didn't get far before she caught up and knocked him down. "He's mine." She dashed on and Joe got up and took aim. His bullet hit close to her feet, making her leap.

"Stay where you are!" he barked as he sprinted past her. He didn't get farther than a dozen feet when the ground flew out from under his feet again and Gabrielle was on top of him. His TRP quivered, pointing at her, while her Sig Sauer stared into his face.

"Is this Costello's gun? Nice work."

"Keep out of my way." She got off him, keeping the Sig aimed.

He sat up, his Springfield worthless in his hand. He couldn't shoot her, which he didn't doubt she knew. He forced her to hold his gaze until her expression changed, and she lowered her gun too.

The air cracked as scattered shots came from somewhere high, hitting at an angle. Kosinski hid in the cabin of the crane. Gabrielle pulled Joe up by his jacket, and they darted for cover. A screech came from above, metal on metal, likely of the crane's spreader beam.

"I'll distract him," Joe said. "Go before I call for backup. Disappear. That's all I can give you."

Gabrielle's gaze was shadowy and soft, and for a few heartbeats Joe let himself imagine the latest revelation was a bad dream. She likely read him because she touched his cheek, as if testing. He let her, at first. But his memory dispelled the illusion, and he pushed her hand away.

Another of Kosinski's blind bullets ricocheted off the siding above.

Wound like a tight spring, unable to stay close to Gabrielle, Joe rolled out from under the car, aiming at the crane's cabin. But the next moment she jerked him back, just as a large metal container released from the crane crashed thunderously between the tracks where Joe was a second before. They scuttled under the protection of the train's oversized wheels.

Something hit Joe's head. Dazed, he turned to be struck by the Sig Sauer. This time he was out cold. Gabrielle pulled him a bit farther along under the car, then into the open, and laid him not far from the rails, shielded on one side by the train and on the other with the landed container.

She took a small plastic bag containing some surgical scalpels and a roll of duct tape out of a pouch on her utility belt and inserted scalpel handles between her right hand's fingers. She taped them to the palm, fashioning a 'Wolverine paw.' When she curled her fist, the blades stuck out like claws. She skittered into the shadow of the next boxcar, firing at the crane's cabin to make sure Kosinski was still there. A bullet cracked above, as worthless as her own. Neither of them could aim. A few more shots rained down, Kosinski trying to buy time to get out of the cabin—a vantage point, but ultimately a trap.

Balled up against a wheel to avoid a ricochet, Gabrielle waited, squinting at the space under the platform. She saw his legs running, shot at them, missed, and was on the move herself. She ran parallel and then slowed to climb over the coupling, dropping further behind Kosinski but on the same side of the cars.

She stopped, aimed low, but Costello's Sig clicked impotently, out of bullets. Barely seeing Kosinski now in the darkness ahead, Gabrielle pushed the empty gun into the holster on her back and sped after him.

He fired at her and, while running, pulled out his spare magazine. A loud metal screech erupted, and the dark mass of the hopper next to him jolted forward at the pull of the unseen engine. Kosinski sprinted next to the train, now moving slug-like. He drew level with the ladder at the end of the car, grabbed the rail with his undamaged left hand, yanked, hooked a foot into the lower rung, and hoisted himself on.

Joe staggered to his feet and loped in the direction of the shots.

Twelve cars ahead, Kosinski leaned out, caught sight of Gabrielle running a few cars behind, fired at her, and smiled in triumph at her short scream. The train was turning right, and he pulled back.

Way behind, Joe heard the shot and the yelp. He ran at full speed.

Kosinski managed to climb on the shaking roof. He lay on his belly, hugged the left edge, and checked the faintly illuminated ground moving below. Then he rotated 180-degrees and peeked over the other side. The imminence of escape exhilarated him. He could now deal with his injury. Moaning with the effort, he curled and unbuttoned his over-shirt.

Joe caught up with the last car, grabbed the end ladder with both hands and pulled himself up while the train chugged through the exit of the yard.

The bandage Kosinski made was sloppy, but it would do. He propped himself on his right elbow, resting the Beretta. He exhaled, his knotted stomach relaxing…

And yowled like an animal as his gun slid into the void. He was staring at a scalpel sticking in the wraps on his stained, bloody tendons. A ghost-like, scowling face rose above the edge. He howled again as he took a swing at Gabrielle with his left arm. She ducked, disappearing from his view and screamed as if she lost her footing.

Crying and cursing, he pulled the scalpel out and crawled away on all fours.

§ § §

Sheppard peeked into the opening of the connex where the locator software led him. The lantern was still on. The sound of distant shots reached him, but this business needed to be attended to first.

"Tom?" he called. No answer. Sheppard climbed in. A quick check confirmed that Tom, although unconscious, was uninjured.

Sheppard took a pocket knife and a bottle of peroxide from the first aid kit he brought with him and poured some on the blade. "Sorry, boy," he said, pulling Tom's pants down. He felt with his fingers, made a small cut, and plucked the RFID chip out.

Gabrielle had placed the tag under Tom's pubic hair when she had him under—not a place he was likely to brush but where it could still be detected in the future, by Tom himself or some intimate friend. If the question about the cut would arise, Sheppard prayed Tom's kidnapper would not be in any condition to answer it.

§ § §

Gabrielle held on, managing to avoid falling under the wheels. Her neck bled, grazed by Kosinski's bullet, but she paid it no mind. She pulled herself up and saw Kosinski at the boxcar's head. He glanced back, his eyes round and white, scrambled to his feet, and took a start. Aided by adrenalin, he leapt on the roof of the next car. For a moment, Gabrielle squatted like a spider, trying to acclimate on the moving, shaking surface while glaring after Kosinski, her clawed hand flexing.

Joe climbed to the train's roof. Gabrielle's silhouette moved doggedly six hoppers away, and Kosinski struggled toward the engine, a few cars farther still.

Joe fired into the air, but neither of the two slowed down or paid him any mind. The train continued to gain speed.

Sheppard's Prius kept an even pace with the train along a truck route. A couple of times his hand crawled to the Ruger rifle on the passenger seat, but he never picked it up. He passed a sign stating an overpass was coming up. He floored the gas and soon overtook the locomotive.

§ § §

Three figures moved perilously atop the speeding train. Joe at the tail but slowly catching up, bleeding but determined. Gabrielle advanced in the middle, and a frantic Kosinski held a narrow and shortening lead. In places where the hoppers joined to the larger containers the distance between the cars was too great, forcing Kosinski to climb down, over the coupling, and up again to the next car's roof. He never risked jumping clear of the train. His mind was numb with fear and pain, his ears filled with wind and song of the wheels gripping and turning below and the increasing drone of the nearing engine.

Kosinski had no plan and only one goal—to live, somehow.

Gabrielle had no plan and only one goal—to kill Kosinski, Viper style.

One last plunge and Kosinski landed on all fours on the back of the locomotive. He crawled over the fans and clung desperately as hot wind rushed from under their lids and nearly blew him off. He reached the long, flat section above the engine. Only the narrow top of the cabin remained ahead, the piping protruding. He had nowhere else to go. He turned around like a cornered rat, and hunkered close to the fans, ready to knock Gabrielle off if she dared to jump into his territory.

She dared—with the scalpel-claw aimed at Kosinski's face—making him lose his nerve, sway back, and swipe at the air in an impotent effort to shove her off. They crouched bug-like, throwing awkward blows. Their exchange lumbering, frenzied, and handicapped, Kosinski shrieked every time Gabrielle's claw connected and ripped into his flesh, opening more and more blood-letting wounds.

The lights of the city faded behind. The train streaked through empty fields.

On the roof of the next car, Joe screamed over the noise, "Down! Now!" and fired into the air again.

§ § §

The sound of Joe's shot penetrated the insulated cabin of the locomotive, where the train's young conductor and the gray-haired engineer peered toward a six-lane grade separation bridge. "Did you hear that?!"

"Look!"

The bridge's lights diffused the darkness, but the blinkers of a car parked a few hundred yards beyond shone brighter. The car seemed to be stuck on the tracks.

The engineer pulled the emergency break.

§ § §

The train shuddered, the horn shrieked, and an earsplitting screech filled the air. The braking knocked Gabrielle off the roof and threw both Kosinski and Joe on their bellies.

Joe's cry at the sight of Gabrielle going over the edge was lost in the noise. He lifted himself on his elbows and saw Kosinski sliding on his ass and kicking at something. Gabrielle must have been trying to hold on. The locomotive likely had a walkway that stopped her fall. Joe fired at Kosinski and heard him howl.

The train rolled under the overpass, and Joe pressed flat again. The inertia of the train slowing propelled him forward. He managed to stop his slide at the front edge of the car and gaped at the sparks flying from the steel wheels in the hole below. The train jumped on the other side, shaking violently. Joe checked the locomotive's roof and saw no one there. He veered to the left, stuck out, saw the empty walkway, and then twisted his head. He couldn't discern the ground far enough back.

Before the train came to a stop, he climbed the hopper's side and jumped down, falling and rolling. His body didn't feel like his own. The emptiness in his chest wouldn't fill with breath. He walked back shakily along the subgrade toward the lights on the overpass, through the sand and sparse grass. In about a hundred yards he spied something lying by the tracks: a body, but not a complete one. He approached on leaden feet.

Cut in two at the hips, intestines trailing on the earth stained black with blood, Kosinski was still alive. The slits of his eyes, silver on his gray face, turned toward Joe, and his mouth opened. Joe thought the man was screaming silently. He wanted to keep on walking, to search for Gabrielle, but his legs divorced him and he went down to his knees. His eyes couldn't leave Kosinski's until the killer shifted his gaze. Joe raised his head.

225

Damien Sheppard stood above. His face bore no triumph or hatred. Only a hard wait.

Kosinski and the Senator watched each other until Kosinski's stare glazed over. Sheppard looked past Joe, who turned and saw Gabrielle kneeling amidst the tall grass about fifty-yards away. Her glistening eyes fastened on his. They were connected in this dim way for a short time he believed to be their last, and he wished he could see her face more clearly.

Then Sheppard went to her, and Joe vomited.

When he raised his head again, Sheppard and Gabrielle were gone. Police sirens and lights approached at the distance. He got up and staggered away from them, toward the locomotive. When he reached it, Sheppard's Prius came into his view, lumbering awkwardly over the tracks. Joe stopped. The Prius wheeled onto the frontage road and sped away.

There was nothing left but wait.

§ § §

"Sheriff Costello!"

Jerry startled awake. He lifted his head from the desk, bewildered by the morning light streaming through the windows. The woman, his charge per the request of Agent Vasquez, was calling to him from inside the holding cell. Jerry's body ached all over and he felt like the worst hangover. Somehow, he got himself up and walked to her. She huddled on the bench in her coat, with a scarf that Jerry didn't remember seeing before wound tightly around her neck, and seemed quite sick as he unlocked her cell. But she was calm and smiled at him.

The front door opened, and an imposing older man walked in. Surprised by his appearance Jerry panicked, realizing he somehow forgot to lock up before he fell asleep yesterday.

"I am Senator Sheppard," the old man greeted Jerry dryly. "I came to collect my friend." He gave Jerry a letter instructing him to immediately release Dr. Lubovich signed by Logan.

"Sorry," Jerry said to Gabrielle. "These FBI people think they can do whatever they please. Are you alright?"

"I'm fine, just tired."

"If you want to issue a complaint…" he said, fearing she would take him on his offer.

"No need." She held her neck. "Agents Vasquez and Gayle were only trying to keep us all safe."

She nearly fell into Sheppard's waiting arms and leaned heavily against him as the two walked out. If not for Jerry's splitting headache, he would feel sorrier for her ordeal and even angrier at Joe Vasquez. He was locking the holding cell when he noticed dark spots on the floor leading to the bench where Gabrielle sat. A small pool of blood coagulated underneath. In his inexperience with the female physiology, the explanation he came up with for the nasty puddle she had left for the janitor shamed and disgusted him.

Chapter 35

Tying Loose Ends

Los Angeles—mid-December

A dozen red roses were delivered to Joe, along with an envelope that had no return address. On the tenth day since coming back to L.A., and also the third day of his post-case, two-weeks off, the only vacationing signs were the stubble on his chin and the glowing cigarette stuck nearly permanently between his lips. He was smoking again.

Joe signed the receipt for the delivery man and carried the flowers and envelop inside. He laid the roses on the kitchen counter, ripped the envelope's ribbon off, and pulled out an old cardboard folder. He stood looking at the label that said 'Emily Howard.' His cell phone started to ring but he was slow to answer. At last he took the call.

"No conspiracy, the killer is dead, case closed," Dante said. "And there is a rumor that someone above—our friend Landaw, I presume—told Cowell you are his best asset, with everything implied. Not bad, Hound." Dante's voice held all the elation Joe lacked. "Lubovich has left the country." He waited but Joe stayed silent. "Want me to try and trace her?"

"What about Sheppard?" Joe asked, instead of an answer.

"Word is he's taking a break from politics for health reasons. You should take care of yourself too, amigo. Last time I saw you, you scared the shit out of me."

They promised to meet up soon, and Joe hung up. He opened the folder. Gabrielle's letter was at the top, written in long hand.

'Dear Joe,' it started. *'For the first time in many years, I am at peace. As you probably guessed, Damien made sure you were assigned to the Craig case. Serendipitously, you were both very perceptive and suitable to our purpose. We fully intended to take advantage of you, but then I got to know you. No one except Bobby had ever touched me so deep, and that's a high mark to measure up to. Growing up, I was unloved and unwanted. Until I met Bobby, my only friend was a dog. And then some fuck shit killed him, and I had nobody. When Damien started with me I was a wretch, an interesting study. But Bobby tried hard to*

229

know me, and he got to really know me—better than even his father, the professional. I'm easy to fall for now, by men who have no idea what I am. And I can have them, as long as I continue my act. But I didn't pretend to Bobby, and he loved me anyway. Do you realize how rare that is? How precious? Damien took me in, but Bobby saved me. And then he died. I am what I am because of him. Except, if he had lived, I would be someone much better.

'We'll never know exactly how he died, but we believe he tried to fight. The fingerprints the cops 'lost' came originally from his abandoned car. Kosinski must have lost his glove while trying to get Bobby out and was too agitated to wipe everything off. Damien and I hunted him for years. The Perry case became a turning point. Kosinski knew we got a fingerprint again, even though he didn't know it was partial. When we didn't go to the police, he asked himself why? He started watching us. However he made the connection, he found out enough. After that, he was no longer willing to run. I helped Blake Johnson, so Kosinski sent us a message, a call to war, by killing him.

'The fact that he went on the offensive was good news because he finally came out of hiding. The problem was we didn't identify him while he knew who we were. However, we were two against one—and after you came into the picture, we were three.

'Instead of waiting for you to burst in on us at any time, I suggested to Damien we bring you in. We could assist you without you knowing, and you could help us.

'We played a dangerous game. The FBI couldn't take Doll-maker alive. If they interrogated him, he would take us down. On the upside, I got to know you. I admire you for your brilliance, your integrity, and even more, for what you think as your weaknesses. It may make you sick that someone like me has such feelings for you, but neither of us can help it. And because I care so much, I'll always stay out of your way. There will be no more cases to concern you or reopen the one you've closed, not in this country anyway. In the eyes of the law, Viper and Doll-maker are now one man, 'removed from circulation' by the brave Agent Vasquez.

'I will not apologize for what I am, Joe. Whatever we think and do, our hearts beat to the drums of our fathers' blood. I envy you and your drum, but I must live with mine. Always yours, Gabrielle.'

Joe picked up the next document, a note bearing Weizlan's signature. *'…during the years preceding his entering politics, Damien Sheppard, at the time a Professor of Psychiatry at the Dallas Graduate Institute, assumed guardianship over his 13-year old patient, Emily Howard, and changed her identity to Gabrielle Lubovich. The child was referred to him to manage psychosis she apparently inherited from her biological father, Samuel Horowitz, a serial killer executed by the state of Texas in…'*

Joe dropped the papers.

In the days following the revelation at the depot, he sleepwalked through his life. He didn't smile or cry. He didn't think. At least he tried not to. The arrival of the package and Gabrielle's letter shattered that eggshell. He slid along the wall to the floor. The tears welled up and he didn't fight them— beggarly and meager, they were a drip, not the pour, the last reserves his tear ducks could squeeze.

She saved him from an explosion and Kosinski knife, and she tried to keep him out of harm's way during their last pursuit. Those were not the actions of a bloodthirsty avenger. No matter what reason said, Gabrielle and Viper would never merge for him. Because he still loved her, and he couldn't love a monster.

When his eyes were dry, he got up, took the flowers from the counter, inhaled the strong aroma of the brazen blossoms, and discarded them into the garbage can. He gathered the papers and carried them past the shelves full of books he no longer read to his mother's room—more of a real office now, orderly and nearly empty, the futon given away the day before, and his mother's desk clean. He sat in the chair and methodically went through the rest of the package's contents. They dated long ago and supported the facts stated in Weizlan's note.

When Joe finished, he lit up and smoked for a while, thinking.

The documents Weizlan stole from the Garfield Municipal Archive allowed him to blackmail Sheppard and acquire tenure at the Institute of Forensic Sciences. Weizlan kept the folder in his office safe until Viper executed him. Joe supposed Gabrielle must have gotten her first taste of killing when she burned, by herself or with Sheppard's assistance, Chris Mattis in his truck. What age was she then? About sixteen, he calculated, so it happened after Bobby's death. Sheppard likely helped her with the planning, preparation, and setting things up to look like an accident. What better schooling for the future avenger of his son than actual practice? Was that his 'therapeutic approach?' Teaching her not to simmer in desperate rage, not to get mad but to get even? Teaching her how it felt to go with the flow of her father's sadistic blood. She became Sheppard's living experiment in an alternative upbringing, his very own killing machine.

The first execution must have been the most difficult, which is why it had to be arson, performed remotely. The next one would be easier and at more close quarters, and then the next would be peanuts, done for the thrill and that great feeling of playing the righteous god. And by then Samuel Horowitz' gene was turned on and killing would become a habit, a need, a compulsion. Viper was born.

Joe wondered at which point she added bloodletting to the repertoire, a tribute to the boy waiting to be avenged.

At last, he remembered the esteemed and mysterious Arthur Landaw. Was Landaw aware of Gabrielle's past or, even more importantly, her noteworthy present? Landaw being a life-long and good enough friend to Sheppard to pull off an acting performance and influence the FBI's investigation, Joe's gut answered in the affirmative. Would Joe ever hear from Agent Parker again? If that happens, it would mean one thing. Even as he tried to steel his mind, the thought of such possibility sent his heart aflutter with a pathetic hope.

He pulled the wire waste basket close and set the papers on fire with his lighter, one after another, dropping them into the basket and watching as the past turned into ashy phyllo dough. The folder itself took a little more effort, but the flames consumed it, too.

Epilogue

It was a rainy day in the beginning of winter, and the dreary light sifted through the ceiling glass of one of the shabby, overcrowded, and disorganized terminals of Charles De Gaulle airport. A long queue of EEC and non-EEC lay-over hopefuls and disembarking passengers stretched to the Customs and Passport counter, past panels offering moot instructions and a group of vacant-looking, uniformed staff puffing on cheap cigarettes under a 'No Smoking' sign. The public, tired from the wait and sick with their own stink, had lost the will to entertain any common civilities, and the customs officer, a Frenchman with a drooping mustache dyed flat black, had done so long before them. He barely looked at the gray and depressing unending arrivals.

But when a pale hand placed papers in front of him, he lifted his eyes. A beautiful face before him instantly brightened his mood. The dark-haired woman could easily be a Parisian, trim and fit in her short, simple dress, with killer legs and the flat stomach of a boy. Even his mustache perked up.

"Business or pleasure, Madam…" he scanned her passport, "…Lubovich."

"Mademoiselle," she corrected him in French. "Which do you think?"

He smiled broadly, the drain of his day forgotten, glancing through her Convention d'Accueil—issued by the request of Institute de Sciences Penales et de Criminologue and signed by no other than the Director of the National Police, Jean Bacar.

"I would guess business, and a serious one. Congratulations on your new job, Mademoiselle. But when in Paris, you must not forget to have fun."

"Merci, Officer…" she read his name tag, "…Benoit. Rest assured, I never forget fun. Especially on the job."

He stamped her papers.

"Here is a small souvenir for you, Messier Benoit." She laid a silver lighter on the counter. "You are a smoker, are you not?"

"Mademoiselle is a detective!" he said, delighted. "Oh, but this is too fancy and expensive. I cannot take it."

"Please, do. I quit smoking as a tribute to a friend."

"Well, in that case, merci beaucoup, Mademoiselle. You are very kind." He took the lighter and felt a little empty as he nodded her through.

She already moved on when he gave in to his impulse and called after her. "Are you going to Paris by taxi or by a bus, Mademoiselle?" He longed to give her detailed directions to any destination, along with tips on the fares and traffic jams—to hell with the waiting queue.

"I'm taking the Reseau Express," she called back, her tone implying she was well rehearsed in her route. "I love trains."

The woman stepped out into the vestibule, and disappeared in the crowd.

Acknowledgments

My deepest gratitude goes to my friend and first editor Alison Brooke Monfort and my publisher Kenneth Tupper for their invaluable input and encouragement, and to my mate George Evans for his continuous support.